PETER HANDKE was born in Griffen, Austria, in 1942. Twenty-four years later, in 1966, his first novel, THE HORNETS, was published. Thus began a literary and theatrical career that has seen him recognized, in less than a decade, as one of the most important writers of postwar Europe.

His first full-length play, KASPAR, premiered in 1968 and was hailed by Max Frisch as "the play of the decade" and compared in importance to WAITING FOR GODOT. Several other plays SELF-ACCUSATION AUDI-ENCE, CON-STAN have been p

His fi world is filled wit or Kafka, Sartre, Camus, a Grillet but also of American gangster films and Westerns. Each new novel reconfirms his stature as one of the most gifted experimenters writing today.

THE HOUR OF THE TRUE SENSIBIL-ITY, his latest novel, is prominent on the West German bestseller list, and will soon be available in an English translation.

THREE BY
PETER HANDKE

PETER HANDKE

 A BARD BOOK/PUBLISHED BY AVON BOOKS

THE GOALIE'S ANXIETY AT THE PENALTY KICK was originally published in German under the title DIE ANGST DES TORMANNS BEIM ELFMETER © SuhrKamp Verlag, Frankfurt am Main, 1970.

SHORT LETTER, LONG FAREWELL was originally published in German under the title DER KURZE BRIEF ZUM LANGEN ABSCHIED © 1972 by Suhrkamp Verlag, Frankfurt am Main, Germany.

A SORROW BEYOND DREAMS was originally published in German under the title WUNSCHLOSES UNGLÜCK © 1972 by Residenz Verlag, Salzburg, Austria.
Quotation from "It's Alright Ma (I'm Only Bleeding)" by Bob Dylan, © 1965 M. Witmark & Sons.
Used by permission of Warner Bros. Music.

AVON BOOKS
A division of
The Hearst Corporation
959 Eighth Avenue
New York, New York 10019

THE GOALIE'S ANXIETY AT THE PENALTY KICK
English Translation Copyright © 1972
by Farrar, Straus & Giroux, Inc.
SHORT LETTER, LONG FAREWELL
English Translation Copyright © 1974
by Farrar, Straus & Giroux, Inc.
A SORROW BEYOND DREAMS
English Translation Copyright © 1974
by Farrar, Straus & Giroux, Inc.

Library of Congress Catalog Card Number: 76-52801
ISBN: 0-380-00968-4

All rights reserved, which includes the right
to reproduce this book or portions thereof in
any form whatsoever. For information address
Farrar, Straus & Giroux, Inc., 19 Union Square West,
New York, New York 10003

First Bard Printing, March, 1977

BARD TRADEMARK REG. U.S. PAT. OFF. AND IN
OTHER COUNTRIES, MARCA REGISTRADA, HECHO EN
U.S.A.

Printed in the U.S.A.

Contents

The Goalie's Anxiety
at the Penalty Kick

TRANSLATED BY MICHAEL ROLOFF

The publishers and the translator express
their thanks to Wayland Schmitt and
Ruth Hein for their help in
preparing the translation.

"The goalie watched as the ball rolled across the line . . ."

*W*HEN Joseph Bloch, a construction worker who had once been a well-known soccer goalie, reported for work that morning, he was told that he was fired. At least that was how he interpreted the fact that no one except the foreman looked up from his coffee break when he appeared at the door of the construction shack, where the workers happened to be at that moment, and Bloch left the building site. Out on the street he raised his arm, but the car that drove past—even though Bloch hadn't been hailing a cab—was not a cab. Then he heard the sound of brakes in front of him. Bloch looked around: behind him there was a cab; its driver started swearing. Bloch turned around, got in, and told the driver to take him to the Naschmarkt.

It was a beautiful October day. Bloch ate a hot dog at a stand and then walked past the stalls to a movie theater. Everything he saw bothered him. He tried to notice as little as possible. Inside the theater he breathed freely.

Afterward he was astonished by the perfectly natural manner of the cashier in responding to the wordless gesture with which he'd put his money on the box-office turntable. Next to the movie screen he noticed the illuminated dial of an electric clock. Halfway through the movie he heard a bell; for a long

5

time he couldn't decide whether the ringing was in the film or in the belfry outside near the Naschmarkt.

Out on the street, he bought some grapes, which were especially cheap at this time of year. He walked on, eating the grapes and spitting out the skins. The first hotel where he asked for a room turned him away because he had only a briefcase with him; the desk clerk at the second hotel, which was on a side street, took him to his room himself. Even before the clerk had gone, Bloch lay down on the bed and soon feel asleep.

In the evening he left the hotel and got drunk. Later he sobered up and tried calling some friends; since most of these friends didn't live in the city and the phone didn't return his coins, Bloch soon ran out of change. A policeman to whom Bloch shouted, thinking he could get his attention, did not respond. Bloch wondered whether the policeman might have misconstrued the words Bloch had called across the street, and he remembered the natural way the movie cashier had spun around the tray with his ticket. He'd been so astonished by the swiftness of her movements that he almost forgot to pick up the ticket. He decided to look up the cashier.

When he got to the movie, the theater's lights were just going out. Bloch saw a man on a ladder exchanging the letters of the film for tomorrow's title. He waited until he could read the name of the next film; then he went back to the hotel.

The next day was Saturday. Bloch decided to stay at the hotel one more day. Except for an American couple, he was alone in the dining room; for a while he listened to their conversation, which he could understand fairly well because he'd traveled with his team to several soccer tournaments in New York; then he quickly went out to buy some newspapers. The papers, because they were the weekend editions, were very heavy; be didn't fold them up but carried them under his arm to the hotel. He sat down at his table, which had been cleared in the meantime, and took out the want-ad sections; this depressed him. Outside he saw two people walking by with thick newspapers. He held his breath until they had passed. Only then did he realize they were the two Americans. Having seen them earlier only at the table in the dining room, he did not recognize them.

At a coffeehouse he sipped for a long time at the glass of water served with his coffee. Once in a while he got up and took a magazine from the stacks lying on the chairs and tables designated for them; once when the waitress retrieved the magazines piled beside him, she muttered the phrase "newspaper table" as she left. Bloch, who could hardly bear looking at the magazines but at the same time could not really put down a single one of them before he had leafed through it completely, tried glancing out at the street now and then; the contrast between the magazine illustrations and the changing views outside soothed him. As he left, he returned the magazines to the table himself.

At the market the stalls were already closed. For a few minutes Bloch casually kicked discarded vegetables and fruit along the ground in front of him. Somewhere between the stalls he relieved himself. Standing there, he noticed that the walls of the wooden stands were black with urine everywhere.

The grape skins he had spat out the day before were still lying on the sidewalk. When Bloch put his money on the cashier's tray, the bill got caught as the turntable revolved; he had a chance to say something. The cashier answered. He said something else. Because this was unusual, the girl looked up. This gave him an excuse to go on talking. Inside the movie, Bloch remembered the cheap novel and the hot plate

7

next to the cashier; he leaned back and began to take in the details on the screen.

Late in the afternoon he took a streetcar to the stadium. He bought standing room but sat down on the newspapers, which he still hadn't thrown away; the fact that the spectators in front of him blocked his view did not bother him. During the game most of them sat down. Bloch wasn't recognized. He left the newspapers where they were, put a beer bottle on top of them, and went out of the stadium before the final whistle, so he wouldn't get caught in the rush. The many nearly empty buses and streetcars waiting outside the stadium—it was a championship game—seemed strange. He sat down in a streetcar. He sat there almost alone for so long that he began to feel impatient. Had the referee called overtime? When Bloch looked up, he saw that the sun was going down. Without meaning anything by it, Bloch lowered his head.

Outside, it suddenly got windy. At just about the time that the final whistle blew, three long separate blasts, the drivers and conductors got into the buses and streetcars and the people crowded out of the stadium. Bloch could imagine the noise of beer bottles landing on the playing field; at the same time he heard dust hitting against the windows. Just as he had leaned back in the movie house, so now, while the spectators surged into the streetcar, he leaned forward. Luckily, he still had his film program. It felt as though the floodlights had just been turned on in the stadium. "Nonsense," Bloch said to himself. He never played well under the lights.

. Downtown he spent some time trying to find a phone booth; when he found an empty one, the ripped-off receiver lay on the floor. He walked on. Finally he was able to make a call from the West Railroad Station. Since it was Saturday, hardly anybody was home. When a woman he used to know finally answered, he had to talk a bit before she understood who he was. They arranged to meet at a restaurant near the station, where Bloch knew there was a juke box. He passed the time until she came putting coins in the juke box, letting other people choose the songs; meanwhile, he looked at the signed photos of soccer players on the walls. The place had been leased a couple of years ago by a forward on the national eleven, who'd then gone overseas as coach of one of the unofficial American teams; now that that league had broken up, he'd disappeared over there. Bloch started talking to a girl who kept reaching blindly behind her from the table next to the juke box, always choosing the same record. She left with him. He tried to get her into a doorway, but all the gates were already locked. When one could be opened, it turned out that, to judge from the singing, a religious service was going on behind an inner door. They found an elevator and got in; Bloch pushed the button for the top floor. Even before the elevator started up, the girl wanted to get out again. Bloch then pushed the button for the second floor; there they got out and stood on the stairs; now the girl became affectionate. They ran upstairs together. The elevator was on the top floor; they got in, rode down, and went out on the street.

Bloch walked beside the girl for a while; then he turned around and went back to the restaurant. The woman, still in her coat, was waiting. Bloch explained to the other girl, who was still at the table next to the juke box, that her friend would not come back, and went out of the restaurant with the woman.

Bloch said, "I feel silly without a coat when you're wearing one." The woman took his arm. To free his arm, Bloch pretended that he wanted to show her something. Then he didn't know what it was he wanted to show her. Suddenly he felt the urge to buy an evening paper. They walked through several streets but couldn't find a newsstand. Finally they took the bus to the South Station, but it was already closed. Bloch pretended to be startled; and in reality he was startled. To the woman—who had hinted, by opening her purse on the bus and fiddling with various things, that she was having her period—he said, "I forgot to leave a note," without knowing what he actually meant by the words "note" and "leave." Anyway, he got into a cab alone and drove to the Naschmarkt.

Since the movie had a late show on Saturdays, Bloch actually arrived too early. He went to a nearby cafeteria and, standing up, ate a croquette. He tried to tell the counter girl a joke as fast as he could; when the time was up and he still hadn't finished, he stopped in the middle of a sentence and paid. The girl laughed.

On the street he ran into a man he knew who asked him for money. Bloch swore at him. As the drunk grabbed Bloch by the shirt, the street blacked out. Startled, the drunk let go. Bloch, who'd been expecting the theater lights to go out, rushed away. In front of the movie house he met the cashier; she was getting into a car with a man. Bloch watched her. When she was in the car, in the seat next to the driver, she answered his look by adjusting her dress on the seat; at least Bloch took this to be a response. There were no incidents; she had closed the door and the car had driven off.

Bloch went back to the hotel. He found the lobby lit up but deserted. When he took his key from the hook, a folded note fell out of the pigeonhole. He opened it: it was his bill. While Bloch stood there in the lobby, with the note in his hand, the desk clerk came out of the checkroom. Bloch immediately asked him for a newspaper and at the same time looked through the open door into the checkroom, where the clerk had evidently been napping on a chair he'd taken from the lobby. The clerk closed the door, so that all Bloch could see was a small stepladder with

a soup bowl on it, and said nothing until he was behind the desk. But Bloch had understood even the
closing of the door as a rebuff and walked upstairs
to his room. In the rather long hall he noticed a
pair of shoes in front of only one door; in his room
he took off his own shoes without untying them and
put them outside the door. He lay down on the bed
and fell asleep at once.

In the middle of the night he was briefly awakened
by a quarrel in the adjoining room; but perhaps his
ears were so oversensitive after the sudden waking
that he only thought the voices next door were quar-
reling. He slammed his fist against the wall. Then he
heard water rushing in the pipes. The water was
turned off; it became quiet, and he fell back to sleep.

Next morning the telephone woke Bloch up. He
was asked whether he wanted to stay another night.
Looking at his briefcase on the floor—the room had
no luggage rack—Bloch immediately said yes and
hung up. After he had brought in his shoes, which had
not been shined, probably because it was Sunday, he
left the hotel without breakfast.

In the rest room at the South Station he shaved
himself with an electric razor. He showered in one
of the shower stalls. While getting dressed, he read
the sports section and the court reports in the newspaper. Afterwards—he was still reading and it was
rather quiet in the adjoining booths—he suddenly felt
good. Fully dressed, he leaned against the wall of the
booth and kicked his foot against the wooden bench.
The noise brought a question from the attendant outside and, when he didn't answer, a knock on the
door. When he still didn't reply, the woman outside
slapped a towel (or whatever it might be) against the
door handle and went away. Bloch finished reading
the paper standing up.

On the square in front of the station he ran into
a man he knew who told him he was going to the sub-

urbs to referee a minor-league game. Bloch thought this idea was a joke and played along with it by saying that he might as well come too, as the linesman. When his friend opened his duffelbag and showed him the referee's uniform and a net bag full of lemons, Bloch saw even those things, in line with the initial idea, as some kind of trick items from a novelty shop and, still playing along, said that since he was coming too, he might as well carry the duffelbag. Later, when he was with his friend on the local train, the duffelbag in his lap, it seemed, especially since it was lunchtime and the compartment was nearly empty, as though he was going through this whole business only as a joke. Though what the empty compartment was supposed to have to do with his frivolous behavior was not clear to Bloch. That this friend of his was going to the suburbs with a duffelbag; that he, Bloch, was coming along; that they had lunch together at a suburban inn and went together to what Bloch called "an honest-to-goodness soccer field," all this seemed to him, even while he was traveling back home alone—he had not liked the game—some kind of mutual pretense. None of that mattered, thought Bloch. Luckily, he didn't run into anyone else on the square in front of the station.

From a telephone booth at the edge of a park he called his ex-wife; she said everything was okay but didn't ask about him. Bloch felt uneasy.

He sat down in a garden café that was still open despite the season and ordered a beer. When, after some time, nobody had brought his beer, he left; besides, the steel tabletop, which wasn't covered by a cloth, had blinded him. He stood outside the window of a restaurant; the people inside were sitting in front of a TV set. He watched for a while. Somebody turned toward him, and he walked away.

In the Prater he was mugged. One thug jerked his jacket over his arms from behind; another butted his head against Bloch's chin. Bloch's knees folded a little, then he gave the guy in front a kick. Finally the two of them shoved him behind a candy stand and finished the job. He fell down and they left. In a rest room, Bloch cleaned off his face and suit.

At a café in the Second District he shot some pool until it was time for the sports news on television. Bloch asked the waitress to turn on the set and then watched as if none of this had anything to do with him. He asked the waitress to join him for a drink. When the waitress came out of the back room, where gambling was going on, Bloch was already at the door; she walked past him but didn't speak. Bloch went out.

Back at the Naschmarkt, the sight of the sloppily piled fruit and vegetable crates behind the stalls seemed like another joke of some kind, nothing to worry about. Like cartoons, thought Bloch, who liked to look at cartoons with no words. This feeling of pretense, of playing around—this business with the referee's whistle in the duffelbag, thought Bloch—went away only when, in the movie, a comic snitched a trumpet from a junk shop and started tooting on it in a perfectly natural way; all this was so casual that it almost seemed unintentional, and Bloch realized that the trumpet and all other objects were stark and unequivocal. Bloch relaxed.

After the movie he waited between the market stalls for the cashier. Some time after the start of the last show, she came out. So as not to frighten her by coming at her from between the stalls, he sat there on a crate until she got to the more brightly lit part of the Naschmarkt. Behind the lowered shutter in one of the stalls, a telephone was ringing; the stand's phone number was written in large numerals on the metal sheet. "No score," Bloch thought at once. He followed the cashier without actually catching up with her. As she got on the bus, he strolled up and stepped aboard after her. He took a seat facing her but left several rows of seats between them. Not until new passengers blocked his view after the next stop was Bloch able to think again. She had certainly looked at him but obviously hadn't recognized him; had the mugging changed his looks that much? Bloch ran his fingers over his face. The idea of glancing at the window to check what she was doing struck him as foolish. He pulled the newspaper from the inside pocket of his jacket and looked down at the letters but didn't read. Then, suddenly, he found himself reading. An eyewitness was testifying about the murder of a pimp who'd been shot in the eye at close range. "A bat flew out of the back of his head and slammed against the wallpaper. My heart skipped a beat." When the sentences went right on about something else, about an entirely different person, with no paragraph, Bloch was startled. "But they should have put a paragraph there," thought Bloch. After his abrupt shock, he was furious. He walked down the aisle toward the cashier and sat diagonally across from her, so that he could look at her; but he did not look at her.

When they got off the bus, Bloch realized that they were far outside the city, near the airport. At this time of night, it was a very quiet area. Bloch walked along beside the girl but not as if he was escorting her or even as if he wanted to. After a while he touched her. The girl stopped, turned, and touched him too, so fiercely that he was startled. For a moment the purse in her other hand seemed more familiar to him than she did.

They walked along together a while, but keeping their distance, not touching. Only when they were on the stairs did he touch her again. She started to run; he walked more slowly. When he got upstairs, he recognized her apartment by the wide-open door.

14

She attracted his attention in the dark; he walked to her and they started in right away.

In the morning, wakened by a noise, he looked out the window and saw a plane coming in for a landing. The blinking lights made him close the curtain. Because they hadn't turned on any lights, the curtain had stayed open. Bloch lay down and closed his eyes.

With his eyes closed, he was overcome by a strange inability to visualize anything. He tried to tell himself the names he knew for each thing in the room, but he couldn't picture anything; not even the plane he had just seen landing, though he might have recognized in his mind, probably from earlier experience, the screeching of its brakes on the runway. He opened his eyes and looked for a while at the corner where the kitchen was: he concentrated on the tea kettle and the wilted flowers drooping in the sink. He had barely closed his eyes again when the flowers and the tea kettle were unimaginable. He resorted to thinking up sentences about the things instead of words for them, in the belief that a story made up of such sentences would help him visualize things. The tea kettle whistled. The flowers were given to the girl by a friend. Nobody took the kettle off the hot plate. "Would you like some tea?" asked the girl. It was no use: Bloch opened his eyes when he couldn't stand it any more. The girl was asleep beside him.

Bloch grew nervous. If the pressure of everything around him when his eyes were open was bad, the pressure of the words for everything out there when his eyes were closed was even worse. "Maybe it's because I just finished sleeping with her," he thought. He went into the bathroom and took a long shower.

The tea kettle was actually whistling when he came back. "The shower woke me up," the girl said. Bloch felt as if she were addressing him directly for the first time. He wasn't quite himself yet, he replied. Were there ants in the teapot? "Ants?" When the boiling water from the kettle hit the bottom of the pot, he didn't see tea leaves but ants, on which he had once poured scalding water. He pulled the curtain open again.

The tea in the open canister seemed—since the light reached it only through the small round hole in the lid—oddly illuminated by reflection from the inner walls Bloch, sitting with the canister at the table, was staring fixedly through the hole. It amused him to be so fascinated by the peculiar glow of the tea leaves while inattentively talking to the girl. Finally he pressed the cap back on the lid, but at the same time he stopped talking. The girl hadn't noticed anything. "My name is Gerda," she said. Bloch hadn't even wanted to know. He asked whether she had noticed anything, but she'd put on a record, an Italian song with electric-guitar accompaniment. "I like his voice," she said. Bloch, who had no use for Italian hits, remained silent.

When she went out briefly to get something for breakfast—"It's Monday," she said—Bloch finally had a chance to study everything carefully. While they ate, they talked a lot. Bloch soon noticed that she talked about the things he'd just told her as if they were hers, but when he mentioned something she had just talked about, he either quoted her exactly or, if he was using his own words, always prefaced the new names with a hesitant "this" or "that," which distanced them, as if he were afraid of making her affairs his. If he talked about the foreman, say, or about a soccer player named Dumm, she could say, almost at once, quite familiarly, "the foreman" and "Dumm"; however, when she mentioned someone she knew called Freddy or a bar called Stephen's Dive, he invariably talked about "this Freddy?" and "that Stephen's Dive?" when he replied. Every word she uttered prevented him from taking any deeper interest, and it upset him that she seemed so free to take over whatever he said.

From time to time, of course, the conversation became as natural for him as for her; he asked a question and she answered; she asked one and he made the obvious reply. "Is that a jet?"—"No, that's a prop plane."—"Where do you live?"—"In the Second District." He even came close to telling her about the mugging.

But then everything began to irritate him more and more. He wanted to answer her but broke off in midsentence because he assumed that she already knew what he had to say. She grew restless and started moving about the room; she was looking for something to do, smiling stupidly now and then. They passed the time by turning records over and changing them. She got up and lay down on the bed; he sat down next to her. Was he going to work today? she wanted to know.

Suddenly he was choking her. From the start his grip was so tight that she'd never had a chance to think he was kidding. Bloch heard voices outside in the hall. He was scared to death. He noticed some stuff running out of her nose. She was gurgling. Finally he heard a snapping noise. It sounded like a stone on a dirt road slamming against the bottom of a car. Saliva had dripped onto the linoleum.

The constriction was so tight that all at once he was exhausted. He lay down on the floor, unable to fall asleep but incapable of raising his head. He heard someone slap a rag against the outside doorknob. He listened. There had been nothing to hear. So he must have fallen asleep after all.

It didn't take him long to wake up; as soon as his eyes were open, he felt exposed; as though there was a draft in the room, he thought. And he hadn't even scraped his skin. Still, he imagined that some kind of lymph fluid was seeping out through all his pores. He was up and had wiped off everything in the room with a dish towel.

He looked out the window: down below, somebody with an armful of coats on hangers was running across the grass toward a delivery truck.

He took the elevator, left the house, and walked straight ahead for a while. Then he took the suburban bus to the streetcar terminal; from there he rode back downtown.

When he got to the hotel, it turned out that his briefcase had already been brought downstairs for safekeeping, since it looked as if he wouldn't be back. While he was paying his bill, the bellboy brought the briefcase from the checkroom. Bloch saw a faint ring on it and realized that a damp milk bottle must have been standing on it; he opened the case while the cashier was getting his change and noticed that the contents had been inspected: the toothbrush handle was sticking out of its leather case; the portable radio was lying on top. Bloch turned toward the bellboy, but he had disappeared into the checkroom. The space behind the desk was quite narrow, so Bloch was able to pull the cashier toward him with one hand and then, after a sharp breath, to fake a slap against his face with the other. The cashier flinched, though Bloch had not even touched him. The bellboy in the checkroom kept quiet. Bloch had already left with his briefcase.

He got to the company's personnel office in time, just before lunch, and picked up his papers. Bloch was surprised that they weren't already there ready for him and that some phone calls still had to be made. He asked to use the phone himself and called his ex-wife; when the boy answered the phone and immediately launched into his rote sentence about his mother not being home, Bloch hung up. The papers were ready by now; he put the income-tax form in his briefcase. Before he could ask the woman about his back pay, she was gone. Bloch counted out on the table the money for the phone call and left the building.

The banks were also closed for the lunch break by now. Bloch waited around in a park until he could withdraw the money from his checking account—he'd never had a savings account. Since that wouldn't take him very far, he decided to return the transistor radio, which was practically brand-new. He took the bus to his place in the Second District and also picked up a flash attachment and a razor. At the store they carefully explained that the goods couldn't be returned, only exchanged. Bloch took the bus back to his room and also stuffed into a suitcase two trophies—of course, they were only copies of cups his team had won, one in a tournament and the other in a championship game—and a gold-plated pendant in the shape of two soccer boots.

When no one came to wait on him in the junk shop, he took out his things and simply put them on the counter. Then he felt that he'd put the things on the counter too confidently, as though he'd already sold them, and he grabbed them back off the counter and hid them in his bag; he would put them back on the counter only after he'd been asked to. On the back of a shelf he noticed a china music box with a dancer striking the familiar pose. As usual when he saw a music box, he felt that he'd seen it before. Without haggling, he simply accepted the first offer for his things.

With the lightweight coat he had taken from his room across his arm, he had then gone to the South Station. On his way to the bus stop, he had run into the woman at whose newsstand he usually bought his papers. She was wearing a fur coat while walking her dog. Even though he usually said something to her, staring all the while at her grimy fingernails, when she handed him his paper and his change, here, away from her stand, she seemed not to know him; at least she didn't look up and hadn't answered his greeting.

Since there were only a few trains to the border each day, Bloch spent the time until the next train sleeping in the newsreel theater. At one point it got very bright and the rustling of a curtain opening or closing seemed ominously near. To see whether the curtain had opened or closed, Bloch opened his eyes. Somebody was shining a flashlight in his face. Bloch knocked the light out of the usher's hand and went into the men's room. It was quiet there; daylight filtered in. Bloch stood still for a while.

The usher had followed him and threatened to call the police. Bloch had turned on the faucet, washed his hands, then pushed the button on the electric dryer and held his hands under the warm air until the usher disappeared.

Then Bloch had cleaned his teeth. He had watched in the mirror how he rubbed one hand across his teeth while the other, loosely clenched into a fist, rested oddly against his chest. From inside the movie house he heard the screaming and horseplay of the cartoon figures.

Bloch remembered that an ex-girlfriend of his ran a tavern in some town near the southern border. In the station post office, where they had phone books for the entire country, he couldn't find her number; there were several taverns in the village, and their owners weren't listed; besides, lifting the phone books—they were all hanging in a row with their spines out—soon proved too much for him. "Face down," he suddenly thought. A cop came in and asked for his papers.

Looking down at the passport and then up at Bloch's face, the cop said that the usher had lodged a complaint. After a while Bloch decided to apologize. But the cop had already returned the passport, with the comment that Bloch sure got around a lot. Bloch didn't watch him go but quickly tipped the phone book back

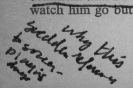

20

into place. Somebody screamed; when Bloch looked up, he saw a Greek workman shouting into the phone in the booth right in front of him. Bloch thought things over and decided to take the bus instead of the train; he turned in his ticket and, after buying a salami sandwich and several newspapers, finally made it to the bus terminal.

The bus was already there, though of course the door was still closed; the drivers stood talking in a group not far away. Bloch sat on a bench; the sun was shining. He ate the salami sandwich but left the papers lying next to him, because he wanted to save them for the long ride.

The luggage racks on both sides of the bus remained quite empty; hardly any of the passengers had luggage. Bloch waited outside so long that the back door was closed. Then he quickly climbed in the front, and the bus started. It stopped again immediately when there was a shout from outside. Bloch did not turn around; a farm woman with a bawling kid had got on. Inside, the kid quieted down; then the bus had taken off.

Bloch noticed that he was sitting on a seat right over a wheel; his feet slipped down off the curve the floor made at that point. He moved to the last row, where, if necessary, he could comfortably look out the back. As he sat down, his eyes met the driver's in the rearview mirror, but there was nothing important about it. The movement Bloch made to stow away the briefcase behind him gave him a chance to look outside. The folding door in the back was rattling loudly.

While the passengers in the other rows of seats all faced the front of the bus, the two rows directly in front of him were turned around to face each other; therefore, most of the passengers seated behind one another stopped talking almost as soon as the bus started, but those in front of him started talking again almost immediately. Bloch found the voices of the people nice; it relaxed him to be able to listen.

21

After a while—the bus was now on the road leading to the highway—a woman sitting next to him showed him that he had dropped some change. "Is that your money?" she asked as she fished a single coin out from between the seat and the backrest. Another coin, an American penny, lay on the seat between them. Bloch took the coins, explaining that he'd probably lost them when he'd turned around. But since the woman had not noticed that he had turned around, she began to ask questions and Bloch went on answering; gradually, although the way they were sitting made it uncomfortable, they began to talk to each other a little.

Between talking and listening, Bloch did not put the change away. The coins had become warm in his hand, as if they had been pushed toward him from a movie box office. The coins were so dirty, he said, because they had been used a little earlier for the coin toss during a soccer game. "I don't understand those things," the woman said. Bloch hastily opened his newspaper. "Heads or tails," she went on, so that Bloch had to close the paper again. Earlier, when he had been in the seat over the wheel, the loop inside his coat collar, which had hung over a hook next to him, had been ripped off when he had abruptly sat down on the dangling coattails. With his coat on his knees, Bloch sat defenseless next to the woman.

The road was bumpier now. Because the back door did not fit tightly, Bloch saw light from outside the bus flash intermittently into the interior through the slit. Without looking at the slit, he was aware of the light flickering over his paper. He read line by line. Then he looked up and watched the passengers up front. The farther away they sat, the nicer it was to look at them. Ater a while he noticed that the flickering had stopped inside. Outside, it had grown dark.

Bloch, who was not used to noticing so many details, had a headache, perhaps also because of the smell from the many newspapers he had with him. Luckily, the bus stopped in a district town, where supper was served to the passengers at a rest stop. While Bloch took a stroll, he heard the cigarette machine crashing again and again in the barroom.

He noticed a lighted phone booth in front of the restaurant. His ears still hummed from the drone of the bus, so the crunch of the gravel by the phone booth felt good. He tossed the newspapers into a trash basket next to the booth and closed himself in. "I make a good target." Once in a movie he had heard somebody standing by a window at night say that.

Nobody answered. Out in the open, Bloch, in the shadow of the phone booth, heard the clanging of the pinball machines through the drawn curtains of the rest stop. When he came into the bar, it turned out to be almost empty; most of the passengers had already gone outside. Bloch drank a beer standing up and went out into the hall: some people were already in the bus, others stood by the door talking to the driver, and more stood farther away in the dark with their backs to the bus. Bloch, who was getting sick of such observations, wiped his hand across his mouth. Why didn't he just look away? He looked away and saw passengers in the hall coming from the rest rooms with their children. When he had wiped his mouth, his hand had smelled of the metal grips on the armrest. "That can't be true," Bloch thought. The driver had got into the bus and, to signal that everybody else should get aboard, had started the engine. "As if you couldn't understand him without that," Bloch thought. As they drove off, sparks from the cigarettes they hastily threw out the window showered the road.

Nobody sat next to him now. Bloch retreated into the corner and put his legs up on the seat. He untied his shoes, leaned against the side window, and looked over at the window on the other side. He held his hands behind his neck, pushed a crumb off the seat with his foot, pressed his arms against his ears, and looked at his elbows in front of him. He pushed the insides of his elbows against his temples, sniffed at his shirtsleeves, rubbed his chin against his upper arm, laid back his head, and looked up at the ceiling lights. There was no end to it any more. The only thing he could think of was to sit up.

The shadows of the trees behind the guard rails circled around the trees themselves. The wipers that lay on the windshield did not point in exactly the same direction. The ticket tray next to the driver seemed open. Something like a glove lay in the center aisle of the bus. Cows were sleeping in the meadows next to the road. It was no use denying any of that.

Gradually more and more passengers got off at their stops. They stood next to the driver until he let them out in front. When the bus stood still, Bloch heard the canvas fluttering on the roof. Then the bus stopped again, and he heard welcoming shouts outside in the dark. Farther on, he recognized a railroad crossing without gates.

Just before midnight the bus stopped at the border town. Bloch immediately took a room at the inn by the bus stop. He asked the girl who showed him upstairs about his girlfriend, whose first name—Hertha—was all he knew. She was able to give him the information: his girlfriend had rented a tavern not far from town. In the room Bloch asked the girl, who was still in the doorway, about the meaning of all that noise. "Some of the guys are still bowling," the girl answered, and left. Without looking around, Bloch undressed, washed his hands, and lay down on the bed. The rumbling and crashing downstairs went on for quite a while. But Bloch had already fallen asleep.

He did not wake up by himself but must have been roused by something. Everything was quiet. Bloch thought about what might have wakened him; after a while he began to imagine that the sound of a newspaper opening had startled him. Or had it been the creaking of the wardrobe? Maybe a coin had fallen out of his pants, hung carelessly over the chair, and had rolled under the bed. On the wall he noticed an engraving that showed the town at the time of the Turkish wars; the townspeople strolled outside the walls; inside them the bell was hanging in the tower so crookedly that it had to be ringing fiercely. Bloch thought about the sexton being yanked up by the bell rope. He noticed that all the townspeople were walking toward the gate in the wall; one child apparently was stumbling because of the dog slinking between his legs. Even the little auxiliary chapel bell was pictured in such a way that it almost tipped over. Under the bed there had been only a burned-out match. Out in the hall, farther away, a key crunched again in a lock; that must have been what had roused him.

At breakfast Bloch heard that a schoolboy who had trouble walking had been missing for two days. The girl talked about this to the bus driver, who had spent the night at the inn before; as Bloch watched through the window, he drove back in the almost-empty bus. Later the girl also left, so that Bloch sat alone in the dining room a while. He piled the newspapers on the chair next to him; he read that the missing boy was not almost crippled but had trouble talking. As soon as she came back, the girl, as though she owed him an explanation, told him that the vacuum cleaner was running upstairs. Bloch didn't know what to say to that. Then empty beer bottles clinked in the crates being carried across the yard outside. The voices of the delivery men in the hall sounded to Bloch as though they came from the TV set next door. The girl had told him that the innkeeper's mother sat in that room and watched the daytime shows.

Later on Bloch bought himself a shirt, some underwear, and several pairs of socks in a general store. The salesgirl, who had taken her time coming out of the rather dim storage room, seemed not to under-

perception of them

stand Bloch, who was using complete sentences in speaking to her; only when he told her word for word the names of the things he wanted did she start to move around again. As she opened the cash-register drawer, she had said that some rubber boots had also just arrived; and as she was handing him his things in a plastic shopping bag, she had asked whether he needed anything else: handkerchiefs? a tie? a wool sweater? At the inn Bloch had changed and stuffed his dirty clothes in the plastic bag. Almost nobody was around in the yard outside and on his way out of town. At a construction site a cement mixer was just being turned off; it was so quiet now that his own steps sounded almost indecent to Bloch. He had stopped and looked at the tarpaulins covering the lumber piles outside a sawmill as if there were something else to hear besides the mumbling of the sawmill workers, who were probably sitting behind the lumber piles during their coffee break.

He had learned that the tavern, along with a couple of farmhouses and the customs shed, stood at a spot where the paved street curved back toward town; a road between the houses, which had once also been paved but recently was covered only with gravel, branched off from the street and then, just before the border, turned into a dirt path. The border crossing was closed. Actually Bloch had not even asked about the border crossing.

He saw a hawk circling over a field. When the hawk hovered at one spot and then dived down, Bloch realized that he had not been watching the hawk fluttering and diving but the spot in the field for which the bird would presumably head; the hawk had caught itself in its dive and risen again.

It was also odd that, while he was walking past the cornfield, Bloch did not look straight down the rows that ran through to the end of the field but saw only an impenetrable thicket of stalks, leaves, and cobs, with here and there some naked kernels showing as well. As well? The brook which the street crossed at that point roared quite loudly, and Bloch stopped.

At the tavern he found a waitress just scrubbing the floor. Bloch asked for the landlady. "She's still asleep," the waitress said. Standing up, Bloch ordered a beer. The waitress lifted a chair off the table. Bloch took the second chair off the table and sat down.

The waitress went behind the bar. Bloch put his hands on the table. The waitress bent down and opened the bottle. Bloch pushed the ashtray aside. The waitress took a cardboard coaster from another table as she passed it. Bloch pushed his chair back. The waitress took the glass, which had been slipped over the neck of the bottle, off the bottle, set the coaster on the table, put the glass on the coaster, tipped the beer into the glass, put the bottle on the table, and went away. It was starting up again. Bloch did not know what to do any more.

Finally he noticed a drop running down the outside of the glass and, on the wall, a clock whose hands were two matches; one match was broken off and served as the hour hand. He had not watched the descending drop but the spot on the coaster that the drop might hit.

The waitress, who by now was rubbing paste wax into the floor, asked if he knew the landlady. Bloch nodded, but only when the waitress looked up did he say yes.

A little girl ran in without closing the door. The waitress sent her back to the entryway, where she scraped her boots and, after a second reminder, shut the door. "The landlady's kid," explained the waitress, who took the child into the kitchen at once. When she came back, she said that a few days ago a man had wanted to see the landlady. "He claimed that he was supposed to dig a well. She wanted to send him away immediately, but he wouldn't let up until she showed him the cellar, and down there he grabbed the spade right away, so that she had to go for help to get him to go away, and she . . ." Bloch barely managed to interrupt her. "The kid has been scared ever since that the well-digger might show up again." But in the meantime a customs guard came in and had a drink at the bar.

Was the missing schoolboy back home again? the waitress asked. The customs guard answered, "No, he hasn't been found yet."

"Well, he hasn't been gone for even two days yet," the waitress said. The guard replied, "But the nights are beginning to get quite chilly now."

"Anyway, he's warmly dressed," said the waitress. The guard agreed that, yes, he was dressed warmly.

"He can't be far," he added. He couldn't have got very far, the waitress repeated. Bloch noticed a damaged set of antlers over the juke box. The waitress explained that it came from a stag that had wandered into the minefield.

From the kitchen he heard sounds that, as he listened, turned into voices. The waitress shouted through the closed door. The landlady answered from the kitchen. They talked to each other like that a while. Then, halfway through an answer, the landlady came in. Bloch said hello.

She sat down at his table, not next to but across from him; she put her hands on her knees under the table. Through the open door Bloch heard the refrigerator humming in the kitchen. The child sat next to it, eating a sandwich. The landlady looked at him as if she hadn't seen him for too long. "I haven't seen you for a long time," she said. Bloch told her a story about his visit here. Through the door, quite far away, he saw the little girl sitting in the kitchen. The landlady put her hands on the table and turned the palms over and back. The waitress brought the drink Bloch had ordered for her. Which "her?" In the kitchen,

which was now empty, the refrigerator rattled.
Through the door Bloch looked at the apple parings
lying on the kitchen table. Under the table there was
a bowl heaped full of apples; a few apples had rolled
off and were scattered around on the floor. A pair
of work pants hung on a nail in the doorframe. The
landlady had pushed the ashtray between herself and
Bloch. Bloch put the bottle to one side, but she put
the match box in front of her and set the glass down
next to it. Finally Bloch pushed his glass and the
bottle to the right of them. Hertha laughed.

The little girl had come back and was leaning against
the back of the landlady's chair. She was sent to get
wood for the kitchen, but when she opened the door
with only one hand, she dropped the logs. The waitress
picked up the wood and carried it into the kitchen
while the child went back to leaning against the back
of the landlady's chair. It seemed to Bloch as if these
proceedings could be used against him.

Somebody tapped against the window from outside
but disappeared immediately. The estate owner's son,
the landlady said. Then some children walked by outside, and one of them darted up and pressed his face
against the glass and ran away again. "School's out,"
she said. After that it got darker inside because a
furniture van had pulled up outside. "There's my furniture," said the landlady. Bloch was relieved that
he could get up and help bring in the furniture.

When they were carrying the wardrobe, one of its
doors swung open. Bloch kicked the door shut again.
When the wardrobe was set down in the bedroom, the
door opened again. One of the movers handed Bloch
the key, and Bloch turned it in the lock. But he wasn't
the proprietor, Bloch said. Gradually, when he said
something new, he himself reappeared in what he said.
The landlady asked him to stay for lunch. Bloch, who
had planned to stay at her place anyway, refused. But
he'd come back this evening. Hertha, who was talking

from the room with the furniture, spoke while he was leaving; anyway, it seemed to him that he had heard her call. He stepped back into the barroom, but all he could see through the doors standing open everywhere was the waitress at the stove in the kitchen while the landlady was putting clothes into the wardrobe in the bedroom and the child was doing her homework at a table in the barroom. Walking out, he had probably confused the water boiling over on the stove with a shout.

Even though the window was open, it was impossible to see into the customs shed; the room was too dark from the outside. Still, somebody must have seen Bloch from the inside; he understood this because he himself held his breath as he walked past. Was it possible that nobody was in the room even though the window was wide open? Why "even though"? Was it possible that nobody was in the room because the window was wide open? Bloch looked back: a beer bottle had even been taken off the windowsill so that they could have a better look at him. He heard a sound like a bottle rolling under a sofa. On the other hand, it was not likely that the customs shed had a sofa. Only when he had gone farther on did it become clear to him that a radio had been turned on in the room. Bloch went back along the wide curve the street made toward the town. At one point he started to run with relief because the street led back to town so openly and simply.

He wandered among the houses for a while. At a café he chose a few records after the owner had turned on the juke box; he had walked out even before all the records had played. Outside he heard the owner unplug the machine. On the benches sat schoolchildren waiting for the bus.

He stopped in front of a fruit stand but stood so far away from it that the owner behind the stand could not speak to him. She looked at him and waited for him to move a step closer. A child who was standing in front of him said something, but the woman did not answer. When a policeman who had come up from behind got close enough to the fruit stand, she spoke to him immediately.

There were no phone booths in the town. Bloch tried to call a friend from the post office. He waited on a bench near the switchboard, but the call did not go through. At that time of day the circuits were busy, he was told. He swore at the postmistress and walked out.

When, outside the town, he passed the public swimming pool, he saw two policemen on bicycles coming toward him. "With capes," he thought. In fact, when the policemen stopped in front of him, they really were wearing capes; and when they got off their bicycles they did not even take the clips off their trousers. Again it seemed to Bloch as if he were watching a music box; as though he had seen all this before. He had not let go of the door in the fence that led to the pool even though it was closed. "The pool is closed," Bloch said.

The policemen, who made the usual remarks, nevertheless seemed to mean something entirely different by them; at least they purposely mispronounced phrases like "got to remember" and "take off" as "goats you remember" and "take-off" and, just as purposely, let their tongues slide over others, saying "whitewash?" instead of "why watch?" and "closed, or" instead of "close door." For what would be the point of their telling him about the goats that, he should remember, had once, when the door had been left open, forced their way into the pool, which hadn't even been officially opened yet, and had soiled everything, even the walls of the restaurant, so that the rooms had to be whitewashed all over again and it wasn't ready on time, which was why Bloch should keep the door closed and stay on the sidewalk? As if to show their contempt for him, the policemen also failed to give their customary

salutes when they drove away—or, anyway, only
hinted at them, as though they wanted to tell Bloch
something by it. They did not look back over their
shoulders. To show that he had nothing to hide, Bloch
stayed by the fence and went on looking in at the
empty pool. "Like I was in an open wardrobe I wanted
to take something out of," Bloch thought. He could not
remember now what he had gone to the public pool
for. Besides, it was getting dark; the lights were already shining on the signs outside the public buildings
at the edge of town. Bloch walked back into town.
When two girls ran past him toward the railroad
station, he called after them. Running, they turned
around and shouted back. Bloch was hungry. He ate
at the inn while the TV set could be heard from the
next room. Later he took a glass in there and watched
until the test pattern came on at the end of the
program. He asked for his key and went upstairs. Half
asleep, he thought he heard a car driving up outside
with its headlights turned off. He asked himself why he
happened to think of a darkened car; he must have
fallen asleep before he figured it out.

Bloch was wakened by a banging and wheezing on
the street, trash cans being dumped into the garbage
truck; but when he looked out, he saw that the folding
door of the bus that was just leaving had closed and,
farther away, that milk cans were being set on the
loading ramp of the dairy. There weren't any garbage
trucks out here in the country; the muddle was starting
all over again.

Bloch saw the girl in the doorway with a pile of
towels on her arm and a flashlight on top of it; even
before he could call attention to himself, she was back
out in the hall. Only after the door was closed did she
excuse herself, but Bloch did not understand her because at the same time he was shouting something to
her. He followed her out into the hall; she was already
in another room. Back in his room, Bloch locked the

door, giving the key two emphatic turns. Later he followed the girl, who by then had moved several rooms farther on, and explained that it had been a misunderstanding. While putting a towel on the sink, the girl answered yes, it was a misunderstanding; before, from far away, she must have mistaken the bus driver on the stairs for him, so she had started into his room thinking that he had already gone downstairs. Bloch, who was standing in the open door, said that that was not what he had meant. But she had just turned on the faucet, so that she asked him to repeat the sentence. Then Bloch answered that there were far too many wardrobes and chests and drawers in the rooms. The girl answered yes, and as far as that went, there were far too few people working at the inn, as the mistaken identification, which could be blamed on her exhaustion, just went to prove. That was not what he meant by his remark about wardrobes, answered Bloch, it was just that you couldn't move around easily in the rooms. The girl asked what he meant by that. Bloch did not answer. She replied to his silence by bunching up the dirty towel—or, rather, Bloch assumed that her bunching up of the towel was a response to his silence. She let the towel drop into the basket; again Bloch did not answer, which made her, so he believed, open the curtains, so that he quickly stepped back into the dim hallway. "That's not what I meant to say," the girl called. She came into the hall after him, but then Bloch followed her while she distributed the towels in the other rooms. At a bend in the hallway they came upon a pile of used bedsheets lying on the floor. When Bloch swerved, a soap box fell from the top of the girl's pile of towels. Did she need a flashlight on the way home? asked Bloch. She had a boyfriend, answered the girl, who was straightening up with a flushed face. Did the inn also have rooms with double doors between them? asked Bloch. "My boyfriend is a carpenter, after all," answered the girl. He'd seen a

33

Why can't the people in this book have normal conversations

movie where a hotel thief got caught between such double doors, Bloch said. "Nothing's ever been taken from our rooms!" said the girl.

Downstairs in the dining room he read that a small American coin had been found beside the cashier, a nickel. The cashier's friends had never seen her with an American soldier, nor were there many American tourists in the country at this time. Furthermore, scribbles had been discovered in the margin of a newspaper, the kind of doodles someone might make while talking. The scribbling plainly was not the girl's; investigations were being made to determine whether it might reveal anything about her visitor.

The innkeeper came to the table and put the registration form in front of him; he said that it had been lying in Bloch's room all the time. Bloch filled out the form. The innkeeper stood off a little and watched him. Just then the chain saw in the sawmill outside struck wood. To Bloch the noise sounded like something forbidden.

Instead of just taking the form behind the bar, which would have been natural, the innkeeper took it into the next room and, as Bloch saw, spoke to his mother; then, instead of coming right back out again, as might be expected since the door had been left open, he went on talking and finally closed the door. Instead of the innkeeper, the old woman came out. The innkeeper did not come out after her but stayed in the room and pulled open the curtains, and then, instead of turning off the TV, he turned on the fan.

The girl now came into the dining room from the other side with a vacuum cleaner. Bloch fully expected to see her casually step out on the street with the machine; instead, she plugged it into the socket and then pushed it back and forth under the tables and chairs. And when the innkeeper closed the curtains in the next room again, and his mother went back into the room, and, finally, the innkeeper turned

34

off the fan, it seemed to Bloch as if everything was falling back into place.

He asked the innkeeper if the local people read many newspapers. "Only the weeklies and magazines," the innkeeper answered. Bloch, who was asking this while leaving, had pinched his arm between the door handle and the door because he was pushing the handle down with his elbow. "That's what you get for that!" the girl shouted after him. Bloch could still hear the innkeeper asking what she meant.

He wrote a few postcards but did not mail them right away. Later, outside the town, when he wanted to stuff them into a mailbox fastened to a fence, he noticed that the mailbox would not be emptied again until tomorrow. Ever since his team, while touring South America, had had to send postcards with every member's signature to the newspapers, Bloch was in the habit, when he was on the road, of writing postcards.

A class of schoolchildren came by; the children were singing and Bloch dropped in the cards. The empty mailbox resounded as they fell into it. But the mailbox was so tiny that nothing could resound in there. Anyway, Bloch had walked away immediately. He walked cross-country for a while. The feeling that a ball heavy with rain was dropping on his head let up. Near the border the woods started. He turned back when he recognized the first watchtower on the other side of the cleared no-man's-land. At the edge of the woods he sat down on a tree trunk. He got up again immediately. Then he sat down again and counted his money. He looked up. The landscape, even though it was flat, curved toward him so firmly that it seemed to dislodge him. He was here at the edge of the woods, the electric power shed was over there, the milk stand was over there, a field was over there, a few people were over there, he was there at the edge of the woods. He sat as still as he could until he was not aware of himself any more. Later he realized that the people in the field were policemen with dogs.

Next to a blackberry bush, half hidden beneath the blackberries, Bloch found a child's bicycle. He stood it upright. The seat was screwed up quite high, as though for an adult. A few blackberry thorns were stuck in the tires, though no air had escaped. The wheel was blocked by a fir branch that had been caught in the spokes. Bloch tugged at the branch. Then he dropped the bicycle, feeling that the policemen might, from far away, see the sun's reflections off the casing of the headlight. But the policemen and their dogs had walked on.

Bloch looked after the figures running down an embankment; the dog's tags and the walkie-talkies glinted. Did the glinting mean anything? Gradually it lost its significance: the headlight casings of cars flashed where the street curved farther away, a splinter from a pocket mirror sparkled next to Bloch, and then the path glimmered with mica gravel. The gravel slid away under the tires when Bloch got on the bicycle.

He rode a little way. Finally he leaned the bicycle against the power shed and went on on foot.

He read the movie ad posted on the milk stand; the other posters under it were tattered. Bloch walked on and saw a boy who had hiccups standing in a farmyard. He saw wasps flying around in an orchard. At a wayside crucifix there were rotting flowers in tin cans. In the grass next to the street lay empty cigarette boxes. Next to the closed window he saw hooks dangling from the shutters. As he walked by an open window, he smelled something decayed. At the tavern the landlady told him that somebody in the house across the street had died yesterday.

When Bloch wanted to join her in the kitchen, she met him at the door and walked ahead of him into the barroom. Bloch passed her and walked toward a table in the corner, but she had already sat down at a table near the door. When Bloch wanted to talk, she had started in. He wanted to show her that the waitress was wearing orthopedic shoes, but the landlady was already pointing to the street, where a policeman was walking past, pushing a child's bicycle. "That's the dumb kid's bike," she said.

The waitress had joined them, with a magazine in her hand; they all looked out the window together. Bloch asked whether the well-digger had reported back. The landlady, who had understood only the words "reported back," started to talk about soldiers. Bloch said "come back" instead, and the landlady talked about the mute schoolboy. "He couldn't even call for help," the waitress said, or rather read from a caption in the magazine. The landlady talked about a movie where some hobnails had been mixed into cake dough. Bloch asked whether the guards on the watchtowers had field glasses; anyway, something was glinting up there. "You can't even see the watchtowers from here," answered one of the two women. Bloch saw that they had flour on their faces from making cake, particularly on their eyebrows and at their hairlines.

He walked out into the yard, but when nobody came after him, he went back inside. He stood next to the juke box, leaving a little room beside him. The waitress, who was now sitting behind the bar, had broken a glass. The landlady had come out of the kitchen at the sound but, instead of looking at the waitress, had looked at him. Bloch turned down the volume control on the back of the juke box. Then, while the landlady was still in the doorway, he turned the volume up again. The landlady walked in front of him through the barroom as though she were pacing it off. Bloch asked her how much rent the estate owner charged for the tavern. At this question Hertha stopped short. The waitress swept the broken glass into a dustpan. Bloch walked toward Hertha, the landlady walked past him into the kitchen. Bloch went in after her.

Since a cat was lying in the second chair, Bloch stood right next to her. She was talking about the estate owner's son, who was her boyfriend. Bloch stood next to the window and questioned her about him. She explained what the estate owner's son did. Without being asked, she went on talking. At the edge of the stove Bloch noticed a second mason jar. Now and then he said, Yes? He noticed a second ruler in the work pants on the doorframe. He interrupted her to ask what number she started counting at. She hesitated, even stopped coring the apple. Bloch said that recently he had noticed that he himself was in the habit of starting to count only at the number 2; this morning, for instance, he'd almost been run down by a car when he was crossing the street because he thought he had enough time until the second car; he'd simply not counted the first one. The landlady answered with a commonplace remark.

Bloch walked over to the chair and lifted it from behind so that the cat jumped down. He sat down but pushed the chair away from the table. In doing this, he bumped against a serving table, and a beer bottle fell down and rolled under the kitchen sofa. Why was he always sitting down, getting up, going out, standing around, coming back in? asked the landlady. Was he doing it to tease her? Instead of answering, Bloch read her a joke from the newspaper under the apple parings. Since from where he sat the paper was upside down, he read so haltingly that the landlady, leaning forward, took over the job. Outside, the waitress laughed. Inside, something fell on the floor in the bedroom. No second sound followed. Bloch, who had not heard a sound the first time either, wanted to go and see; but the landlady explained that earlier she had heard the little girl waking up; she had just go out of bed and would probably come in any minute now and ask for a piece of cake. But Bloch then actually heard a sound like whimpering. It turned out that the child had fallen out of bed in her sleep and couldn't figure out where she was on the floor next to the bed. In the kitchen the girl said there were some flies under her pillow. The landlady explained to Bloch that the neighbor's children, who, because of the death in their family, were sleeping over here for the duration of the wake, passed the time by shooting the rubber rings from mason jars at flies on the wall; in the evening they put the flies that had fallen on the floor under the pillow.

After a few things had been pressed into the girl's hand—the first one or two she dropped again—she gradually calmed down. Bloch saw the waitress come out of the bedroom with her hand cupped and toss the flies into the garbage can. It wasn't his fault, he said. He saw the baker's truck stop in front of the neighbor's house and the driver put two loaves on the doorstep, the dark loaf on the bottom, the white one on top. The landlady sent the little girl to meet the driver at the door; Bloch heard the waitress running water over her hand at the bar; lately he was always apologizing, the landlady said. Really? asked Bloch. Just then the little girl came into the kitchen with two loaves. He also saw the waitress wiping her hands on her apron as she walked toward a customer. What did he want to drink? Who? Nothing right now, was the answer. The child had closed the door to the barroom.

"Now we're alone," said Hertha. Bloch looked at the kid standing by the window looking at the neighbor's house. "That doesn't count," she said. Bloch took this as a hint that she had something to tell him, but then he realized that what she had meant was that he should start talking. Bloch could not think of anything. He said something obscene. She immedi-

39

ately sent the child out of the room. He put his hand next to hers. She told him off, softly. Roughly, he grabbed her arm but let go again immediately. Outside on the street he bumped into the kid, who was poking a piece of straw at the plaster wall of the house.

He looked through the open window into the neighbor's house. On a trestle table he saw the corpse; next to it stood the coffin. A woman sat on a stool in the corner and dunked some bread into a cider jar; a young man lay asleep on his back on a bench behind the table; a cat lay on his stomach.

As Bloch came into the house, he almost fell over a log in the hallway. The woman came to the door; he stepped inside and talked with her. The young man had sat up but did not say anything; the cat had run out. "He had to keep watch all night," the woman said. In the morning she had found him quite drunk. She turned around to the dead man and said a prayer. Now and then she changed the water in the flowers. "It happened very quickly," she said. "We had to wake up our little boy so that he could run into town." But then the kid hadn't even been able to tell the priest what had happened, and so the bells hadn't been tolled. Bloch realized that the room was being heated; after a while the wood in the stove had collapsed. "Go get some more wood," said the woman. The young man came back with several logs, some under each arm, which he dropped next to the stove so hard that the dust flew.

He sat down at the table, and the woman threw the logs into the stove. "We already lost one of our kids; he had pumpkins thrown at him," she said. Two old women came by the window and called in. On the windowsill Bloch noticed a black purse. It had just been bought; the tissue paper stuffing had not even been taken out yet. "All of a sudden he gave a loud snort and died," the woman said.

Bloch could see into the barroom of the tavern across the street; the sun, which was quite low by now, shone in so deeply that the bottom part of the room, especially the surfaces of the freshly waxed floorboards and the legs of the chairs, tables, and people, glowed as though of themselves. In the kitchen he saw the estate owner's son, who, leaning against the door with his arms across his chest, was talking to the landlady, who, presumably, was still sitting farther away at the table. The deeper the sun sank, the deeper and more remote these pictures seemed to Bloch. He could not look away; only the children running back and forth on the street swept away the impression. A child came in with a bunch of flowers. The woman put the flowers in a tumbler and set the glass at the foot of the trestle. The child just stood there. After a while the woman handed her a coin and she went out.

Bloch heard a noise as if somebody had broken through the floorboards. But it was just the logs in the stove collapsing again. As soon as Bloch had stopped talking to the woman, the young man had stretched out on the bench and fallen back to sleep. Later several women came and said their beads. Somebody wiped the chalk marks off the blackboard outside the grocery store and wrote instead: oranges, caramels, sardines. The conversation in the room was soft; the children outside were making a lot of noise. A bat had caught itself in the curtain; roused by the squeaking, the young man had leaped up and rushed toward it instantly, but the bat had already flown off.

It was the kind of dusk when no one felt like turning on the lights. Only the barroom of the tavern across the street was faintly lit by the light of the juke box; but no records were playing. The kitchen was already dark. Bloch was invited to stay for supper and ate at the table with the others.

Although the window was now closed, gnats flew around the room. A child was sent to the tavern to get coasters; they were then laid over the glasses so the gnats wouldn't fall in. One woman remarked that she had lost the pendant from her necklace. Everybody started to look for it. Bloch stayed at the table. After a while he was seized by a need to be the one who found it, and he joined the others. When the pendant was not to be found in the room, they went on looking for it in the hall. A shovel fell over—or, rather, Bloch caught it just before it fell over completely. The young man was shining the flashlight, the woman came with a kerosene lamp. Bloch asked for the flashlight and went out in the street. Bent over, he moved around in the gravel, but nobody came out after him. He heard somebody shout in the hall that the pendant had been found. Bloch refused to believe it and went on looking. Then he heard that they were starting to pray again behind the window. He put the flashlight on the outside of the windowsill and went away.

Back in town, Bloch sat down in a café and looked on during a card game. He started to argue with the player he was sitting behind. The other players told Bloch to get lost. Bloch went into the back room. A slide lecture was going on there. Bloch watched for a while. It was a lecture on missionary hospitals in Southeast Asia. Bloch, who was interrupting loudly, started to argue with people again. He turned around and walked out.

He thought about going back inside, but he could not think of anything to say if he did. He went to the second café. There he asked to have the fan turned off. What's more, the lights were much too dim, he said. When the waitress sat down with him, he soon pretended that he wanted to put his arm around her; she realized that he was only pretending and leaned back even before he could make it clear to her that he was just pretending. Bloch wanted to justify himself by really putting his arm around the waitress,

42

but she had already stood up. When Bloch wanted to get up, the waitress walked away. Now Bloch should have pretended that he wanted to follow her. But he had had enough, and he left the café.

In his room at the inn he woke up just before dawn. All at once, everything around him was unbearable. He wondered whether he had wakened just because at a certain moment, shortly before dawn, everything all at once became unbearable. The mattress he was lying on had caved in, the wardrobes and bureaus stood far away against the walls, the ceiling overhead was unbearably high. It was so quiet in the half-dark room, out in the hall, and especially out on the street, that Bloch could not stand it any longer. A fierce nausea gripped him. He immediately vomited into the sink. He vomited for a while, with no relief. He lay back down on the bed. He was not dizzy; on the contrary, he saw everything with excruciating stability. It did not help to lean out the window and look along the street. A tarpaulin lay motionless over a parked car. Inside the room he noticed the two water pipes along the wall; they ran parallel to each other, cut off above by the ceiling and below by the floor. Everything he saw was cut off in the most unbearable way. The nausea did not so much elate him as depress him even more. It seemed as though a crowbar had pried him away from what he saw—or, rather, as though the things around him had all been pulled away from him. The wardrobe, the sink, the suitcase, the door: only now did he realize that he, as if compelled, was thinking of the word for each thing. Each glimpse of a thing was immediately followed by its word. The chair, the clothes hangers, the key. It had become so quiet earlier that no noises could distract him now; and because it had grown, on the one hand, so light that he could see the things all around him and, on the other hand, so quiet that no sound could distract him from them, he had seen the things as though they were, at the same time, advertisements for themselves. In fact, his nausea was the same kind of nausea that had sometimes been brought on by certain jingles, pop songs, or national anthems that he felt compelled to repeat word for word or hum to himself until he fell asleep. He held his breath as though he had hiccups. When he took another breath, it came back. He held his breath again. After a while this began to help, and he fell asleep.

The next morning he could not imagine any of that any more. The dining room had been straightened up, and a tax official walked around while the innkeeper told him the prices of everything. The innkeeper showed the official the receipt for a coffeemaker and the freezer; the fact that the two men were discussing prices made his state during the night seem all the more ridiculous to Bloch. He had put the newspapers aside after quickly leafing through them and was now listening only to the tax official, who was arguing with the innkeeper about an ice-cream freezer. The innkeeper's mother and the girl joined them; all of them talked at once. Bloch broke in to ask what the furnishings for one room in the inn might cost. The innkeeper answered that he had bought the furniture quite cheap from nearby farmers who had either moved away or left the country altogether. He told Bloch a price. Bloch wanted that price broken down item by item. The innkeeper asked the girl for the inventory list for a room and gave the price he had paid for each item as well as the price he thought he could get for a chest or a wardrobe. The tax official, who had been taking notes up to that point, stopped writing and asked the girl for a glass of wine. Bloch, satisfied, was ready to leave. The tax official explained that whenever he saw an item, say a washing machine, he always asked the price immediately, and then when he saw the item again, say a washing machine of the same make, he would recognize it not by its external features, that is, a washing machine by the knobs which regulated the wash cycle, but by what the item, say a washing machine, had cost when he first saw it, that is, by its price. The price, of course, he remembered precisely, and that way he could recognize almost any item. And what if the item was worthless, asked Bloch. He had nothing to do with items that had no market value, the tax official replied, at least not in his work.

The mute schoolboy still had not been found. Though the bicycle had been impounded and the surrounding area was being searched, the shot that might have been the signal that one of the policemen had come across something had not been fired. Anyway, in the barbershop where Bloch had gone, the noise of the hair dryer behind the screen was so loud that he could not hear anything from outside. He asked to have the hair at the back of his neck clipped. While the barber was washing his hands, the girl brushed off Bloch's collar. Now the hair dryer was turned off and he heard paper rustling behind the screen. There was a bang. But it was only a curler that had fallen into a metal pan behind the screen.

Bloch asked the girl if she went home for lunch. The girl answered that she didn't live in town, she came every morning by train; for lunch she went to a café or stayed with the other girl here in the shop. Bloch asked whether she bought a round-trip ticket every day. The girl told him that she was commuting on a weekly ticket. "How much is a weekly ticket?" Bloch asked immediately. But before the girl could answer, he said that it was none of his business. Nevertheless, the girl told him the price. From behind the screen the other girl said, "Why are you asking if it's none of your business?" Bloch, who was already standing up waiting for his change, read the price list next to the mirror, and went out.

He noticed that he had an odd compulsion to find
out the price of everything. He was actually relieved to
see the prices of newly arrived goods marked on the
window of a grocery store. On a fruit display in front
of the store a price tag had fallen over. He set it right.
The movement was enough to bring somebody out to
ask if he wanted to buy something. At another store
a rocking chair had been covered by a long dress. A
tag with a pin stuck through it lay on the chair next to
the dress. Bloch was long undecided whether the price
was for the chair or for the dress; one or the other
must not be for sale. He stood so long in front of them
that, again, somebody came out and questioned him.
He questioned back. He was told that the price tag
with the pin must have fallen off the dress; it was
clear, wasn't it, that the tag couldn't have anything to
do with the chair; naturally, that was private property.
He had just wanted to ask, said Bloch, moving on. The
other person called after him to tell him where he
could buy that kind of rocking chair. In the café
Bloch asked the price of the juke box. It didn't belong
to him, said the owner, he just leased it. That's not
what he meant, Bloch answered, he just wanted to
know the price. Not until the owner had told him the
price was Bloch satisfied. But he wasn't sure, the
owner said. Bloch now began to ask about other things
in the café that the owner had to know the prices of
because they were his. The owner then talked about
the public swimming pool, which had cost much more
than the original estimate. "How much more?" Bloch
asked. The owner didn't know. Bloch became impatient. "And what was the estimate?" asked Bloch.
Again the owner didn't have the answer. Anyway, last
spring a corpse had been found in one of the changing
booths; it must have been lying there all winter. The
head was stuck in a plastic shopping bag. The dead
man had been a gypsy. Some gypsies had settled in
this region; they'd built themselves little huts at the

edge of the woods with the reparation money they'd
received for being confined in the concentration camps.
"It's supposed to be very clean inside," the owner
said. The policemen who had questioned the inhabitants during their search for the missing boy had
been surprised by the freshly scrubbed floors and the
general neatness of the rooms everywhere. But it was
just that neatness, the owner went on, that actually fed
their suspicions, for the gypsies certainly wouldn't have
scrubbed the floors without good reason. Bloch didn't
let up and asked whether the reparations had been
enough to cover the costs of building the huts. The
owner couldn't say what the reparations had amounted
to. "Building materials and labor were still cheap in
those days," the owner said. Curiously, Bloch turned
over the sales slip that was stuck to the bottom of the
beer glass. "Is this worth anything?" he asked, reaching into his pocket and setting a stone on the table.
Without picking up the stone, the owner answered that
you could find stones like that at every step around
here. Bloch said nothing. Then the owner picked up
the stone, let it roll around the hollow of his hand, and
set it back on the table. Finished! Bloch promptly put
the stone away.

In the doorway he met the two girls from the
barbershop. He invited them to go with him to the
other café. The second girl said that the juke box there
didn't have any records. Bloch asked what she meant.
She told him that the records in the juke box were no
good. Bloch went ahead and they followed after him.
They ordered something to drink and unwrapped their
sandwiches. Bloch leaned forward and talked with
them. They showed him their I.D. cards. When he
touched the plastic covers, his hands immediately
began to sweat. They asked him if he was a soldier.
The second one had a date that night with a traveling
salesman; but they'd make it a foursome because there
was nothing to talk about when there were only two

of you. "When there are four of you, somebody will say something, then somebody else. You can tell each other jokes." Bloch did not know what to answer. In the next room a baby was crawling on the floor. A dog was bounding around the child and licking its face. The telephone on the counter rang; as long as it was ringing, Bloch stopped listening to the conversation. Soldiers mostly didn't have any money, one of the girls said. Bloch did not answer. When he looked at their hands, they explained that their fingernails were so black because of the hairsetting lotion. "It doesn't help to polish them, the rims always stay black." Bloch looked up. "We buy all our dresses ready-made." "We do each other's hair." "In the summer it's usually getting light by the time we finally get home." "I prefer the slow dances." "On the trip home we don't joke around as much any more, then we forget about talking." She took everything too seriously, the first girl said. Yesterday on the way to the train station she had even looked in the orchard for the missing schoolboy. Instead of handing back their I.D. cards, Bloch just put them down on the table, as if it hadn't been right for him to look at them. He watched the dampness of his fingerprints evaporate from the plastic. When they asked him what he did, he told them that he had been a soccer goalie. He explained that goal-keepers could keep on playing longer than fielders. "Zamora was already quite old," said Bloch. In answer, they talked about the soccer players they had known personally. When there was a game in their town, they stood behind the visiting team's goal and heckled the goalie to make him nervous. Most goalies were bowlegged.

Bloch noticed that each time he mentioned something and talked about it, the two of them countered with a story about their own experiences with the same or a similar thing or with a story they had heard about it. For instance, if Bloch talked about the ribs he had broken while playing, they told him that a few days ago one of the workers at the sawmill had fallen off a lumber pile and broken his ribs; and if Bloch then mentioned that his lips had had to be stitched more than once, they answered by talking about a fight on TV in which a boxer's eyebrows had been split open; and when Bloch told how once he had slammed into a goalpost during a lunge and split his tongue, they immediately replied that the schoolboy also had a cleft tongue.

Besides, they talked about things and especially about people he couldn't possibly know as though he did know them, was one of their group. Maria had hit Otto over the head with her alligator bag. Uncle had come down in the cellar, chased Alfred into the yard, and beaten the Italian kitchen maid with a birch rod. Edward had let her out at the intersection, so that she had to walk the rest of the way in the middle of the night; she had to go through the Child Murderer's Forest, so that Walter and Karl wouldn't see her on the Foreigners' Path, and she'd finally taken off the dancing slippers Herr Friedrich had given her. Bloch, on the other hand, explained, whenever he mentioned a name, whom he was talking about. Even when he mentioned an object, he used a description to identify it.

When the name Victor came up, Bloch added, "a friend of mine," and when he talked about an indirect free kick, he not only described what an indirect free kick was but explained, while the girls waited for the story to go on, the general rules about free kicks. When he mentioned a corner kick that had been awarded by a referee, he even felt he owed them the explanation that he was not talking about the corner of a room. The longer he talked, the less natural what he said seemed to Bloch. Gradually it began to seem that every word needed an explanation. He had to watch himself so that he didn't get stuck in the middle of a sentence. A couple of times when he

becoming more and more detached from normal communication

thought out a sentence even while he said it, he made a slip of the tongue; when what the girls were saying ended exactly as he thought it would, he couldn't answer at first. As long as they had gone on with this familiar talk, he had also forgotten the surroundings more and more; he had even stopped noticing the child and the dog in the next room; but when he began to hesitate and did not know how to go on and finally searched for sentences he might still say, the surroundings became conspicuous again, and he noticed details everywhere. Finally he asked whether Alfred was her boyfriend; whether the birch rod was always kept on top of the wardrobe; whether Herr Friedrich was a traveling salesman; and whether perhaps the Foreigners' Path was called that because it led past a settlement of foreigners. They answered readily; and gradually, instead of bleached hair with dark roots, instead of the single pin at the neck, instead of a black-rimmed fingernail, instead of the single pimple on the shaved eyebrow, instead of the split lining of the empty café chair, Bloch once again became aware of contours, movements, voices, exclamations, and figures all together. And with a single sure rapid movement he also caught the purse that had suddenly slipped off the table. The first girl offered him a bite of her sandwich, and when she held it toward him he bit into it as though this was the most natural thing in the world.

Outside, he heard that the schoolchildren had been given the day off so that they could all look for the boy. But all they found were a couple of things that, except for a broken pocket mirror, had nothing to do with the missing boy. The plastic cover of the mirror had identified it as the property of the mute. Even though the area where the mirror was discovered had been carefully searched, no other clues were found. The policeman who was telling Bloch all this added that the whereabouts of one of the gypsies had remained unknown since the day of the disappearance.

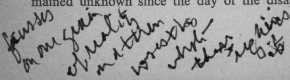

Bloch was surprised that the policeman bothered to stop across the street to shout all this information over to him. He called back to ask if the public pool had been searched yet. The policeman answered that the pool was locked; nobody could get in there, not even a gypsy.

Outside town, Bloch noticed that the cornfields had been almost completely trampled down, so that yellow pumpkin blossoms were visible between the bent stalks; in the middle of the cornfield, always in the shade, the pumpkins had only now begun to blossom. Broken corncobs, partially peeled and gnawed by the schoolchildren, were scattered all over the street; the black silk that had been torn off the cobs lay next to them. Even in town Bloch had watched the children throwing balls of the black fibers at each other while they waited for the bus. The cornsilk was so wet that every time Bloch stepped on it, it squished as though he were walking across marshy ground. He almost fell over a weasel that had been run over; its tongue had been driven quite far out of its mouth. Bloch stopped and touched the long slim tongue, black with blood, with the tip of his shoe; it was hard and rigid. He shoved the weasel to the curb with his foot and walked on.

At the bridge he left the street and walked along the brook in the direction of the border. Gradually, the brook seemed to become deeper; anyway, the water flowed more and more slowly. The hazelnut bushes on both sides hung so far over the brook that the surface was barely visible. Quite far away, a scythe was swishing as it mowed. The slower the water flowed, the muddier it seemed to become. Approaching a bend, the brook stopped flowing altogether, and the water became completely opaque. From far away there was the sound of a tractor clattering as though it had nothing to do with any of this. Black bunches of overripe blackberries hung in the thicket. Tiny oil flecks floated on the still surface of the water.

Bubbles could be seen risiing from the bottom of the water every so often. The tips of the hazelnut bushes hung into the brook. Now there was no outside sound to distract attention. The bubbles had scarcely reached the surface when they disappeared again. Something leaped out so quickly that you couldn't tell if it had been a fish.

When after a while Bloch moved suddenly, a gurgling sound ran through the water. He stepped onto a footbridge that led across the brook and, motionless, looked down at the water. The water was so still that the tops of the leaves floating on it stayed completely dry.

Water bugs were dashing back and forth, and above them one could see, without lifting one's head, a swarm of gnats. At one spot the water rippled ever so slightly. There was another splash as a fish leaped out of the water. At the edge, you could see one toad sitting on top of another. A clump of earth came loose from the shore, and there was another bubbling under the water. The minute events on the water's surface seemed so important that when they recurred they could be seen and remembered simultaneously. And the leaves moved so slowly on the water that you felt like watching them without blinking, until your eyes hurt, for fear that you might mistake the movement of your eyelids for the movement of the leaves. Not even the branches almost dipping into the muddy water were reflected in it.

Outside his field of vision something began to bother Bloch, who was staring fixedly at the water. He blinked as if it was his eyes' fault but did not look around. Gradually it came into his field of vision. For a while he saw it without really taking it in; his whole consciousness seemed to be a blind spot. Then, as when in a movie comedy somebody casually opens a crate and goes right on talking, then does a double-take and rushes back to the crate, he saw below him in the water the corpse of a child.

He had then gone back to the street. Along the curve with the last houses before the border a policeman on a motorbike came toward him. Bloch had already seen him in the mirror that stood beside the curve. Then he really appeared, sitting up straight on his bike, wearing white gloves, one hand on the handlebars, the other on his stomach; the tires were spattered with mud. The policeman's face revealed nothing. The longer Bloch looked after the figure of the policeman on the bike, the more it seemed to him that he was slowly looking up from a newspaper and through a window out into the open: the policeman moved farther and farther away and mattered less and less to him. At the same time, it struck Bloch that what he saw while looking after the policeman looked for a moment like a simile for something else. The policeman disappeared from the picture, and Bloch's attention grew completely superficial. In the tavern by the border, where he went next, he found no one at first, though the door to the barroom was open.

He stood there for a while, then opened the door again and closed it carefully from the inside. He sat down at a table in the corner and passed the time by pushing the little balls used for keeping score in card games back and forth. Finally he shuffled the deck of cards that had been stuck between the rows of balls and played by himself. He became obsessed with playing; a card fell under the table. He bent down and saw the landlady's little girl squatting under another table, between the chairs that had been set all around it. Bloch straightened up and went on playing; the cards were so worn that each single card seemed swollen to him. He looked into the room of the neighbor's house, where the trestle table was now empty; the casement windows stood wide open. Children were shouting on the street outside, and the girl under the table quickly pushed away the chairs and ran out.

The waitress came in from the yard. As if she were answering his sitting there, she said the landlady had gone to the castle to have the lease renewed. The waitress had been followed by a young man dragging two crates of beer bottles, one in each hand; even so, his mouth was not closed. Bloch spoke to him, but the waitress said he shouldn't, the guy couldn't talk when he was pulling such heavy loads. The young man, who, it seemed, was slightly feeble-minded, had stacked the crates behind the bar. The waitress said to him: "Is he pouring the ashes on the bed again instead of into the brook? Has he stopped jumping the goats? Has he started cutting open pumpkins again and smearing the stuff all over his face?" She stood next to the door, holding a beer bottle, but he did not answer. When she showed him the bottle, he came toward her. She gave him the bottle and let him out. A cat dashed in, leaped at a fly in the air, and gulped down the fly at once. The waitress had closed the door. While the door had been open, Bloch had heard the phone ringing in the customs shed next door.

Following close behind the young man, Bloch then went up to the castle. He walked slowly because he did not want to catch up with him; he watched him as he pointed excitedly up into a pear tree and heard him say, "Swarm of bees," and at first believed that he saw a swarm of bees hanging there, until he realized, after looking at the other trees, that it was just that the trunks had thickened at some points. He saw the young man hurl the beer bottle up into the tree, as if to prove that it was bees that he saw. The dregs of the beer sprayed against the trunk, the bottle fell onto a heap of rotting pears in the grass; flies and wasps immediately swarmed up out of the pears. While Bloch walked alongside the young man, he heard him talking about the "bathing nut" he'd seen swimming in the brook yesterday; his fingers had been all shriveled up, and there was a big bubble of foam in front of his mouth. Bloch asked him if he himself knew how to swim. He saw the young man force his mouth open wide and nod emphatically, but then he heard him say, "No." Bloch walked ahead and could hear that he was still talking but did not look back again.

Outside the castle, he knocked on the window of the gatekeeper's cottage. He went up so close to the pane that he could see inside. There was a tub full of plums on the table. The gatekeeper, who was lying on the sofa, had just wakened; he made signs that Bloch did not know how to answer. He nodded. The gatekeeper came out with a key and opened the gate but immediately turned around again and walked ahead. "A gatekeeper with a key!" thought Bloch; again it seemed as if he should be seeing all this only in a figurative sense. He realized that the gatekeeper planned to show him through the building. He decided to clear up the confusion but, even though the gatekeeper did not say much, he never had the chance. There were fishheads nailed all over the entrance door. Bloch had started to explain, but he must have missed the right moment again. They were inside already.

In the library the gatekeeper read to him from the estate books how many shares of the harvest the peasants used to have to turn over to the lord of the manor as rent. Bloch had no chance to interrupt him then, because the gatekeeper was just translating a Latin entry dealing with an insubordinate peasant. " 'He had to depart from the estate,' " the gatekeeper read, " 'and some time later he was discovered in the forest, hanging by his feet from a branch, his head in an anthill.' " The estate book was so thick that the gatekeeper had to use both hands to shut it. Bloch asked if the house was inhabited. The gatekeeper answered that visitors were not allowed into the private quarters. Bloch heard a clicking sound, but it was just the gatekeeper locking the estate book back up. " 'The darkness in the fir forests,' " the gatekeeper recited from memory, " 'had caused him to take leave of his senses.' " Outside the window there was a sound like a heavy apple coming loose from a branch. But nothing hit the ground. Bloch looked out the window and saw the estate owner's son in the garden carrying a long pole; at the tip of the pole hung a sack with metal prongs that he used to yank apples off the tree and into the sack, while the landlady stood on the grass below with her apron spread out.

In the next room, panels of butterflies were hung. The gatekeeper showed him how splotchy his hands had become from preparing them. Even so, many butterflies had fallen off the pins that had held them in place; underneath the cases Bloch saw the dust on the floor. He stepped closer and inspected those butterflies that were still held in place by the pins. When the gatekeeper closed the door behind him, something fell to the floor outside his field of vision and pulverized even while it fell. Bloch saw an Emperor moth that seemed almost completely overgrown with a woolly green film. He did not bend forward or step back. He read the labels under the empty pins. Some of the butterflies had changed so much that they could be recognized only by the descriptions. " 'A corpse in the living room,' " recited the gatekeeper, standing in the doorway to the next room. Outside, someone screamed, and an apple hit the ground. Bloch, looking out the window, saw that an empty branch had snapped back. The landlady put the apple that had fallen to the ground on the pile of other damaged apples.

Later on, a school class from outside the town joined them, and the gatekeeper interrupted his tour to begin it all over again. Bloch took this chance to leave.

Out on the street, at the stop for the mail bus, he sat on a bench that, as a brass plate on it attested, had been donated by the local savings bank. The houses were so far away that they could hardly be distinguished from each other; when bells began to toll, they could not be seen in the belfry. A plane flew overhead, so high that he could not see it; only once did it glint. Next to him on the bench there was a dried-up snail spoor. The grass under the bench was wet with last night's dew; the cellophane wrapper of a cigarette box was fogged with mist. To his left he saw . . . To his right there was . . . Behind him he saw . . . He got hungry and walked away.

Back at the tavern, Bloch ordered the cold plate. The waitress, using an automatic bread-slicer, sliced bread and sausage and brought him the sausage slices on a plate; she had squeezed some mustard on top. Bloch ate; it was getting dark already. Outside, a child had hidden himself so well while playing that he had not been found. Only after the game was over did Bloch see him walk along the deserted street. He pushed the plate aside, pushed the coaster aside as well, pushed the salt shaker away from himself.

The waitress put the little girl to bed. Later the child came back into the barroom in her nightgown and ran around among the customers. Every so often, moths fluttered up from the floor. After she came back, the landlady carried the child back into the bedroom.

The curtains were pulled shut and the barroom filled up. Several young men could be seen standing at the bar; every time they laughed, they took one step backward. Next to them stood girls in nylon coats, as if they wanted to leave again immediately. When one of the young men told a story, the others could be seen to stiffen up just before they all screamed with laughter. The people who sat preferred to sit against the wall. The mechanical hand in the juke box could be seen grabbing a record and the tone arm coming down on it, and some people who were waiting for their records could be heard quieting down; it was no use, it didn't change anything. And it didn't change anything that you could see the wristwatch slip out from under the sleeve and down to the wrist when the waitress let her arm drop, that the lever on the coffee machine rose slowly, and that you could hear somebody hold a match box to his ear and shake it before opening it. You saw how completely empty glasses were repeatedly brought to the lips, how the waitress lifted a glass to check whether she could take it away, how the young men pummeled each other's faces in fun. Only when somebody shouted for his check did things become real again.

Bloch was quite drunk. Everything seemed to be out of his reach. He was so far away from what happened around him that he himself no longer appeared in what he saw and heard. "Like aerial photographs," he thought while looking at the antlers and horns on the wall. The noises seemed to him like static, like the coughing and clearing of throats during radio broadcasts of church services.

Later the estate owner's son came in. He was wearing knickers and hung his coat so close to Bloch that Bloch had to lean to one side.

The landlady sat down with the estate owner's son, and could be heard as she asked him, after she had sat down, what he wanted to drink and then shouted the order to the waitress. For a while Bloch saw them both drinking from the same glass; whenever the young man said something, the landlady nudged him in the ribs; and when she wiped the flat of her hand across his face, he could be seen snapping and licking at it. Then the landlady had sat down at another table, where she went on with her routine motions by fingering another young man's hair. The estate owner's son had stood up again and reached for his cigarettes in the coat behind Bloch. When Bloch shook his head in answer to a question about whether the coat bothered him, he realized that he had not lifted his eyes from one and the same spot for quite a while. Bloch shouted, "My check!" and everybody seemed to become serious again for a moment. The landlady, whose head was bent backward because she was just opening a bottle of wine, made a sign to the waitress, who was standing behind the bar washing glasses, which she put on the foam-rubber mat that soaked up the water, and the waitress walked toward him, between the young men standing at the bar, and gave him his change, with fingers that were cold, and as he stood up, he put the wet coins in his pocket immediately; a joke, thought Bloch; perhaps the sequence of events seemed so laborious to him because he was drunk.

He stood up and walked to the door; he opened the door and went outside—everything was all right.

Just to make sure, he stood there for a while. Every once in a while somebody came out to relieve himself. Others, who were just arriving, started to sing along as soon as they heard the juke box, even when they were still outside. Bloch moved off.

Back in town; back at the inn; back in his room. "Eleven words altogether," thought Bloch with relief. He heard bath water draining out overhead; anyway, he heard gurgling and then, finally, a snuffling and smacking.

He must have just dropped off when he woke up again. For a moment it seemed as if he had fallen out of himself. He realized that he lay in a bed. "Not fit to be moved," thought Bloch. A cancer. He became aware of himself as if he had suddenly degenerated. He did not matter any more. No matter how still he lay, he was one big wriggling and retching; his lying there was so sharply distinct and glaring that he could not escape into even one picture that he might have compared himself with. The way he lay there, he was something lewd, obscene, inappropriate, thoroughly obnoxious. "Bury it!" thought Bloch. "Prohibit it, remove it!" He thought he was touching himself unpleasantly but realized that his awareness of himself was so intense that he felt it like a sense of touch all over his body; as though his consciousness, as though his thoughts, had become palpable, aggressive, abusive toward himself. Defenseless, incapable of defending himself, he lay there. Nauseatingly his insides turned out; not alien, only repulsively different. It had been a jolt, and with one jolt he had become unnatural, had been torn out of context. He lay there, as impossible as he was real; no comparisons now. His awareness of himself was so strong that he was scared to death. He was sweating. A coin fell on the floor and rolled under the bed: a comparison? Then he had fallen asleep.

Waking up again. "Two, three, four," Bloch started to count. His situation had not changed, but he must have grown used to it in his sleep. He pocketed the coin that had fallen under the bed and went downstairs. When he put on an act, one word still nicely yielded the next. A rainy October day; early morning; a dusty windowpane; it worked. He greeted the innkeeper; the innkeeper was just putting the newspapers into their racks; the girl was pushing a tray through the service hatch between the kitchen and dining room: it was still working. If he kept up his guard, it could go on like this, one thing after another; he sat at the table he always sat at; he opened the newspaper he opened every day; he read the paragraph in the paper that said an important lead in the Gerda T. case was being followed into the southern part of the country; the doodles in the margin of the newspaper that had been found in the dead girl's apartment had furthered the investigation. One sentence yielded the next sentence.

And then, and then, and then . . . For a little while it was possible to look ahead without worrying.

After a while, although he was still sitting in the dining room listing the things that went on out on the street, Bloch caught himself becoming aware of a sentence, "For he had been idle too long." Since that sentence looked like a final sentence to Bloch, he thought back to how he had come to it. What had come before it? Oh, yes, earlier he had thought, "Surprised by the shot, he'd let the ball roll right through his legs." And before this sentence he had thought about the photographers who annoyed him behind the cage. And before that, "Somebody had stopped behind him but had only whistled for his dog." And before that sentence? Before that sentence he had thought about a woman who had stopped in a park, had turned around, and had looked at something behind him the way one looks at an unruly child. And before that? Before that, the innkeeper had talked about the mute schoolboy, who'd been found dead right near the border. And before the schoolboy he had thought of the ball that had bounced up just in front of the goal line. And before the thought of the ball, he had seen the market woman jump up from her stool on the street and run after a schoolboy. And the market woman had been preceded by a sentence in the paper: "The carpenter was hindered in his pursuit of the thief by the fact that he was still wearing his apron." But he had read the sentence in the paper just when he thought of how his jacket had been pulled down over his arms during a mugging. And he had come to the mugging when he had bumped his shin painfully against the table. And before that? He could not remember any more what had made him bump his shin against the table. He searched the sequence for a clue about what might have come before: did it have to do with the movement? or with the pain? or with the sound of table and shin? But it did not go any further back. Then he noticed, in the paper in front of him, a picture of an apartment door that, because there was a corpse behind it, had had to be broken open. So, he thought, it all started with this apartment door, until he had brought himself back to the sentence, "He had been idle too long."

Everything had gone well for a while after that: the lip movements of the people he talked to coincided with what he heard them say; the houses were not just façades; heavy sacks of flour were being dragged from the loading ramp of the dairy into the storage room; when somebody shouted something far down the street, it sounded as though it actually came from down there. The people walking past on the sidewalk across the street did not appear to have been paid to walk past in the background; the man with the adhesive tape under his eye had a genuine scab; and the rain seemed to fall not just in the foreground of the picture but everywhere. Bloch then found himself under the projecting roof of a church. He must have got there through a side alley and stopped under the roof when it started to rain.

Inside the church he noticed that it was brighter than he had expected. So, after quickly sitting down on a bench, he could look up at the painted ceiling. After a while he recognized it: it was reproduced in the brochure that was placed in every room at the inn. Bloch, who had brought a copy because it also contained a sketchy map of the town and its vicinity with all its streets and paths, pulled out the brochure and read that different painters had worked on the background and foreground of the picture; the figures in the foreground had been finished long before the other painter had finished filling in the background. Bloch looked from the page up into the vault; because he did not know them, the figures—they probably represented people from the Bible—bored him; still, it was pleasant to look up at the vault while it rained harder and harder outside. The painting stretched all the way across the ceiling of the church. The background represented the sky, almost cloudless and an almost even blue; here and there a few fluffy clouds could be seen; at one spot, quite far above the figures, a bird had been painted. Bloch guessed the exact area the painter had had to fill with paint. Would it have been hard to paint such an even blue? It was a blue that was so light that white had probably been mixed into the color. And in mixing them didn't you have to be careful that the shade of blue didn't change from day to day? On the other hand, the blue was not absolutely even but changed within each brush stroke. So you couldn't just paint the ceiling an even blue but actually had to paint a picture. The background did not become a sky because the paint was blindly slapped on the plaster base—which, moreover, had to be wet—with as big a brush as possible, maybe even with a broom, but, Bloch reflected, the painter had to paint an actual sky with small variations in the blue which, nevertheless, had to be so indistinct that nobody would think they were a mistake in the mixing. In fact, the background did not look like a sky because you were used to imagining a sky in the background but because the sky had been painted there, stroke by stroke. It had been painted with such precision, thought Bloch, that it almost looked drawn; it was much more precise, anyway, than the figures in the foreground. Had he added the bird out of sheer rage? And had he painted the bird right at the start or had he only added it when he was quite finished? Might the background painter have been in some kind of despair? Nothing indicated this, and such an interpretation immediately seemed ridiculous to Bloch. Altogether it seemed to him as if his preoccupation with the painting, as if his walking back and forth, his sitting here and there, his going out, his coming in, were nothing but excuses. He stood up. "No distractions," he muttered to himself. As if to contradict himself, he went outside, walked straight across the street into an entryway, and stood there defiantly among the empty milk bottles—not that anyone came to ask him to account for his presence there—until it stopped raining. Then he went to a café and sat there for a while with his legs stretched out— not that anyone did him the favor of stumbling over them and starting a fight.

When he looked out, he saw a segment of the marketplace with the school bus; in the café he saw, to the left and to the right, segments of the walls, one with an unlit stove with a bunch of flowers on it, the one on the other side with a coat rack with an umbrella hanging from it. He noticed another segment with the juke box with a point of light slowly wandering through it before it stopped at the selected number, and next to it a cigarette machine with another bunch of flowers on top; then still another segment with the café owner behind the bar and next to him the waitress for whom he was opening a bottle, which the waitress put on the tray; and, finally, a segment of himself with his legs stretched out, the dirty tips of his wet shoes, and also the huge ashtray on the table and next to it a vase, which was smaller, and the filled wine glass on the next table, where nobody was sitting right now. His angle of vision onto the square corresponded, as he realized now that the school bus had left, almost exactly with the angle on picture postcards; here a segment of the memorial column by the fountain; there, at the edge of the picture, a segment of the bicycle stand.

Bloch was irritated. Within the segments themselves he saw the details with grating distinctness: as if the parts he saw stood for the whole. Again the details seemed to him like nameplates. "Neon signs," he thought. So he saw the waitress's ear with one earring as a sign of the entire person; and a purse on a nearby table, slightly open so that he could recognize a polka-dotted scarf in it, stood for the woman holding the coffee cup who sat behind it and, with her other hand, pausing only now and then at a picture, rapidly leafed through a magazine. A tower of ice-cream dishes dovetailed into each other on the bar seemed a simile for the café owner, and the puddle on the floor by the coat rack represented the umbrella hanging above it. Instead of the heads of the customers, Bloch saw the dirty spots on the wall at the level of their heads. He was so irritated that he looked at the grimy cord that the waitress was just pulling to turn off the wall lights—it had grown brighter outside again—as if the entire lighting arrangement was designed especially to tax his strength. Also, his head hurt because he had been caught in the rain.

The grating details seemed to stain and completely distort the figures and the surroundings they fitted into. The only defense was to name the things one by one and use those names as insults against the people themselves. The owner behind the bar might be called an ice-cream dish, and you could tell the waitress that she was a hole through the ear lobe. And you also felt like saying to the woman with the magazine, "You Purse, you," and to the man at the next table, who had finally come out of the back room and, standing up, finished his wine while he paid, "You Spot on Your Pants," or to shout after him as he set the empty glass on the table and walked out that he was a fingerprint, a doorknob, the slit in the back of his coat, a rain puddle, a bicycle clip, a fender, and so on, until the figure outside had disappeared on his bicycle . . . Even the conversation and especially the exclamations—"What?" and "I see"—seemed so grating that one wanted to repeat the words out loud, scornfully.

Bloch went into a butcher shop and bought two salami sandwiches. He did not want to eat at the tavern because his money was running low. He looked over the sausages dangling together from a pole and pointed at the one he wanted the girl to slice. A boy came in with a note in his hand. At first the customs guard thought the schoolboy's corpse was a mattress that had been washed up, the girl had just said. She took two rolls out of a carton and split them in half without separating them completely. The bread was so stale that Bloch heard them crunch as the knife cut into them. The girl pulled, the rolls apart and put the sliced meat inside. Bloch said that he had time and she should take care of the child first. He saw the boy silently holding the note out. The girl leaned forward and read it. Then the chunk she was hacking off the meat slipped off the board and fell on the stone floor. "Plop," said the child. The chunk had stayed where it had fallen. The girl picked it up, scraped it off with the edge of her knife, and wrapped it up. Outside, Bloch saw the schoolchildren walking by with their unbrellas open, even though it had stopped raining. He opened the door for the boy and watched the girl tear the skin off the sausage end and put the slices inside the second roll.

Business was bad, the girl said. "There aren't any houses except on this side of the street where the shop is, so that, first of all, nobody lives across the street who could see from there that there is a shop here and, second of all, the people going by never walk on the other side of the street, so they pass by so close that they don't see that there is a store here, especially since the shop window isn't much bigger than the living-room windows of the houses next door."

Bloch wondered why the people didn't walk on the other side of the street as well, where there was more room and where it was sunnier. Probably everybody feels some need to walk right next to the houses, he said. The girl, who had not understood him because he had become disgusted with talking in the middle of the sentence and had only mumbled the rest,

miss you
victim in the
mun ication

laughed as though all she had expected for an answer
was a joke. In fact, when a few people passed by the
shop window, it got so dark in the shop that it did
seem like a joke.

"First of all . . . second of all . . ." Bloch repeated
to himself what the girl had said; it seemed uncanny
to him how someone could begin to speak and at the
same time know how the sentence would end. Outside, he ate the sandwiches while he walked along. He
bunched up the waxed paper they were wrapped in
and was ready to throw it away. There was no trash
basket nearby. For a while he walked along with the
balled-up paper, first in one direction and then in another. He put the paper in his coat pocket, took it out
again, and finally threw it through a fence into an
orchard. Chickens came running from all directions
at once but turned back before they had pecked the
paper ball open.

In front of him Bloch saw three men walk diagonally across the street, two in uniform and the one
in the middle in a black Sunday suit with a tie hanging
over his shoulder, where it had been blown either by
the wind or by fast running. He watched as the policemen led the gypsy into the police station. They
walked next to each other as far as the door, and
the gypsy, it seemed, moved easily and willingly between the two policemen and talked with them; when
one of the policemen pushed open the door, the other
did not grab the gypsy but just touched his elbow
lightly from behind. The gypsy looked back over his
shoulder at the policeman and gave a friendly smile;
the collar under the knot of the gypsy's tie was open. It
seemed to Bloch as if the gypsy was so deeply trapped
that all he could do when he was touched on the arm
was look at the policeman with helpless friendliness.

Bloch followed them into the building, which also
housed the post office; for just a moment he believed
that if anybody saw him eating a sandwich out in

Bloch in the custody of the policemen of his sense

87

public, they could not possibly think that he was involved in anything. "Involved"? He could not even let himself think that he had to justify his presence here, while they were bringing in the gypsy, by any action such as, say, eating salami sandwiches. He could justify himself only when he was questioned and accused of something; and because he had to avoid even thinking that he might be questioned, he also could not let himself think about how to prepare justifications in advance for this possibility—this possibility did not even exist. So if he was asked whether he had watched while the gypsy was being brought in, he would not have to deny it and pretend that he had been distracted because he was eating a sandwich but could admit that he had witnessed the event. "Witnessed"? Bloch interrupted himself while he waited in the post office for his phone connection; "admit"? What did these words have to do with this event, which for him was of no significance. Didn't they give it a significance he was making every effort to deny? "Deny?" Bloch interrupted himself again. He had to keep his guard up against words that transformed what he wanted to say into some kind of statement.

His call had gone through. Absorbed in avoiding the impression that he was prepared to make a statement, he caught himself wrapping a handkerchief over the receiver. Slightly disconcerted, he put the handkerchief back in his pocket. How had he come from the thought of unguarded talk to the handkerchief? He was told that the friend he was calling had to stay quartered with his team in a training camp until the important match on Sunday and could not be reached by phone. Bloch gave the postmistress another number. She asked him to pay for the first call first. Bloch paid and sat on a bench to wait for the second call. The phone rang and he stood up. But it was only a birthday telegram arriving. The postmistress wrote it down and confirmed it word by word. Bloch walked

back and forth. One of the mailmen had returned
from his route and was now loudly reporting to the
girl. Bloch sat down. Outside on the street, now that
it was early afternoon, there was no distraction. Bloch
had become impatient but did not show it. He heard
the mailman say that the gypsy had been hiding all
this time near the border in one of those lean-to shelters the customs guards used. "Anyone can say that,"
said Bloch. The mailman turned toward him and
stopped talking. What he claimed to be the latest
news, Bloch went on, anybody could have read yesterday, the day before yesterday, even the day before
the day before yesterday, in the papers. What he
said didn't mean anything, nothing at all, nothing
whatsoever. The mailman had turned his back to
Bloch even while Bloch was still talking and was now
speaking quietly with the postmistress, in a murmur that
sounded to Bloch like those passages in foreign films
that are left untranslated because they are supposed to be incomprehensible anyway. Bloch couldn't
reach them any more with his remark. All at once
the fact that it was in a post office that he "couldn't
reach anybody any more" seemed to him not like a
fact at all but like a bad joke, like one of those word
games that, say, sportswriters play, which he had
always loathed. Even the mailman's story about the
gypsy had seemed to him crudely suggestive, a clumsy
insinuation, like the birthday telegram, whose words
were so commonplace that they simply could not
mean what they said. And it wasn't only the conversation that was insinuating; everything around him
was also meant to suggest something to him. "As
though they winked and made signs at me," thought
Bloch. For what was it supposed to mean that the lid
of the inkwell lay right next to the well on the blotter
and that the blotter on the desk had obviously been
replaced just today, so only a few impressions were
legible on it? And wouldn't it be more proper to say

"so that" instead of "so"? So *that* the impressions would therefore be legible. And now the postmistress picked up the phone and spelled out the birthday telegram letter by letter. What was she hinting at by that? What was behind her dictating "All the best," "With kind regards": what was that supposed to mean? Who was behind the cover name "your loving grandparents?" Even that morning Bloch had instantly recognized the short slogan "Why not phone?" as a trap.

It seemed to him as if the mailman and the postmistress were in the know. "The postmistress and the mailman," he corrected himself. Now the loathsome word-game sickness had struck even him, and in broad daylight. "Broad daylight"? He must have hit on that phrase somehow. That expression seemed witty to him, in an unpleasant way. But were the other words in the sentence any better? If you said the word "sickness" to yourself, after a few repetitions you couldn't help laughing at it. "A sickness strikes me": silly. "I am stricken by a sickness": just as silly. "The postmistress and the mailman"; "the mailman and the postmistress"; "the postmistress and the mailman": one big joke. Have you heard the one about the mailman and the postmistress? "Everything seems like a heading," thought Bloch: "THE BIRTHDAY TELEGRAM," "THE INKWELL LID," "THE SCRAPS OF BLOTTER ON THE FLOOR." The rack where the various rubber stamps hung looked as if it had been sketched. He looked at it for a long time but did not figure out what was supposed to be funny about the stand. On the other hand, there had to be a joke in it: otherwise, why should it look sketched to him? Or was it another trap? Was the thing there so that he would make a slip of the tongue? Bloch looked somewhere else, looked at another place, and looked somewhere else again. Does this ink pad mean anything to you? What do you think of when you see this filled-out check? What do you asssociate with that drawer's being open? It seemed to Bloch that he should take inventory of the room, so that the objects he paused at or that he left out during his count could serve as evidence. The mailman hit the flat of his hand against the big bag that was still hanging from his shoulder. "The mailman hits the bag and takes it off," thought Bloch, word for word. "Now he puts it on the table and walks into the package room." He described the events to himself like a radio announcer to the public, as if this was the only way he could see them for himself. After a while it helped.

He stopped pacing because the phone rang. As always when the phone rang, he felt he had known it would a moment before it did. The postmistress picked up the phone and then pointed to the booth. Already inside the booth, he asked himself whether perhaps he had misunderstood her gesture, if perhaps it had been meant for no one in particular. He picked up the receiver and asked his ex-wife, who had started by giving only her first name, as though she knew it was him, to send some money to general delivery. A peculiar silence followed. Bloch heard some whispering that wasn't meant for him. "Where are you?" the woman asked. He'd got cold feet and now he was high and dry, Bloch said and laughed as though he had said something extremely witty. The woman didn't answer. Bloch heard more whispering. It was very difficult, said the woman. Why? asked Bloch. She hadn't been talking to him, answered the woman. "Where should I send the money?" His pockets would be empty soon if she didn't give him a hand, Bloch said. The woman kept quiet. Then the phone was hung up at her end.

"The snows of yesteryear," Bloch thought, unexpectedly, as he came out of the booth. What was that supposed to mean? In fact, he had heard that the underbrush was so tangled and thick at the border that patches of snow could be found at certain spots even during the early summer. But that was not what he had meant. Besides, people had no business in the underbrush. "No business"? How did he mean that? "The way I said it," thought Bloch.

At the savings bank he traded in the American dollar bill he had carried with him for a long time. He also tried to exchange a Brazilian bill, but the bank did not trade that currency; besides, they didn't know the exchange rate.

When Bloch came in, the bank teller was counting out coins, wrapping them up in rolls, and stretching rubber bands around the rolls. Bloch put the dollar bill on the counter. Next to it there was a music box; only when he gave it a second look did Bloch recognize it as a contribution box for some charity. The teller looked up but went on counting. Before he had been asked to, Bloch slid the bill under the partition through to the other side. The teller was lining up the rolls in a single row next to him. Bloch bent down and blew the bill in front of the teller, and the teller unfolded the bill, smoothed it with the edge of his hand, and ran his fingertips over it. Bloch saw that his fingertips were quite black. Another teller came out of the back room; to witness something, thought Bloch. He asked to have the change—in which there was not even one bill—put in an envelope and shoved the coins back under the partition. The official, in the same way he had lined up the piles earlier, stuffed the coins into an envelope and pushed the envelope back to Bloch. Bloch thought that if everybody asked to have their money put in envelopes, the savings bank would eventually go broke. They could do the same thing with everything they bought: maybe the heavy demand for packaging would slowly but surely drive businesses bankrupt? Anyway, it was fun to think about.

In a stationery store Bloch bought a tourist map of the region and had it well wrapped. He also bought a pencil; the pencil he asked to have put in a paper bag. With the rolled-up map in his hand, he walked on; he felt more harmless now than before, when his hands had been empty.

Outside the town, at a spot where he had a full view of the area, he sat down on a bench and, using the pencil, compared the details on the map with the items in the landscape in front of him. Key to the symbols; these circles meant a deciduous forest, those triangles a coniferous one, and when you looked up from the map, you were astonished that it was true. Over there, the terrain had to be swampy; over there, there had to be a wayside shrine; over there, there had to be a railroad crossing. If you walked along this dirt road, you had to cross a bridge here, then had to come across a wagon trail, then had to walk up a steep incline, where, since somebody might be waiting on top, you had to turn off the path and run across this field, had to run toward this forest—luckily, a coniferous forest—but someone might possibly come at you out of the forest, so that you had to double back and then run down this slope toward this farmhouse, had to run past this shed, then run along this brook, had to leap over it at this spot because a jeep might come at you here, then zigzag across this field, slip through this hedge onto the street where a truck was just going by, which you could stop and then you were safe. Bloch stopped short. "If it's a question of murder, your mind jumps from one thing to another," he had heard somebody say in a movie.

He was relieved to discover a square on the map that he could not find in the landscape: the house that had to be there wasn't there, and the street that curved at this spot was in reality straight. It seemed to Bloch that this discrepancy might be helpful to him.

He watched a dog running toward a man in a field; then he realized that he was not watching the dog any more but the man, who was moving like somebody

73

trying to block somebody else's way. Now he saw a little boy standing behind the man, and he realized that he was not watching the man and the dog, as would have been expected, but the boy, who, from this distance, seemed to be fidgeting; but then he realized that it was the boy's screaming that seemed like fidgeting to him. In the meantime, the man had grabbed the dog by the collar and all three, dog, man, and boy, had walked off in the same direction. "Who was that meant for?" thought Bloch.

On the ground in front of him a different picture: ants approaching a crumb of bread. He realized once again that he wasn't watching the ants but, on the contrary, the fly sitting on the bread crumb.

Everything he saw was conspicuous. The pictures did not seem natural but looked as if they had been made specifically for the occasion. They served some purpose. As you looked at them, they jumped out at you. "Like call letters," thought Bloch. Like commands. When he closed his eyes and looked again afterwards, everything seemed to be different. The segments that could be seen seemed to glimmer and tremble at their edges.

From a sitting position, Bloch, without really getting up, had immediately walked away. After a while he stopped, then immediately broke into a run from a standing position. He got off to a quick start, suddenly stopped short, changed direction, ran at a steady pace, then changed his step, changed his step again, stopped short, then ran backward, turned around while running backward, ran forward again, again turned around to run backward, went backward, turned around to run forward, after a few steps changed to a sprint, stopped short, sat down on a curbstone, and immediately went back to running from a sitting position.

When he stopped and then walked on, the pictures seemed to dim from the edges; finally they had turned completely black except for a circle in the middle.

"Like when somebody in a movie looks through a telescope," he thought. He wiped the sweat off his legs with his trousers. He walked past a cellar where, because the cellar door was half open, tea leaves shimmered in a peculiar way. "Like potatoes," Bloch thought.

Of course the house in front of him had only one story, the shutters were fastened, the roof tiles were covered with moss (another one of those words!), the door was closed, PUBLIC SCHOOL was written above it, in the garden somebody was chopping wood, it had to be the school janitor, of course, and in front of the school naturally there was a hedge; yes, everything was in order, nothing was missing, not even the sponge underneath the blackboard in the dusky classroom and the chalk box next to it, not even the semicircles on the outside walls underneath the windows and the other marks that, in explanation, confirmed that these scratches were made by window hooks; in every respect it was as though everything you saw or heard confirmed to you that it was true to its word.

In the classroom the lid of the coal bucket was open, and in the bucket itself the handle of the coal shovel could be seen (an April fool's joke), and the floor with the wide boards, the cracks still wet from mopping, not forgetting the map on the wall, the sink next to the blackboard, and the corn husks on the windowsill: one single, cheap imitation. No, he would not let himself be tricked by April fool's jokes like these.

It was as if he were drawing wider and wider circles. He had forgotten the lightning rod next to the door, and now it seemed to him like a cue. He was supposed to start. He helped himself out by walking around the school back to the yard and talking with the janitor in the woodshed. Woodshed, janitor, yard: cues. He watched while the janitor put a log on the chopping block and lifted up the ax. He said a couple of words from the yard; the janitor stopped, answered, and as he hit the log, it fell to one side before he had struck it, and the ax hit the chopping block so that the pile of unchopped logs in the background collapsed. Another one of those cues. But the only thing that happened was that he called to the janitor in the dim woodshed, asking whether this was the only classroom for the whole school, and the janitor answered that for the whole school there was only this classroom.

No wonder the children hadn't even learned to read by the time they left school, the janitor said suddenly, slamming the ax into the chopping block and coming out of the shed: they couldn't manage even to finish a single sentence of their own, they talked to each other almost entirely in single words, and they wouldn't talk at all unless you asked them to, and what they learned was only memorized stuff that they rattled off by rote; except for that, they couldn't use whole sentences. "Actually, all of them, more or less, have a speech defect," said the janitor.

What was that supposed to mean? What reason did the janitor have for that? What did it have to do with him? Nothing? Yes, but why did the janitor act as if it had something to do with him?

Bloch should have answered, but he did not let himself get involved. Once he got started, he would have to go on talking. So he walked around the yard a while longer, helped the janitor pick up the logs that had been flung out of the shed during the chopping, and then, little by little, wandered unobtrusively back out onto the street and was able to make his getaway with no trouble.

He walked past the athletic field. It was after work, and the soccer team was practicing. The ground was so wet that drops sprayed out from the grass when a player kicked the ball. Bloch watched for a while, but it was getting dark, and he left.

In the restaurant at the railroad station he ate a croquette and drank a couple of glasses of beer. On the platform outside, he sat on a bench. A girl in spike heels walked back and forth in the gravel. A phone rang in the traffic supervisor's office. A railroad official stood in the door, smoking. Somebody came out of the waiting room and stopped again immediately. There was more rattling in the office, and loud talking, like somebody talking into a telephone, could be heard. It had grown dark by now.

It was fairly quiet. Here and there someone could be seen drawing on a cigarette. A faucet was turned on sharply and was turned off again at once—as though somebody had been startled. Farther away people were talking in the dark; faint sounds could be heard, as in a half-sleep: ah ee. Somebody shouted: "Ow!" There was no way to tell whether a man or a woman had shouted. Very far away someone could be heard saying, very distinctly, "You look worn out." Between the railroad tracks, just as distinctly, a railroad worker could be seen standing and scratching his head. Bloch thought he was asleep.

An incoming train could be seen. You could watch a few passengers getting off, looking as if they were undecided whether to get off or not. A drunk got off last of all and slammed the door shut. The official on the platform could be seen as he gave a signal with his flashlight, and then the train was leaving.

In the waiting room Bloch looked at the schedule. No more trains stopped at the station today. Anyway, it was late enough now to go to the movies.

Some people were already in the lobby of the movie house. Bloch sat with them, his ticket in his hand. More and more people came. It was pleasant to hear so many sounds. Bloch went out in front of the theater, stood out there with some other people, then went back into the movie house.

In the movie somebody shot a rifle at a man who

was sitting far away at a campfire with his back turned. Nothing happened; the man did not fall over, just sat there, did not even look to see who had fired. Some time passed. Then the man slowly sank to one side and lay there without moving. That's the trouble with these old guns, the gunman said to his partner; no impact. But the man had actually been dead all the time he sat there at the campfire.

After the movie he rode out to the border with two men in a car. A stone slammed against the bottom of the car. Bloch, who was in the back seat, became alert again.

Since this had been pay day, he could not find a single empty table at the tavern. He sat down with some other people. The landlady came and put her hand on his shoulder. He understood and ordered drinks for the whole table.

To pay, he put a folded bill on the table. Somebody next to him unfolded the bill and said that another one might be tucked inside it. Bloch said, "So what?" and refolded the bill. The man unfolded the bill again and pushed an ashtray on top of it. Bloch reached into the ashtray and, underhand, threw the butts into the man's face. Somebody pulled his chair out from under him, so that he slid under the table.

Bloch jumped up and in a flash slammed his forearm against the chest of the man who had pulled away his chair. The man fell against the wall and groaned loudly because he couldn't catch his breath. A couple of men twisted Bloch's arms behind his back and shoved him out the door. He did not fall, just staggered around and ran right back in.

He swung at the man who had unfolded the bill. A kick hit him from behind, and he fell against the table with the man. Even while they were falling, Bloch slugged away at him.

Sombeody grabbed him by the legs and hauled him

away. Bloch kicked him in the ribs, and he let go. A few others got hold of Bloch and dragged him out. On the street they put a headlock on him and marched him back and forth like that. They stopped in front of the customs shed with him, pushed his head against the doorbell, and went away.

A guard came out, saw Bloch standing there, and went back inside. Bloch ran after the men and tackled one of them from behind. The others rushed him. Bloch stepped to one side and butted his head into somebody's stomach. A few more people came out from the tavern. Somebody threw a coat over his head. He hit him in the shins, but somebody else was tying the arms of the coat together. Then they swiftly beat him down and went back into the tavern.

Bloch got loose from the coat and ran after them. One of them stopped but did not turn around. Bloch charged him; the man just walked away, and Bloch sprawled on the ground.

After a while he got up and went into the tavern. He wanted to say something, but when he moved his tongue, the blood in his mouth bubbled. He sat down at one of the tables and pointed with his finger to show that he wanted a drink. The waitress brought him a bottle of beer without the glass. He thought he saw tiny flies running back and forth on the table, but it was just cigarette smoke. He was too weak to lift the beer bottle with one hand; so he clutched it with both hands and bent over so that it didn't have to be lifted too high. His ears were so sensitive that at times the cards didn't fall but were slammed on the next table, and at the bar the sponge didn't fall but slapped into the sink; and the landlady's daughter, with clogs on her bare feet, didn't walk through the barroom but clattered through the barroom; the wine didn't flow but gurgled into the glasses; and the music didn't play but boomed from the juke box.

79

He heard a woman scream in fright, but in a tavern a woman's scream didn't mean anything; therefore, the woman could not have screamed in fright. Nevertheless, he had been jolted by the scream; it was only because of the noise, because the scream had been so shrill.

Little by little the other details lost their significance: the foam in the empty beer bottle meant no more to him then the cigarette box that the man next to him tore open just enough so that he managed to extract a single cigarette with his fingernails. Nor did the used matches lying loose everywhere in the cracks between the floorboards occupy his attention any more, and the fingernail impressions in the putty along the windowframe no longer seemed to have anything to do with him. Everything left him cold now, stood once more in its place; like peacetime, thought Bloch. The stuffed grouse above the juke box no longer forced one to draw conclusions; and the flies sleeping on the ceiling did not suggest anything any more.

You could see a man combing his hair with his fingers, you could see girls walking backward as they danced, you could see men standing up and buttoning their coats, you could hear cards sloshing as they were shuffled, but you didn't have to dwell on it any more.

Bloch got tired. The tireder he got, the more clearly he took in everything, distinguished one thing from another. He saw how the door invariably stayed open when somebody went out, and how somebody else always got up and shut the door again. He was so tired that he saw each thing by itself, especially the contours, as though there was nothing to the things but their contours. He saw and heard everything with total immediacy, without first having to translate it into words, as before, or comprehending it only in terms of words or word games. He was in a state where everything seemed natural to him.

Later the landlady sat down with him, and he put

his arm around her so naturally that she did not even seem to notice. He dropped a couple of coins into the juke box as though it were nothing and danced effortlessly with the landlady. He noticed that every time she said something she added his name to it.

It wasn't important any more that he could see the waitress clasping one hand with the other, nor was there anything special about the thick curtains, and it was only natural that more and more people left. They could be heard as they relieved themselves out on the street and then walked away.

It got quieter in the barroom, so that the records in the juke box played very distinctly. In the pause between records people talked more softly or almost held their breath; it was a relief when the next record came on. It seemed to Bloch that you could talk about these occurrences as things that recurred forever; the course of a single day, he thought; things that you wrote about on picture postcards. "At night we sit in the tavern and listen to records." He got tireder and tireder, and outside the apples were dropping off the trees.

When nobody but him was left, the landlady went into the kitchen. Bloch sat there and waited until the record was over. He turned off the juke box, so that now only the kitchen light was still on. The landlady sat at the table and did her accounts. Bloch approached her, a coaster in his hand. She looked up when he came out of the barroom and looked at him while he approached her. It was too late when he remembered the coaster; he wanted to hide it quickly, before she saw it, but the landlady looked away from him and at the coaster in his hand and asked him what he was doing with it, if perhaps she had written a bill on it that hadn't been paid. Bloch dropped the coaster and sat down next to the landlady, not doing one thing smoothly after the other but hesitating at each move. She went on counting, talked with him while she did, then cleared away the money. Bloch said he'd just forgotten about the coaster in his hand; it hadn't meant anything.

She asked him to have a bite with her. She set a wooden board in front of him. There was no knife, he said, though she had set the knife next to the board. She had to bring the laundry in from the garden, she said, it was just starting to rain. It wasn't raining, he corrected her, it was only dripping from the trees because there was a little wind. But she had gone out already, and since she left the door open, he could see that it was actually raining. He saw her come back and shouted that she had dropped a shirt, but it turned out that it was only a rag for the floor, which had been lying in the entryway all along. When she lit the candle on the table, he saw the wax dripping on a plate because she had tilted the candle slightly in her hand. She should watch out, he said, wax was dripping onto the clean plate. But she was already setting the candle in the spilled wax, which was still liquid, and pressed it down until it stood by itself. "I didn't know that you wanted to put the candle on the plate," Bloch said. She started to sit down where there was no chair, and Bloch shouted, "Watch out!" though she had just squatted to pick up a coin that had fallen under the table while she was counting. When she went into the bedroom to take care of the girl, he immediately asked for her; once when she left the table he even called after her to ask where she was going.

She turned on the radio on the kitchen cabinet; it was nice to watch her walking back and forth while the music came out of the radio. When somebody in a movie turned on the radio, the program was instantly interrupted for a bulletin about a wanted man.

While they sat at the table, they talked to each other. It seemed to Bloch that he could not say any-

ky is to keep contact?

thing serious. He cracked jokes, but the landlady took everything he said literally. He said that her blouse was striped like a soccer jersey and wanted to go on, but she asked him whether he didn't like her blouse, what bothered him about it. It did no good to assure her that he had only made a joke and that the blouse went very nicely with her pale skin; she went on to ask if her skin was too pale for him. He said, jokingly, that the kitchen was furnished almost like a city kitchen, and she asked why he said "almost." Did people there keep their things cleaner? Even when Bloch made a joke about the estate owner's son (he'd proposed to her, hadn't he?), she took him literally and said the estate owner's son wasn't available. He tried to explain, using a comparison, that he had not meant it seriously, but she took the comparison literally as well. "I didn't mean anything by it," Bloch said. "You must have had a reason for saying it," the landlady answered. Bloch laughed. The landlady asked why he was laughing at her.

The little girl called from the bedroom. She went in and calmed her down. When she came back, Bloch had stood up. She stood in front of him and looked at him for a while. But then she talked about herself. Because she was standing so close to him, he could not answer and took a step backward. She did not follow him, but hesitated. Bloch wanted to touch her. When he finally moved his hand, she looked to one side. Bloch let his hand drop and pretended that he had made a joke. The landlady sat on the other side of the table and went on talking.

He wanted to say something, but then he could not think of what it was he wanted to say. He tried to remember: he could not remember what it was about, but it had something to do with disgust. Then a movement of the landlady's hand reminded him of something else. He could not think of what it was this time either, but it had something to do with shame.

83

s of movements and things did not
f other movements and things but of sen-
eelings, and he did not remember the feel-
they were from the past but relived them
a____ning in the present: he did not remember
shame and nausea but only felt ashamed and nau-
seated now that he remembered without being able to
think of the things that had brought on shame and
nausea. The mixture of nausea and shame was
so strong that his whole body started to itch.

A piece of metal knocked against the windowpane
outside. The landlady answered his question by saying that it was the wire from the lightning rod that
had come loose. Bloch, who had seen a lightning rod
at the school, immediately concluded that this repeti-
tion was intentional; it could be no accident that
he ran across a lightning rod two times in a row. Altogether he found everything alike; all things reminded
him of each other. What was the meaning of the repeated appearances of lightning rods? How should he
interpret the lightning rod? "Lightning rod"? Surely
that was just another word game? Did it mean that
he was safe from harm? Or did it indicate that he
should tell the landlady everything? And why were
the cookies on the wooden plate fish-shaped? What did
they suggest? Should he be "mute as a fish"? Was
he not permitted to talk? Was that what the cookies
on the wooden plate were trying to tell him? It was
as if he did not see any of this but read it off a
posted list of regulations.

Yes, they were regulations. The dishrag hanging
over the faucet told him to do something. Even the
cap of the bottle left on the table, which by now had
been cleared, summoned him to do something.
Everything fell into place: everywhere he saw a sum-
mons: to do one thing, not to do another. Everything
was spelled out for him, the shelf where the spice
boxes were, a shelf with jars of freshly made jam . . .

things repeated themselves. Bloch noticed that for quite a while he had stopped talking to himself: the landlady was at the sink gathering bits of bread out of the saucers. You had to clean up after him all the time, she said, he didn't even shut the table drawer when he took out the silverware; he just left books he had looked through open, he took off his coat and just let it drop.

Bloch answered that he really felt that he would let everything drop. It wouldn't take much for him to let go of this ashtray in his hand, it even surprised him to see that the ashtray was still in his hand. He had stood up, still holding the ashtray in front of him. The landlady looked at him. He stared at the ashtray a while, then he put it down. As if in anticipation of the insinuations all around him, which repeated themselves, Bloch repeated what he had said. He was so helpless that he repeated it once more. He saw the landlady shake her arm over the sink. She said that a piece of apple had slipped up her sleeve and now it didn't want to come out. Didn't want to come out? Bloch imitated her by shaking his own sleeve. It seemed to him that if he imitated everything, he would stay on the safe side, so to speak. But she noticed it immediately and mimicked his imitation of her.

As she did that, she came near the refrigerator, on top of which there was a bakery carton. Bloch watched her as she, still mimicking him, touched the carton from behind. Since he was watching her so intently, she shoved her elbow back once more. The carton began to slip and slowly tipped over the rounded edges of the refrigerator. Bloch could still have caught it, but he watched until it hit the floor.

While the landlady bent down to pick up the carton, he walked one way and then another; wherever he stopped he shoved things into the corner—a chair, a lighter on the stove, an egg cup on the kitchen table. "Is everything all right?" he asked. He asked her what he wanted her to ask him. But before she could answer, something knocked on the window in a way the wire from a lightning rod would never knock against a pane. Bloch had known it a moment beforehand.

The landlady opened the window. A customs guard was outside asking to borrow an umbrella for the walk back to town. Bloch said that he might as well go along with him, and the landlady handed him the umbrella which hung under the work pants on the doorframe. He promised to bring it back the next day. As long as he hadn't brought it back, nothing could go wrong.

On the street he opened the umbrella; the rain immediately rattled so loudly that he did not hear whether she had answered him. The guard came running along the wall of the house to get under the umbrella, and they started off.

They were only a few steps away when the light in the tavern was turned off and it became completely dark. It was so dark that Bloch put his hand over his eyes. Behind the wall that they were just passing he heard the snorting of cows. Something ran past him. "I almost stepped on a hedgehog just then!" the guard exclaimed.

Bloch asked how he could have seen a hedgehog in the dark. The guard answered, "That's part of my profession. Even if all you see is one movement or hear just one noise, you must be able to identify the thing that made that movement or sound. Even when something moves at the very edge of your vision, you must be able to recognize it, in fact even be able to determine what color it is, though actually you can recognize colors only at the center of your retina." They had passed the houses by the border by now and were walking along a short cut beside the brook. The path was covered with sand of some kind, which became brighter as Bloch grew more accustomed to the dark.

"Of course, we're not kept very busy here," the

guard said. "Since the border has been mined, there's no smuggling going on here any more. So your alertness slips, you get tired and can't concentrate any more. And then when something does happen, you don't even react."

Bloch saw something running toward him and stepped behind the guard. A dog brushed past him as it ran past.

"And then if somebody suddenly steps in front of you, you don't even know how you should grab hold of him. You're in the wrong position from the start and when you finally get yourself right, you depend on your partner, who is standing next to you, to catch him, and all along your partner is depending on you to catch him yourself—and the guy you're after gives you the slip." The slip? Bloch heard the customs guard next to him under the umbrella take a deep breath.

Behind him the sand crunched. He turned around and saw that the dog had come back. They walked on, the dog running alongside sniffing at the backs of his knees. Bloch stopped, broke off a hazelnut twig by the brook, and chased the dog away.

"If you're facing each other," the guard went on, "it's important to look the other guy in the eyes. Before he starts to run, his eyes show which direction he'll take. But you've also got to watch his legs at the same time. Which leg is he putting his weight on? The direction that leg is pointing is the direction he'll want to take. But if the other guy wants to fool you and not run in that direction, he'll have to shift his weight just before he takes off, and that takes so much time that you can rush him in the meantime."

Bloch looked down at the brook, whose roaring could be heard but which could not be seen. A heavy bird flew up out of a thicket. Chickens in a coop could be heard scratching and pecking their beaks against the boards.

"Actually, there aren't any hard-and-fast rules,"

said the guard. "You're always at a disadvantage because the other guy also watches to see how you're reacting to him. All you can ever do is react. And when he starts to run, he'll change his direction after the first step and you're the one whose weight is on the wrong foot."

Meanwhile, they had come back to the paved road and were approaching the edge of town. Here and there they stepped on wet sawdust which the rain had swept out to the street. Bloch asked himself whether the guard went into so much detail about something that could be said in one sentence because he was really trying to say something else by it. "He spoke *from memory,*" thought Bloch. As a test, he himself started to talk at great length about something that usually required only one sentence, but the guard seemed to think that this was completely natural and didn't ask him what he was driving at. So the guard seemed to have meant what he said before quite literally.

In the center of town some people who had been taking a dance lesson came toward them. "Dance lessons"? What did that phrase suggest? One girl had been searching for something in her "purse" as she passed, and another had been wearing boots with "high tops." Were these abbreviations for something? He heard the purse snapping shut behind him; he almost closed up his umbrella in reply.

He held the umbrella over the customs guard as far as the municipal housing project. "So far I have only a rented apartment, but I'm saving up to buy one for myself," said the guard, standing on the staircase. Bloch had come in too. Would he like to come up for a drink? Bloch refused but stood still. The lights went off again while the guard was going up the stairs. Bloch leaned against the mailboxes downstairs. Outside, quite high up, a plane flew past. "The mail plane," the guard shouted down into the dark, and pushed the light switch. It echoed in the stairwell. Bloch had quickly gone out.

At the inn he learned that a large tourist group had arrived and had been put up on cots in the bowling alley; that's why it was so quiet down there tonight. Bloch asked the girl who told him about this if she wanted to come upstairs with him. She answered, gravely, that that was impossible tonight. Later, in his room, he heard her walk down the hall and go past his door. The rain had made the room so cold that it seemed to him as if damp sawdust had been spread all over. He set the umbrella tip-down in the sink and lay on the bed fully dressed.

Bloch got sleepy. He made a few tired gestures to make light of his sleepiness, but that made him even sleepier. Various things he had said during the day came back to him; he tried to get rid of them by breathing out. Then he felt himself falling asleep; as before the end of a paragraph, he thought.

He woke up gradually and realized that somebody was breathing loudly in the next room and that the rhythm of the breathing was forming itself into sentences in his half-sleep; he heard the exhale as a long-drawn-out "and," and the extended sound of the inhale then transformed itself inside him into sentences that—after the dash that corresponded to the pause between the inhale and the exhale—invariably attached themselves to the "and." Soldiers with pointed dress shoes stood in front of the movie house, and a vase was on the TV set, and a truck filled with sand whizzed past the bus, and a hitchhiker had a bunch of grapes in his other hand, and outside the door somebody said, "Open up, please."

"Open up, please." Those last three words did not fit at all into the breathing from next door, which became more and more distinct while the sentences were slowly beginning to fade out. He was wide awake now. Somebody knocked on the door again and said, "Open up, please." He must have been wakened by that, since the rain had stopped.

He sat up quickly, a bedspring snapped back into place, the chambermaid was outside the door with the breakfast tray. He hadn't ordered breakfast, he could barely manage to say before she had excused herself and knocked on the door across the hall.

Alone in the room, he found everything rearranged. He turned on the faucet. A fly immediately fell off the mirror into the sink and was washed down at once. He sat down on the bed: just now that chair had been to his right, and now it was to his left. Was the picture reversed? He looked at it from left to right, then from right to left. He repeated the look from left to right; this look seemed to him like reading. He saw a "wardrobe," "then" "a" "wastebasket," "then" "a" "drape"; while looking from right to left, however, he saw ⊐ , next to it the ⊓ , under it the ⊖ , next to it the ▭ , on top of it his ▭; and when he looked around, he saw the ▯ , next to it the ⊿ and the ⊙ . He sat on the ⊔ , under it there was a ▬, next to it a ▭. He walked to the ▦: ▦ ▦:

Bloch closed the curtains and went out.

The dining room downstairs was filled with the tourists. The innkeeper led Bloch into the other room, where the innkeeper's mother was sitting in front of the TV set with the curtains closed. The innkeeper opened the curtains and stood next to Bloch; once Bloch saw him standing to his left; then, when he looked up again, it was the other way around. Bloch ordered breakfast and asked for the newspaper. The innkeeper said that the tourists were reading it just now. Bloch ran his fingers over his face; his cheeks seemed to be numb. He felt cold. The flies on the floor were crawling so slowly that at first he mistook them for beetles. A bee rose from the windowsill but fell back immediately. The people outside were leaping over the puddles; they were carrying heavy shopping bags. Bloch ran his fingers all over his face.

The innkeeper came in with the tray and said that the newspaper still wasn't free. He spoke so softly that Bloch also spoke softly when he answered. "There's no hurry," he whispered. The screen of the TV set was dusty here in the daylight, and the window that the schoolchildren looked through as they walked past was reflected in it. Bloch ate and listened to the show. The innkeeper's mother moaned from time to time.

Outside he noticed a stand with a bag full of newspapers. He went outside, dropped a coin into the slot next to the bag, and then took out a paper. He had so much practice in opening papers that he read the description of himself even as he was going inside. He had attracted a woman's attention on the bus because some change had fallen out of his pocket; she had bent down for it, and had noticed that it was American money. Subsequently, she had heard that similar coins had been found beside the dead cashier. No one took her story seriously at first, but then it turned out that her description matched the description given by one of the cashier's friends who, when he called for the cashier in his car the night before the murder, had seen a man standing near the movie house.

Bloch sat back down in the other room and looked at the picture they had drawn of him according to the woman's description. Did that mean that they did not know his name yet? When had the paper been printed? He saw that it was the first edition, which usually came out the evening before. The headline and the picture looked to him as if they had been pasted onto the paper; like newspapers in movies, he thought: there the real headlines were also replaced by headlines that fitted the film; or like those headlines you could have made up about yourself in penny arcades.

The doodles in the margin had been deciphered as the word "Dumm" and, moreover, with a capital at the beginning; so it was probably a proper name. Was a person named Dumm involved in the matter? Bloch remembered telling the cashier about his friend Dumm, the soccer player.

When the girl cleared the table, Bloch did not close the paper. He learned that the gypsy had been released, that the mute schoolboy's death had been an accident. The paper carried only a school picture of the boy because he had never been photographed alone.

A cushion that the innkeeper's mother was using as a backrest fell from the armchair onto the floor. Bloch picked it up and went out with the paper. He saw the inn's copy lying on the card table; the tourists had left by now. The paper—it was the weekend edition— was so thick that it did not fit into the rack.

When a car drove past him, he stupidly—for it was quite bright out—wondered why its headlights were turned off. Nothing in particular happened. He saw the boxes of apples being poured into sacks in the orchards. A bicycle that passed him slid back and forth in the mud. He saw two farmers shaking hands in a store doorway; their hands were so dry that he heard them rustling. Tractors had left muddy tracks from the dirt paths on the asphalt. He saw an old woman bent over in front of a display window, a finger to her lips. The parking spaces in front of the stores were emptying; the customers who were still arriving came in through the back doors. "Suds" "poured" "over" "the doorsteps." "Featherbeds" "were lying" "behind" "the windowpanes." The blackboards listing prices were carried back into the stores. "The chickens" "pecked at" "grapes that had been dropped." The turkeys squatted heavily in the wire cages in the orchards. The salesgirls stood outside the doors and put their hands on their hips. The owner stood inside the dark store, absolutely still behind the scale. "Lumps of yeast" "lay" "on the counter."

Bloch stood against the wall of a house. There was an odd sound when a casement window that was ajar next to him opened all the way. He had walked on immediately.

He stopped in front of a brand-new building that was still unoccupied but already had glass in its windows. The rooms were so empty that the landscape on the other side could be seen through the windows. Bloch felt as though he had built the house himself. He himself had installed the wall outlets and even set in the windowpanes. The crowbar, the sandwich wrapping, and the plastic food container had also been put on the windowsill by him.

He took a second look: no, the light switches stayed light switches, and the garden chairs in the landscape behind the house stayed garden chairs.

He walked on because—

Did he have to give a reason for walking, so that—?

What did he have in mind when—? Did he have to justify the "when" by—? Did this go on until—? Had he reached the point where—?

Why did anything have to be inferred from the fact

that he was walking here? Did he have to give a reason for stopping here? Why did he have to have something in mind when he walked past a swimming pool?

These "so thats," "becauses," and "whens" were like regulations; he decided to avoid them in order not to—

It was as if a window that was slightly ajar was gently opened beside him. Everything thinkable, everything visible, was occupied. It was not a scream that startled him but a sentence upside down at the top of a series of normal sentences. Everything seemed to have been newly named.

The stores were already closed. The window displays, now that nobody was walking back and forth in front of them any more, looked too full. Not a single spot was without at least a stack of cans on it. A half-torn receipt hung out of the cash register. The stores were so crowded that . . .

"The stores were so crowded that you couldn't point to anything any more because . . ." "The stores were so crowded that you couldn't point to anything any more because the individual items hid each other." The parking spaces were now completely empty except for the bicycles of the salesgirls.

After lunch Bloch went to the athletic field. Even from far away he heard the spectators' screaming. When he got there, the reserves were still playing a pregame match. He sat on a bench at the sidelines and read the paper as far as the supplements. He heard a sound as if a chunk of meat had fallen on a stone floor; he looked up and saw that the wet heavy ball had smacked off a player's head.

He got up and walked away. When he came back, the main match had already started. The benches were filled, and he walked beside the playing field to the space behind the goal. He did not want to stand too close behind the goal, and he climbed up the bank to the street. He walked along the street as far as the corner flag. It seemed to him that a button was coming off his jacket and popping on the street; he picked up the button and put in in his pocket.

He started talking to some man who was standing next to him. He asked which teams were playing and about their standings in the league. They shouldn't play the ball so high in a strong wind like this, he said.

He noticed that the man next to him had buckles on his shoes. "I don't know either," the man answered. "I'm a salesman, and I'm here for only a few days."

"The men are shouting much too much," Bloch said. "A good game goes very quietly."

"There's no coach to tell them what to do from the sidelines," answered the man. It seemed to Bloch as though they were talking to each other for the benefit of some third party.

"On a small field like this you have to decide very quickly when to pass," he said.

He heard a slap as if the ball had hit a goalpost. Bloch told about how he had once played against a team whose players were all barefoot; every time they kicked the ball, the slapping sound had gone right through him.

"In the stadium I once saw a player break his leg," the salesman said. "You could hear the cracking sound all the way up in the top rows."

Bloch saw the other spectators around him talking to each other. He did not watch the one who happened to be speaking but always watched the one who was listening. He asked the salesman whether he had ever tried to look away from the forward at the beginning of a rush and, instead, to look at the goalie the forwards were rushing toward.

"It's very difficult to take your eyes off the forwards and the ball and watch the goalie," Bloch said. "You have to tear yourself away from the ball; it's a completely unnatural thing to do." Instead of seeing the ball, you saw how the goalkeeper ran back and forth with his hands on his thighs, how he bent to the left and right and screamed at his defense. "Usually you don't notice him until the ball has been shot at the goal."

They walked along the sideline together. Bloch heard panting as though a linesman were running past them. "It's a strange sight to watch the goalie running back and forth like that, without the ball but expecting it," he said.

He couldn't watch that way for very long, answered the salesman; you couldn't help but look back at the forwards. If you looked at the goalkeeper, it seemed as if you had to look cross-eyed. It was like seeing somebody walk toward the door and instead of looking at the man you looked at the doorknob. It made your head hurt, and you couldn't breathe properly any more.

"You get used to it," said Bloch, "but it's ridiculous."

A penalty kick was called. All the spectators rushed behind the goal.

"The goalkeeper is trying to figure out which corner the kicker will send the ball into," Bloch said. "If he knows the kicker, he knows which corner he usually goes for. But maybe the kicker is also counting on the goalie's figuring this out. So the goalie goes on figuring that just today the ball might go into the other corner. But what if the kicker follows the goalkeeper's thinking and plans to shoot into the usual corner after all? And so on, and so on."

Boch saw how all the players gradually cleared the penalty area. The penalty kicker adjusted the ball. Then he too backed out of the penalty area.

"When the kicker starts his run, the goalkeeper unconsciously shows with his body which way he'll throw himself even before the ball is kicked, and the kicker can simply kick in the other direction," Bloch said. "The goalie might just as well try to pry open a door with a piece of straw."

The kicker suddenly started his run. The goalkeeper, who was wearing a bright yellow jersey, stood absolutely still, and the penalty kicker shot the ball into his hands.

Short Letter,
Long Farewell

TRANSLATED BY RALPH MANHEIM

"And once when they were strolling outside the town gate on a warm but overcast morning, Iffland said that this would be good weather to go away in—and indeed, the weather seemed made for travel: the sky lay close to earth and the objects round about were dark, as though to confine the traveler's attention to the road he was going to travel."

Karl Philipp Moritz, *Anton Reiser*

The
Short Letter

*J*EFFERSON Street is a quiet thoroughfare in Providence. It circles around the business section, changes its name to Norwich Street in the South End, and leads into the old Boston Post Road. Here and there Jefferson Street widens into small squares bordered by beech and maple trees. On one of these, Wayland Square, there is a good-sized building in the style of an English manor house, the Wayland Manor Hotel. When I arrived there at the end of April, the desk clerk took a letter from my pigeon-hole and handed it to me along with my key. Before entering the elevator, I tore open the envelope, which, come to think of it, was barely sealed. The letter was short: "I am in New York. Please don't look for me. It would not be nice for you to find me."

As far back as I can remember, I seem to have been born for horror and fear. Before the American bombers came, someone carried me into the house; firewood was scattered all over the yard in the quiet sunlight. Drops of blood glistened on the side steps where hares were butchered on weekends. In a dusk more terrifying than black night, I stumbled, my arms swinging ridiculously, along the edge of the woods sunk in darkness; only the lichen on the outermost tree trunks still shimmered faintly; from time to time I stopped still and cried out in a voice made pathetically feeble by shame; then, when I was too horror-stricken to feel ashamed, I bellowed into the woods from the bottom of my soul, bellowed for someone who had gone into the woods that morning and hadn't come out; and again the fluffy feathers of fleeing chickens lay scattered all over the yard and the house walls in the sunlight.

As I entered the elevator, the old Negro operator told me to watch my step, and I stumbled a little over the slightly raised floor of the car. The Negro closed the door and the inner gate and set the elevator in motion with a lever.

There must have been a service elevator beside the passenger elevator, because, as we slowly rose, a tinkling as of piled cups kept pace with us and continued unchanged all the way up. I raised my eyes from my letter and studied the elevator operator, who stood bent over the lever in the dark corner and did not look at me. His deep-blue uniform made him almost invisible except for his white shirt . . . Suddenly, as often happens to me when I am in a room with other people and no one has said anything for a while, I was sure that in another second the Negro would go mad and fling himself at me. I took the newspaper I had bought that morning before leaving Boston out of my coat pocket, and, by pointing at the headlines, tried to explain to the elevator operator that because various European currencies had just been revalued I would have to spend all my American money on my trip, since if I changed it back again on my return to Europe I would receive much less for it than I had paid. The elevator operator nodded and pointed at the pile of papers under the seat, on top of which lay the coins he had received for the papers he had already sold; the *Providence Journal* under the seat carried the same headlines as my *Boston Globe*.

Relieved that the elevator operator had communicated with me, I reached into my trouser pocket for a banknote, so as to hand it to him as soon as he opened my room door and put down my suitcase. But once in the room, I saw to my surprise that what I had in my hand was a ten-dollar bill. I shifted it to my other hand and, without taking my wad of bills from my pocket, rummaged for a dollar bill. When I thought I had found one, I transferred it directly from my pocket to the elevator operator. It was a five-dollar bill and instantly the Negro closed his hand over it. "I haven't been here long enough," I said aloud when I was alone. Still in my overcoat, I went into the bathroom and looked more at the mirror than at myself. I saw a few hairs on my coat collar and said, "I must have shed these hairs in the bus." I sat down on the edge of the bathtub, disconcerted because I had started talking to myself for the first time since I was a child. By talking rather loudly to himself, the child had provided himself with a companion. But here, where I had decided for once to observe rather than participate, I was at a loss to see why I was doing it. I began to giggle and finally, in a fit of exuberance, punched myself in the head so hard that I almost toppled into the bathtub.

The bottom of the tub was covered with crisscrossing, light-colored strips of something that looked like adhesive tape; they were supposed to prevent the bather from slipping. Between the sight of the adhesive tape and the thought of my conversation with myself I instantly saw a correspondence which was so incomprehensible that I stopped giggling and went back into the room.

In front of the window, which faced a rural-looking area with a sprinkling of small houses, there were tall birch trees. The leaves on the trees were still tiny and the sun shone through. I opened the window, pulled up an easy chair, and sat down; I put my feet on the radiator, which must have been hot early in the morning and was still slightly warm. The easy chair had casters; I rolled back and forth and looked at the envelope. It was a light-blue hotel envelope; on the back was printed "Delmonico's, Park Avenue at Fifty-ninth Street, New York." But the postmark said "PHILADELPHIA, PA."; the letter had been mailed there five days before. I saw the letters *p.m.* in the postmark, and said aloud, "In the afternoon."

"Where did she get the money for the trip?" I asked. "She must have a lot of money, I'm sure a room in that place costs thirty dollars." Delmonico's was known to me chiefly from musicals: country people danced in from the street and dined with rustic awkwardness in separated stalls. "On the other hand, she has no idea of money, not the usual idea in any case. Children always go in for swapping and she's never got over it, to her money is just something to be swapped. She loves everything that can be easily used up or at least easily exchanged, and money gives her both possibilities in one." I looked out as far as I could and saw a church that was obscured by the haze rising from a textile mill; according to my map, it must have been the Baptist church. "Her letter took a long time to get here," I said. "Could she have died in the meantime?" Once toward evening I had climbed a rocky hill to look for my mother. She had spells of melancholy, and I thought she must have jumped off it, or perhaps just let herself fall. I stood on the hilltop and looked down at the village in the early dusk. I saw nothing in particular, but a group of women, who had put down their shopping bags as if something frightening had happened and were soon joined by someone else, gave me the idea of looking for scraps of clothing on the ledges below me. I was unable to open my mouth, the air hurt me; everything in me had shriveled with fear. Then the lights went on in the village below, and a few cars went by with their headlights on. Up on the cliff it grew very still, only the crickets were still chirping. I felt heavier and heavier. The lamps went on in the gas station at the end of the village. But it was still light! The people in the street began to walk faster. While taking short steps back and forth on the hilltop, I saw someone moving very slowly among them and recognized my mother, who had recently taken to doing everything very slowly. And when she crossed the street, it was not directly, as usual, but in a long diagonal.

I rolled my chair to the bedside table and called Delmonico's Hotel in New York. It wasn't until I gave Judith's maiden name that they found her in the register. She had checked out five days before, without leaving a forwarding address; and, oh yes, she had forgotten a camera in her room: should they send it to her address in Europe? I said I would be in New York next day and pick it up myself. "Yes," I repeated after hanging up, "I am her husband." To avoid giggling again, I rolled back to the window.

Without getting up I took off my coat and leafed through the traveler's checks which, having heard a good deal about all the mugging in America, I had procured before leaving Austria. The bank clerk, to be sure, had promised to take the checks back at the same rate, but now that the revaluation had been announced, he could hardly be held to his promise. "How can I spend all of three thousand dollars over here?" I asked. It had been pure caprice to exchange so much. Then and there I decided to spend the money living as lazily and frivolously as possible. I called Delmonico's again to reserve a room for the next day. When they told me none was available, I asked them to reserve one at the Waldorf Astoria, the first place that entered my head, but then I changed my mind and, thinking of F. Scott Fitzgerald, whose books I was reading at the time, switched to the Algonquin on Forty-fourth Street, where he had often stayed. At the Algonquin there was still a room to be had.

Then, as I was running water for a bath, it occurred to me that Judith must have drawn what money was left in my account. "I shouldn't have given her that power of attorney," I said, though I didn't really mind; actually I was amused and curious to know what would happen next, but only for a moment, because the last time I had seen her, stretched out on her bed one afternoon, she had become inaccessible and had looked at me in such a way that I stopped still on my way to her, knowing that I could no longer help her.

I stretched out in the tub and read the end of Fitzgerald's *The Great Gatsby*. It is a love story about a man who buys a house on a bay for the sole purpose of seeing the lights go on every evening in a house on the other side of the bay, where the woman he loves is living with another man. For the great Gatsby's delicacy, his sense of shame, was as great as his obsession with his love, while the woman grew more cowardly as her love grew more desperate and shameless.

"Yes," I said, "on the one hand I have a strong sense of shame; on the other hand, where my feelings for Judith are concerned, I am cowardly. In my dealings with her I have always been afraid to come out of my shell. I see now that my sense of shame, which I have clung to because I thought it preserved me from putting up with everything, is a kind of cowardice. The great Gatsby's delicacy applied only to the formal aspect of the love that possessed him. He was polite. I would like to be as polite and ruthless as he was, if it's not too late."

I opened the stopper while still sitting in the bath. I closed my eyes and leaned back as the water slowly flowed out, and it seemed to me as though with the leisurely ebbing of the water I myself were growing smaller, until finally I dissolved altogether. It was not until I felt cold because I was lying in the waterless tub that I became aware of myself again and stood up. I took hold of my member, first with the towel, then with my bare hand, and began to masturbate. It took a long time; now and then I opened my eyes and looked at the frosted-glass bathroom window on which the shadows of birch leaves were moving up and down. When the sperm finally came, my knees buckled. Then I washed myself, sprayed out the bathtub, and dressed.

I lay on the bed awhile, unable to think of anything. For a moment this was painful, then I found it pleasant. I wasn't sleepy, only unthinking. From time to time I heard, at some distance from the window, a sound like a combined thud and crash, followed by the cries of the students who were playing baseball on the Brown University campus.

I stood up, washed a pair of socks with the hotel soap, and went down the stairs to the lobby. The elevator operator was sitting on a stool beside the elevator, with his head propped on his hands. I went out; it was late afternoon; the cab drivers on the square, who were chatting as they sat in their drivers' seats waiting, called out to me as I passed. When I had gone some distance, I noticed that my reluctance to answer them with so much as a gesture had cheered me up.

"This is my second day in America," I said, stepping off the sidewalk into the roadway and then back onto the sidewalk. "I wonder if I've already changed." Involuntarily I cast a glance over my shoulder as I walked, then looked at my wrist watch impatiently. As happens occasionally when something I've read makes me want to have the same experiences for myself, the great Gatsby now commanded me to transform myself instantly. Suddenly the impulse to become different from what I was became a physical need. How, I wondered, could I show the feelings the great Gatsby had made possible in me, and act on them in my environment? They were feelings of warmth, attentiveness, serenity, and happiness, and I sensed that I had to banish forever my predisposition to fear and panic. My new feelings could be acted upon: never again would I be parched with terror! But where was the environment in which I would finally show that I'm capable of being different? For the present I had left my old environment behind me; in my new environment I was still incapable of being anything more than a someone who made use of public conveniences, walked on streets, rode on buses, lived in hotels, and sat on bar stools. Nor did I wish to be anything more, because to do so I should have had to show off. I believed that I had finally rid myself of the need to get attention by showing off. Nevertheless, determined to be alert and open to my surroundings, I quickly looked away from everyone who approached me on the sidewalk, soured by the sight of another face, disgusted as usual with everything that was not myself. Once, as I proceeded down Jefferson Street, I caught myself thinking of Judith and chased her away in the time it took to expel my breath and take a few steps; otherwise my mind was empty of human inhabitants, and my whole body was filled with a hot anger that became almost murderous because I could direct it neither at myself nor at anything else.

I turned into a side street. The street lamps had come on and the sky was very blue. The sun had set and the grass under the trees sparkled in the afterglow. A slow rain of blossoms fell from the bushes of the front gardens. Not far away, the door of a big American car slammed. I went back to Jefferson Street and had a ginger ale in a snack bar that didn't serve alcoholic beverages. When the ginger ale was gone, I waited until the two lumps of ice in my glass had melted, then drank the water; it tasted bitter, but pleasantly so after the sweet ginger ale. On the wall beside every table there was a box with which one could operate the jukebox without getting up. I put in a quarter and selected Otis Redding's "Sitting on the Dock of the Bay." I thought of the great Gatsby and became more self-assured than ever before in my life: to the point that I lost all awareness of myself. I would do many things differently. I would become unrecognizable! I ordered a hamburger and a Coca-Cola. I felt tired and yawned. In the middle of my yawn, I felt a hollow inside me; instantly it filled with the image of a deep black forest, and once again, like a recurrence of fever, the thought that Judith was dead came over me. The image of the forest grew still darker when I looked into the gathering darkness outside the snack bar, and my horror became so great that I suddenly turned back into an inert object. I couldn't eat any more, I could only drink in short sips. I ordered another Coca-Cola and sat there with pounding heart.

My sense of horror and the need to change as quickly as possible and get rid of it made me impatient. The time passed so slowly that I looked at my wrist watch again. My old hysterical time sense took hold of me. Years before, I had once seen a fat woman bathing in the sea; every ten minutes I turned to look at her, because I seriously thought she must have grown thinner in the meantime. And now in the snack bar I kept looking at a man with a scab on his forehead, eager to know if the scab had finally gone away.

Judith had no sense of time, I thought. True, she never forgot an appointment, but she was always late, like the women in jokes. Her feeling simply didn't tell her that the time had come. She seldom knew what day it was. If anyone told her the time, it frightened her; whereas I went to the phone almost every hour to find out what time it was. She always cried out, "Oh, it's so late!" She never said, "Oh, it's so early!" She was incapable of thinking that it could ever be time to do this or that. I said to her, "Maybe it's because you've moved so often ever since you were a child, because you've lived in so many places. You always know where you were before, but never *when* you were there. And the fact is that your sense of direction is much better than mine; I often get lost. Or maybe it's because you had a job with fixed working hours much too soon. But to tell you the honest truth, I'm certain that if you have no feeling for time it's simply because you have no feeling for other people." She answered, "No, that's not true, it's only for myself that I have no feeling." "In addition," I said, "you have no money sense." She agreed: "No, I have no head for figures." "And even your sense of direction makes me dizzy," I went on. "When you go up to a house, you always say you're going *down;* long after we've stepped out of the house, you say the car is *outside;* and when you drive downtown, you say it's uptown, because the street goes north."

On the other hand, I now thought, it's my exaggerated sense of time, meaning perhaps my exaggerated feeling for myself, that prevents me from achieving the attentive detachment I'm aiming at.

I stood up, this reminiscence was too silly. I took my check to the cashier and stupidly, without a word, put down a banknote; that was the way I felt at the moment, and I was glad that this gesture required little change in my attitude. As I was leaving, an at first angry, then euphoric revulsion toward all the concepts, definitions, and abstractions in terms of which I had just been thinking made me stop still for a moment. I tried to belch; the Coca-Cola helped. Outside, a chubby-cheeked crew-cut student wearing sneakers and Bermuda shorts that revealed his fat thighs came toward me; I looked at him in horror, aghast at the thought that someone might still dare to make a general statement about this individual figure, that someone might classify him and set him down as a representative of something else. Involuntarily I said hello and looked at him without embarrassment. He too said hello. He was an image that had suddenly come to life, and now I knew why for some time I had been able to read only stories about individuals. Take the cashier at the snack bar! Her hair was bleached, the black roots peeped out, and beside her she had a small upright American flag. What of it? Nothing at all. In retrospect her face actually began to gleam and took on the obstinate look of a saint. I turned back to the fat student. A likeness of Al Wilson, the singer in the Canned Heat Show, was printed on the back of his shirt. Wison was short and stocky. He had pimples that you could see clearly on TV, and wore glasses. A few months before, he had been found dead in his sleeping bag outside his house in Laurel Canyon near Los Angeles. In a delicate high voice he had sung "On the Road Again" and "Going up the Country." I felt differently about him than about Jimi Hendrix or Janis Joplin, who, like rock music in general, were beginning to leave me cold; I still ached with his death, and his short life, which I then thought I understood, often came back to me in painful half-waking thoughts. On my way back to the hotel two lines I had often put together occurred to me:

> "I say goodbye to Colorado" and
> "It's so nice to walk in California."

Next to the barbershop in the basement of the hotel there was a bar; I sat at a table in the dark, eating potato chips and drinking tequila; from time to time the waitress brought a fresh bag of potato chips and emptied it into my plate. Two men were sitting at the next table; I listened to their conversation long enough to find out that they were businessmen from the nearby city of Fall River. The waitress sat down with them and I watched the three of them attentively but without curiosity. Their table was rather too small for three; in between the whiskey glasses, which the waitress perhaps intentionally neglected to remove, they were playing poker dice. Except for them it was almost silent in the room—only a small ventilator over the bar was purring gently—and I could hear the clicking when the dice struck the glasses; now and then the tape that was being rewound behind the bar made a flapping sound. I noticed that little by little I was beginning to take in the surroundings without any sense of strain.

The waitress signaled me to move to their table, but I didn't accept the invitation until one of the businessmen drew up another chair and pointed to it. At first I only watched; then I joined in the game, but soon stopped because one of my dice kept falling on the floor. I ordered another tequila. The waitress brought the bottle from the bar and turned on the tape recorder. Back at the table she sprinkled salt over the back of her hand, licked it off, spilling a few grains on the table, and took a sip of tequila from my glass. On the bottle there was a picture of an agave in the middle of a desert with glittering yellow sand. From the tape recorder came Western music: a male chorus sang the song of the U.S. Cavalry, then came a postlude without voices, in which the trumpets dropped out little by little until in the end only a harmonica was playing softly. The waitress told me her son was in the army, and I said I'd like to join in the dice game again.

Then something strange happened to me: I needed a particular number; when I tipped the cup, all the dice except one came instantly to rest; while this one was rolling between the glasses, the number I needed flashed up at me and vanished; when the dice stopped rolling, another number was on top. But the brief appearance of my number had made such a strong impression that I felt as if my number had really come up—not now but AT SOME OTHER TIME.

This other time was not the future or the past, it

was in essence a time OTHER than the time in which I ordinarily lived and thought forward and backward. I was filled with a sense of ANOTHER time, in which there must be places different from any present place, in which everything must have a different meaning than in my present consciousness, in which feelings were different from present feelings, so that I myself at that very moment was in the same state as the lifeless earth on the day when, for the first time after thousands of years of rain, a raindrop fell that did not instantly evaporate. Quickly as it passed, this feeling was so penetrating and painful that it was echoed in a brief, unthinking glance from the waitress, which I at once recognized to be unblinking though not rigid, infinitely wide-eyed, infinitely awake, and at the same time infinitely spent, a glance so full of longing as to tear the retina and provoke a faint cry, the glance of ANOTHER woman at that OTHER TIME. There had to be something more than the life I had been living up until now! I looked at my watch, paid my check, and went up to my room.

I slept a sound dreamless sleep, but all night my whole body was suffused with a feeling of expectant happiness, which left me only toward morning. Then I began to dream and awoke feeling ill at ease. My socks were laid out on the radiator and there was an irregular gap at one side of the window curtain, which was imprinted with scenes from American history: jiggling in the breeze, Sir Walter Raleigh was smoking a cigar in his Virginia colony; the Pilgrim Fathers, tight-packed aboard the *Mayflower,* were landing in Massachusetts; George Washington was listening, while Benjamin Franklin read the Constitution; on their way from the Missouri to the mouth of the Columbia River, Captains Lewis and Clark were shooting Blackfoot Indians (one of the Indians, on a hill far in the distance, was still holding his arm half upraised in the direction of the rifle barrel); and to one side of the battlefield at Appomattox, Abraham Lincoln, leaning slightly backward, was holding out his hand to a Negro.

I opened the curtain but did not look out. The sun shone in on the floor and warmed my bare feet. When I saw the Bible on the bedside table, I thought of the story about Judith cutting Holofernes' head off. "She has always stepped, or rather stumbled, on my feet," I said. "In fact, she was always stumbling over something. She hopped and danced along, and then she stumbled. Then she would start hopping again and bump into someone who was coming toward her, and a little later she would slip and jab herself with a knitting needle she always carried around, though she seldom finished knitting anything and always had to unravel it.

"And yet she's efficient," I went on while taking my bath, while shaving, while dressing and packing; "she could drive nails without ever bending one, lay carpets, paper walls, cut clothes, make wooden benches, hammer out bumps in the car, but when engaged in these activities she kept slipping, stumbling and trampling on other things, until I couldn't bear to look. And her gestures! Once she came into the room and wanted me to turn off the record player: standing rigidly in the doorway, she jerked her head slightly in the direction of the record player. Another time the doorbell rang: she got there before I did and saw a letter lying on the doormat. She left the door ajar; when I arrived she opened it again so as to let me pick up the letter. She did it without thinking, but my hand slipped. I slapped her in the face. Luckily my aim was bad, it was only a glancing blow, and we soon made up."

I paid the hotel bill with a traveler's check and hailed a taxi, which here in Providence was not yet yellow but black as in England, and drove to the Greyhound bus terminal.

During the ride through New England I had time

for . . . for what? I thought. I soon got sick of looking out, because the color of the Greyhound bus windows gave the landscape a somber look. From time to time we stopped at a toll station and the driver handed a few coins out the window to a toll-taker. Whe I opened the window to get a better view, someone told me an open window upset the air-cooling system and I closed it again. The closer we came to New York, the more written advertisements gave way to pictures: gigantic overflowing beer mugs, a catchup bottle as big as a lighthouse, a life-size picture of a jet plane flying above the clouds. Beside me, peanuts were eaten and cigarettes smoked, and though drinking was prohibited, beer cans were passed secretly from mouth to mouth. Since I seldom looked up, I saw no faces, only activities. On the floor lay walnut and peanut shells, some wrapped in chewing-gum paper. I began to read Gottfried Keller's *Green Heinrich*.

Heinrich Lee's father had died when he was five years old. All he remembered about his father was how one day the man had pulled up a potato plant and shown him the tubers. Because the boy was always dressed in green, he soon came to be known as Green Heinrich.

The bus took the Bruckner Expressway through the Bronx, turned off to the right, and crossed the Harlem River to Manhattan. As it made its way slowly, but as fast as possible, down Fifth Avenue through Harlem, the people in the bus brought their Kodaks and movie cameras into play. It was Saturday, the black inhabitants of Harlem were taking the air on sidewalks bordered by wrecked cars and tumble-down tenements, only the ground floors of which were still inhabited. Some were reading the paper, boys were playing baseball and girls badminton in the street. The usual signs such as HAMBURGERS and PIZZA seemed strangely out of place. The bus drove on past Central Park and finally turned into a dark bus terminal on Forty-first Street. There I took a cab, which was now yellow, and drove to the Hotel Algonquin.

The Algonquin was a narrow, not very tall building with small rooms; when I closed the door to my room, an intervening crack remained, as if the door had often been tugged at. As I passed, I saw signs of scratching on some of the locks. This time I succeeded in giving the Japanese who carried my suitcase a dollar bill without incident.

The room was on a court; so, apparently, was the kitchen, for I saw steam rising from the ventilators and heard the rattling of dishes and cutlery. It was very cool in the room, the air conditioning roared, and because I had been conveyed all day with no effort on my part, I began to shiver while sitting on the bed to calm myself. I tried to turn off the air conditioning but couldn't find a switch. I called the desk and they shut it off from down below. The roaring stopped. In the silence the room seemed to get bigger. I lay down on the bed and ate the grapes out of the fruit bowl that I found on the bedside table.

At first I thought it was the grapes that were bloating me so. My torso swelled up, while my head and limbs shrank into animal appendages, a bird's skull and a fish's fins. In the middle I was crushed by the heat, at the extremities I was freezing. There ought to be some way of pushing back these excrescences! A vein in my hand quivered furiously; my nose began to burn, as though it had collided violently with something, and it was only then that I realized that my fear of death had taken body again now that I had been set down after a long trip, not fear of my own death but an almost insane fear of other people's sudden death. My nose suddenly cooled off, the quivering vein in my hand relaxed, and before me I saw the image of a dark, breathlessly still deep-sea valley without a living soul in it.

I called the hotel in Providence and asked if there was a message for me; there wasn't. I gave them the address of my hotel in New York. Then, wishing to provide another forwarding address, I leafed through the Philadelphia section of my guidebook and chose at random the Barclay Hotel on Rittenhouse Square. I called the desk again and asked the clerk to book me a train ticket to Philadelphia. Then I rang Delmonico's Hotel and asked if my wife had picked up her camera in the meantime; she hadn't. I said I would be there myself in an hour. I waited a few minutes, dialed zero, and said I wished to make a call to Europe. The hotel operator connected me with the overseas operator, and I gave him my mother's phone number in Austria. Was it a person-to-person call or would I speak to anyone who answered? The latter, the operator informed me, would cost much less. "I don't care who answers," I said. It was a relief to be playing the part of an unknown interlocutor: in such a role you could lose yourself completely. The operator asked me for my number and, when I had read it off the phone, told me to hang up.

I sat still, looking at the empty clothes hangers in the closet that I had opened on coming in. Now I could hear loud voices from the kitchen. By then it must have been early afternoon. From time to time phones rang in other rooms. Then mine rang loudly; the overseas operator told me to hold on. The telephone crackled: I spoke into it but received no answer. For a long time I heard only a buzzing and a soft hissing sound. Then some more crackling, followed by the same sounds as before, but not quite the same, and, sure enough, a moment later came a long-drawn-out signal that was repeated several times. I held on. The Vienna operator answered, and I heard the overseas operator giving her my number. I heard the number being dialed in Vienna; again there was a ringing, and I heard a woman on another line laughing and saying

121

in Austrian dialect, "I know!" And then another woman: "You don't know a thing." The ringing broke off, and as though disguising his voice the boy next door shouted his name into the phone. I tried to tell him who and where I was, but he was so confused, as if awakened out of a sound sleep, that he could only repeat, "She's taking the last bus! She's taking the last bus!" Quickly but for no particular reason, very quietly, I hung up. Then I saw another image: by the side of a forest path stood a hunter's blind and beside the blind a cross, and in front of the cross marsh grass was slowly springing up.

"I'll never get used to the telephone," I said. "It wasn't till I went to the university that I made my first call from a phone booth. I started doing a good many things when I was too old to take them for granted. That's why there are so many things I can't get used to. When once in a blue moon I'd get to the point of feeling unreflectingly at ease with somebody, I always had to start all over again the next day. Today life with a woman sometimes strikes me as an artificial state of affairs, as absurd as a filmed novel. I feel that I'm overdoing it when I order something for her in a restaurant. Often when I'm walking *beside* her or sitting *beside* her, I feel as though a mime were doing it and I were only pretending."

The phone rang again; the receiver was still moist because I had held it so long while waiting. The hotel operator told me what my conversation had cost and asked me whether to put the seven dollars on my hotel bill. I was delighted: that made seven dollars less. I asked where in the neighborhood I could get out-of-town newspapers. Only then did it occur to me that in Europe it was already night. The operator suggested Times Square, and I went out.

I walked east on Forty-fourth Street. "No, west!" I turned around and went in the opposite direction, thinking I would come to Broadway. I had crossed

Fifth and Madison Avenues before I realized that I had not really turned around. I must only have imagined that I had turned around and gone in the opposite direction. However, because I felt turned around, I stood still and thought it over until my head was spinning. Then I went down Madison Avenue to Forty-second Street. There I turned, proceeded slowly, and actually reached Broadway at Times Square.

I bought the *Philadelphia Inquirer* and looked through it at the newsstand. There was no mention of Judith. Since I hadn't expected to find anything, I put my paper back on the pile, bought some German papers, and read them while drinking American beer at a bar. I soon noticed that I had already read them on the plane to Boston. I had only glanced through them, but I must have absorbed them, because I now remembered every detail.

I walked east on Forty-second Street and turned north at Park Avenue. I felt as I had for a period in the past when in telling someone what I had just been doing I compulsively described all the partial actions of which the total action was composed. If I went into a house, I never said, "I went into the house," but, "I wiped my shoes, turned the door handle, pushed the door, went in, and closed the door behind me"; or if I had written someone a letter, I always (instead of saying, "I wrote him a letter") said, "I took out a clean sheet of paper, removed the cap from my fountain pen, wrote the letter, folded it, put it in an envelope, addressed the envelope, affixed a stamp, and dropped my letter in the mailbox." In unfamiliar surroundings, as I am now, I tried to deceive my own sense of ignorance and inexperience by dissecting the few activities within my reach as though speaking of momentous undertakings. And now in very much the same way I crossed Fifth Avenue and Madison Avenue, walked up and over to Park Avenue and up Park to Fifty-

ninth Street, stepped under a marquee, pushed a revolving door, and entered Delmonico's.

The desk clerk had the camera ready for me. He
handed it to me without looking at my passport. It was
the large Polaroid camera I had once bought at an
airport, where it cost much more than it would have
anywhere else. By the number on the paper tab sticking out of one side, I saw that Judith had taken a few
pictures. So she had seen something she wanted to remember. That struck me as so auspicious an omen
that on leaving the hotel I felt utterly carefree.

It was a bright day and the wind made it seem even
brighter; the clouds were racing across the sky. Out on
the street I stopped and looked around. Two girls were
standing in a phone booth outside the hotel. One was
talking into the phone; from time to time the other
leaned over and took up the conversation, meanwhile
pushing her hair back behind one ear. At first the
sight of them merely arrested my attention, then it
cheered me, and I took genuine pleasure in watching
the two of them in the tiny booth, as one or the other
kept pushing the door open with her foot, as they
laughed, passed the receiver back and forth, exchanged
whispers, inserted another coin, and continued to take
turns in bending over the phone, while outside the
booth the steam from the sewer poured out of the
street gratings and drifted off across the asphalt. The
sight relieved me of all burdens. I watched them in a
paradisiacal state of lightness, a state in which one has
no desire but to see, and in which to see is to know.
Then I went back down Park Avenue until it changed
its name to Park Avenue South, and on to Eighteenth
Street.

I went into the Elgin Theatre, where one of Johnny
Weissmuller's *Tarzan* pictures was playing. From the
start I had a feeling that I was seeing something forbidden, but something I could visualize in advance. A

small airplane was flying low over the jungle. An interior view of the plane disclosed a man, a woman, and a baby. The plane roared and jiggled strangely as a real plane would never do. Suddenly the jiggling sparked a memory of the bench on which I had seen this same film as a child. "They're on their way to Nairobi," I said aloud. But the name of the city was not mentioned. "And now they're going to crash!" The parents held each other in an embrace; then the plane was seen from outside, whirling downward and vanishing among the trees. It fell with a crash, and no, not smoke but air bubbles rose from a twilight landscape, which later, when that part of the picture came along, I recognized as the pond beneath whose surface Tarzan, with a knife between his teeth, and the orphaned baby, who had grown in the meantime to be a boy, were breathing out air bubbles at long intervals while slowly swimming about as though lost in a dream. Immediately after the plane crash, my memory, which subsequently hardened into a firm image, began, by a mysterious process of anticipation, to move in the rhythm of the air bubbles which, later, released by the two swimmers, rose to the surface of the water.

Although the picture otherwise bored me, I did not leave. Comics don't amuse me any more, I thought; they stopped amusing me long before I came over here. For a time I read a lot of comics. What I should have avoided was comic books. One adventure begins and ends and another starts right in. I remember a bad night I had had after reading *Peanuts;* each one of my dreams stopped after four frames and was followed by a new dream, which in turn consisted of four frames. I had the feeling that in every fourth frame my feet were pulled out from under me and I fell flat on my face. And then another adventure story started up! The same with the movies. I wouldn't want to see any more silent comedies, I thought. Their praise of clumsiness would no longer flatter me. The heroes who can't walk

down the street without having their hats blown into
the paths of steamrollers, or bow to a lady without
pouring coffee on her skirt, had come to strike me more
and more as exemplars of an inhuman life that
survives only in the minds of children: breathless,
floundering, distorted figures who also distort their surroundings, whose only desire is to *look up* at the world,
at things and people. On the one hand, Chaplin's
scornful *Schadenfreude,* on the other, the way he cud-
dles up to himself and mothers himself; Harry
Langdon's way of rolling in and attaching himself to
people. Only Buster Keaton, with that obstinate alert
look of his, searched frantically for a way out, though
he would never know what was happening to him. I
still liked to look at his face, and it was also nice when
Marilyn Monroe combined a frown, a helpless grin,
and the candid gaze of Stan Laurel.

When I came out of the movie theater, it was getting dark. Wondering what to do next, I walked rather
slowly. In front of me a tall girl was also walking
slowly, as though propelled by her dangling handbag.
She had black hair and was wearing blue jeans, but
because of her relaxed movements they didn't look like
blue jeans; they neither creased at the buttocks at every step, nor did they, as usual, bag behind the knees.
She looked around—and kept on walking, as slowly as
before. Suddenly I was overcome with excitement because I knew I was going to speak to her. We walked
along almost side by side, then she took the lead, then
I overtook her. By the time we reached Broadway, I
was so excited that I wanted to topple her over on the
street. But when at last I spoke to her, I only asked if
she would have a drink with me.

She said, "Why not?" but then it was over. Both of
us still flushed with the excitement of our meeting, we
just walked on side by side. If we had speeded up as if
we were going somewhere, our hurried movements

might have excited us still more and driven us into a doorway; but as it was, we just went on about as slowly as before and had to start in again from the beginning. Nevertheless I tried to take hold of her. She took it as an unintentional collision.

We went into a cafeteria. When I saw we would have to wait on ourselves, I wanted to leave, but she had already taken her place in line. I too took a tray and put a sandwich on it. We sat down at a table. I ate my sandwich, and she drank coffee. She asked me my name, and without knowing why I was lying I told her it was Wilhelm. That made me feel better and I offered her a bite of my sandwich. She broke off a piece. After a while she stood up, said she had a headache, waved her hand vaguely, and left.

I got myself a bottle of beer and sat down again. Through the narrow curtained door I looked out at the street. The visible area was so small that the movements I saw in it took on a particular clarity; the people who traversed it seemed to move very slowly, as though displaying themselves; it was as if they were not passing the doorway but strolling back and forth in front of it. Women's breasts had never seemed so beautiful and so provocative. The sight of these women was almost painful, and yet I was glad that I wanted only to watch them strolling back and forth, so pleased with themselves in the light of the big electrc signs. A woman came to a stop in the doorway, apparently looking for something. It was frightening how much I wanted to go out to her, but a moment later I thought, "What could I do with her? It would be irresponsible." And then I relaxed. It had become so impossible for me to imagine myself caressing a woman that the mere thought of holding out my hand to one made me feel desperately tired.

Someone had left a newspaper on the next table; I picked it up and began to read. I read what had hap-

pened and what was yet to happen, page after page
with an increasing sense of well-being. A baby had
been born on the Long Island Rail Road; a gas station attendant was walking on his hands from Mont-
gomery, Alabama, to Savannah, Georgia. In the
Nevada desert the cactus was already in bloom. Whatever I saw in print aroused a compulsive sympathy
in me; I felt drawn to every place or person mentioned; even the judge who had an obstreperous
defendant chained to his chair, though I couldn't ap-
prove, left me with an uncanny sense of well-being.
I felt a kinship with everyone I read about. A woman
columnist wrote that she would hide her head in shame
if she had conscientious objectors for sons; looking
at her picture, I was unable to ward off a quick feeling
of affinity; and when a captain testified in court that
looking down on the rice paddy from a helicopter he
had seen something that looked like a group of women
and children but might equally well have been "a
man and two water buffaloes," the mere reading of the
words gave me a pang of regret that I hadn't been in
the captain's place. Every human being and even more
so every place that was still unknown to me became,
as I read, so congenial to me that I was stricken with
wanderlust. Reading about a telegraph office in Mon-
tana and a street in an army camp in Virginia, I instantly wanted to be there and stay awhile; otherwise,
I felt, I would be missing something that could never
be retrieved.

Such feelings were not new to me; even as a child,
I would suddenly, in the middle of an argument or
fight, be taken with a feeling that everything was all
right; I would stop arguing or let myself be thrown;
or when running away from someone, screaming
for all I was worth, I would stop running and perhaps
even sit down, looking at my pursuer so innocently
that he usually passed me by as if he had actually been
chasing someone else. If I was bawling someone out,

I could seldom keep it up very long; just to be talking put me in a friendly mood, I stopped, and we made up. In the early years when Judith and I started shouting at each other, our quarrel soon became, for me at least, a quotation about a quarrel, not because I found the bone of contention trivial, but because the fact of talking or shouting gave me a sudden sense of the ridiculous. Later on, I continued to feel in the midst of our hostilities that I might just as well burst out laughing the next moment, and sometimes I actually couldn't help laughing, but by then we were getting on each other's nerves so badly that any unilateral interruption of a quarrel, even a conciliatory laugh, could only have been taken as an insult by the other. It frightened me that here in New York, while reading the paper, I should again, after so long a time, feel so strangely attracted to everything and everybody; but at the moment I didn't want to worry about it. Besides, the feeling didn't last; when I began to think about it, it was gone and forgotten. Once out in the street, I was alone again.

I wandered about aimlessly but full of curiosity. On Times Square I looked at some albums of nude photographs; the latest news was spelled out for me in electric lights on the Allied Chemical Building. I looked at the clock and set my watch. The square was so bright that I was blind for a moment when I turned into one of the dark side streets. I had read in the paper that a restaurant in Central Park had just reopened after being destroyed by fire, and that some of the charred beams had been used in the new interior. While I was walking along looking for a cab to take me there, someone offered me a ticket for a musical. I was going to ignore him, but then it occurred to me that the cast included Lauren Bacall, who many years ago, playing the part of a strong young woman in Howard Hawks's picture *To Have and Have Not,* had leaned over the piano-player's shoulder in a waterfront dive and sung a song in a deep, husky voice. I gave the man twenty dollars and, ticket in hand, hurried to the theater.

My seat was in the front row, right over the booming orchestra. Like everyone else I had my coat in my lap. Lauren Bacall was the oldest on the stage, even the men looked younger. She no longer lounged or slunk as she had in the waterfront dive, but was very sprightly in her movements. In one number, she and a group of young, rather long-haired men, with chains around their necks, danced on tables. Even while sinking with weariness, she had, in mid-collapse, to jump up again and do something different. To keep the attention of the audience from flagging, each of her movements had to be canceled out by the next movement. While telephoning, she had to slip into her shoes, so as to be able to run off the moment she hung up, and after every sentence she spoke she changed her posture, or at least shifted her legs. She had rather large eyes, and her eyeballs went along with each one of her gestures. In each new scene she appeared in an entirely different outfit, though she could hardly have had time to change. I only felt good about her once—when she was doing nothing but holding out a whiskey glass with her long arm. The rest of the time I had the impression that, with her movie career behind her, it no longer amused her to make a living with gestures that were not her own. It was like watching a man who is doing work that is beneath him and who is sure to feel offended at being watched. I thought of Judith: her routine movements were composed of the many little poses that Lauren Bacall's body was running through like a machine. In a dress shop, I thought, she quite unintentionally adopted the gestures of a lady of fashion: she would stop in the entrance and look around but not at anyone; only when the salesgirl approached her did she focus her eyes, as though startled at her presence. But on the stage she was transformed: the simplicity of her movements was not the unthinking negligence with which simple people saunter about even on the stage; rather, they expressed relief that on the stage it became possible for her to be serious. Everywhere else she might act up and put on airs, but on the stage she calmed down, became selflessly attentive to others, and played her part so naturally that afterward one almost forgot her.

A police car outside the theater drove through my thoughts with its wailing siren that the orchestra made almost inaudible. A page from somebody's program floated very slowly down from the balcony, and the fluttering paper made me feel certain that at that very moment Judith was sitting carefree in a restaurant, eating but already lifting her little finger to order something else, and that she was too engrossed in what she was doing to think of other things. From time to time the conductor bobbed up in the orchestra pit! The actors' trousers were so beautifully pressed! And the way Lauren's rival picked the olive out of her martini and licked it before popping it into her mouth! Nothing could possibly have happened to her. It was inconceivable that she should not be enjoying herself somewhere. On my money! I was getting hungry; I left in the intermission and took a cab to the restaurant in Central Park.

The trees in the park rustled softly, as though it were going to rain soon. In the restaurant even the menus had artifically charred corners, and on the cloakroom desk there was a guest book with print as luminous as that of half-burned newspapers. Outside, a police siren was wailing again. One of the waiters drew the curtain over the window where he was standing, another went to the door and stood with folded arms looking out. The siren was very shrill, and for a moment the ice cubes trembled in the glass of water that had been put on my table as soon as I sat down. Only a few people were still at the tables and their faces were half in shadow. The room was almost empty and so large that while the siren faded away in the distance I began to feel very tired. As I sat motionless, something began to move back and forth in my head in a rhythm resembling that of my wanderings about New York that day. Once it stopped, then for a long while it ran straight ahead, then it zigzagged, then it circled awhile and subsided. It was neither an image nor a sound, only a rhythm that now and then pretended to be one or the other. It was only then that I saw inside me the city that up until then I had almost overlooked.

A city, which during the day I had merely passed by, caught up with me. Rows of houses and streets took form from the vibrations, the sudden stops, the jolts and crisscrossings it had left in me. Then the vibrations became sounds, the surge and roar of a torrent sweeping over a quiet flooded plain. The heavily curtained windows were no barrier to the sounds and images, because they were in my head; now and then they paled into mere vibrations and rhythms, but soon my head so speeded their pace that they sounded and flared up again: the streets became longer, the buildings taller than ever, and horizons moved spasmodically farther and farther into the distance. Nevertheless, it was pleasant: the pattern of New York spread out peacefully inside me and didn't oppress me. I sat there relaxed yet alive with curiosity, ate the roast lamb to which I had treated myself, drank California red wine that made me thirstier with every swallow, and the compressed, still-rumbling city became for me a gentle panorama of nature. Everything that I had hitherto seen close up, plate glass, stop signs, flagpoles, electric signs, now expanded, because for hours I had been unable to look into the distance, into a landscape that was open as far as the eye could see. I wanted to lie down in it and read a book.

When I had finished eating, I kept looking through the menu and read the names of dishes as insatiably as I had once read the lives of saints in my prayer book. A steak Alamo, a Louisiana pullet, a bear hock à la Daniel Boone, a cutlet à la Uncle Tom. The few diners were still there and were now talking in loud voices. A newsboy came in and threw a few papers on the cloakroom desk. A heavily made-up old woman went from table to table with flowers. A waiter deftly poured cognac over a soufflé at the table of a corpulent couple, the lady struck a match for him, he took it with a bow, and held it over the frying pan. The soufflé flared up and the couple clapped their hands. The waiter smiled, transferred the soufflé to a plate, and served it to the lady. Then with his napkin he took a bottle of white wine out of the ice bucket and poured it, holding his free arm behind his back. A pianist turned up from somewhere and began to play softly. A cook stuck his head through the kitchen window and listened. I ordered another carafe of red wine and drank it up, but made no move to leave.

A waiter went into the kitchen and came back chewing. The cloakroom attendant laid out a game of solitaire. She had a pin in her mouth and, while playing, stirred a cup of coffee that was perched on the rail. Then she put the spoon down, let the pin drop out of her mouth, and drank her coffee at one gulp. She swirled the cup to dissolve the residue of sugar, tipped it into her mouth, and went on with her solitaire. Two women came in from outside, one waved a long glove at the waiters, the other sat down at the piano. The pianist changed over to another tune, and she sang:

133

*"In the days of old, in the days of gold,
In the days of forty-nine."*

Long after midnight I walked back to the hotel,
where I sat down in the Blue Bar and drank Kentucky
whiskey. I drank slowly and didn't get drunk. I found
some picture postcards of the hotel on a table and
wrote to a lot of people, including some I had never
written to before. I got airmail stamps out of the vending machine in the lobby and dropped my cards in
the hotel mailbox. I went back to the bar, sat down
in a big leather swivel armchair, and held my glass in
front of me on the palm of my hand. From time to
time I bent over and took a sip. The bartender came
over and put an ash tray on a table at which an old
woman was sitting. From time to time she giggled;
after each giggle she took a notebook out of her
quilted bag and wrote something with a little silver
ballpoint pen. Finally, for the second time that night,
I felt tired, took another picture postcard from the
pile, and went up to my room. On my way I addressed
the card and dropped it into the mail slot on my landing. On the way down it rattled once or twice.

When I got to my room there was a sheet of white
paper on the floor. Thinking it was a message for
me, I picked it up. But it was only the hotel manager's
card, which had been on top of the fruit bowl. I
called the desk again and asked them to turn the air
conditioning back on. Then I went to bed without washing and opened *Green Heinrich*.

I read how at school Heinrich Lee acquired his
first enemy. A schoolmate encouraged him to bet on
everything that stirred in nature: what fence post a
bird would sit on, how low a tree would bend in
the wind, whether every fifth or every sixth wave in
the lake would be a big one. Heinrich developed
betting fever; he lost and couldn't pay up. The two
friends, now enemies, met for the last time on a nar-

row mountain path. Neither said a word; they just flung themselves on each other and fought bitterly. With deadly calm Heinrich clutched his enemy and punched him rhythmically in the face. But every time he punched him he felt a furious pain; never in all his life was he to suffer more deeply. Soon he had to leave school and move to the country. There for the first time he found freedom in nature and began to sketch it with a pleasure he had never before experienced.

I had grown up in the country and it was hard for me to imagine that nature could free anyone from anything. It had only oppressed me; at any rate, it had been distasteful to me. I detested stubble fields, fruit trees, and pastures, there was something repulsive about them. I saw them from too close at hand: in the stubble fields I ran barefoot; when I climbed trees, the bark scraped my skin; in the pastures I went about in rubber boots, chasing pissing cows in the rain. Only now did it dawn on me that I had been so keenly aware of these little annoyances because I had never been able to move about freely in nature: the fruit trees belonged to other people that I had to run away from, across the fields, and my only reward for tending the cows was rubber boots that I needed only for tending the cows. Because I was driven into nature as a child, because nature was my place of work, I never developed an eye for it; at the most, I was curious about crevices, hollow trees, holes in the ground, anything I could disappear into, especially underground caves. I was also attracted by underbrush, corn fields, hazelnut thickets, sunken lanes, and gullies. But to nature I preferred houses and streets, where there were more forbidden things to be done. When the wind ruffled a wheat field, it only annoyed me by blowing my hair in my face. Later on, to be sure, I often thought of wheat fields *waving in the wind* to persuade myself that nature hadn't really been so distasteful to me, and to tell the truth, it was distasteful to me only because in my nature days I could never do as I pleased.

I put the book down and lay in the dark. The air conditioning purred softly, and I watched myself gradually falling asleep. The bathroom door turned into a white house on a hill. Someone was trying to breathe through his nose, and at the foot of a cliff far below me a dog whimpered in answer. I turned over on the other side and immediately rolled down a slope. I fell into the dry bed of a brook—it was full of clothes hangers and chopped-up rubber boots—and curled up to sleep. The rain was pouring down, a flash flood was approaching with an uproar, but never got to me. "I've forgotten to sign the register!"

Next morning, shortly before noon, I went to Pennsylvania Station and took a Penn Central train to Philadelphia.

. Thinking back, I can't understand it; that day passed as quickly for me as the days in horror films. You stepped into a subterranean station, escalators carried you farther and farther down; pushed forward by the last step of the escalator, you passed through an open door, and it was only after you had sat down and were moving that you knew for sure you were on a train. For a few minutes it was dark outside the windows, while the train was passing through the tunnel under the Hudson River; when it rose to the surface in New Jersey, you were in a twilight landscape and the gloom was deepened by the tinted windows. In the car it was bright, the pages of your book almost glittered when you turned them; but each time you looked out, the clouds seemed darker than ever and the land below them emptier: garbage heaps instead of houses, yellow smoke on the horizon but no chimneys, a car without tires lying upside down in a fallow field, scraggly woods in which trees uprooted by the wind hung withering on the leafy green branches of their neighbors, here and there on the sand hills, scraps of parachute silk—sea gulls that had flown inland by mistake. The railroad line had recently gone into bankruptcy, and many of the way stations had been closed down. You passed through cities that seemed depopulated because the houses faced away from the tracks. After two hours, rows of soot-covered houses with boarded-up windows on which skulls and crossbones had been painted closed in on the right of way and it became so dark in the car that you didn't notice it when the train entered the tunnel leading to the subterranean Philadelphia station.

More escalators; a large square you could step right out into without going down any steps. I looked to see if anyone had come to meet me. I said, "There's no need for you to hide. You were watching me from behind one of those pillars in the station, weren't you? I have no desire to find you." "Don't blackmail me with myself," I said. "I don't scare easily, not any more at least. I'm no longer defenseless against fear." Two Quakers in long black coats and flat broad-brimmed hats crossed the square to an open car beside which a young Negro chauffeur, with a small radio in his shirt pocket, was standing. A marine, whom I had seen on the train, came running after the Quakers and showed them something. They only smiled; one of them made a negative gesture, while the other got into the car. Then he got out again and pointed at me. I was frightened. They motioned to me and I went slowly toward them. The marine raised his arm and brandished my camera; I had left it in the train.

I crossed the square with the marine. Neither of us knew where he was going, each was following the other. In front of a statue of William Penn I took his picture and he put it in his pocket when it was dry. In return, he took out a newspaper clipping and unfolded it, holding it firmly by the edges like an important document. It was a story about his return to his home town of Red Wing, Minnesota. He had been welcomed by the American Legion and had made a speech which, according to the clipping, had been simple but had won all hearts with its easy good humor. "Actually," said the marine, "I only talked about the time Bob Hope and his girls entertained us, and I told a few of his jokes. But everybody was in a good humor and nobody asked any questions." And he went on, "Then later on I showed Red Wing how to rock. First I practiced at home with my girl, then one night I picked 'Jailhouse Rock' on the jukebox; we began to dance as if it was a waltz and then all of a sudden I threw her over my shoulder." "I admire Elvis Presley," said the marine. "He spent more than two years in the army and now he's back in business again. I'm not crazy about being a marine, but it's my job. One time I saw a reed growing in shallow water. There were a few other reeds nearby, but they all moved. This one reed didn't move. We had to kill somebody now and then or we'd have been killed ourselves." The marine had a round face with large nostrils. He wore glasses, and dandruff had fallen on them from his eyebrows. His lips were very pale; he had a gold tooth and spoke softly. At the end of every sentence he went into a singsong and his voice went up, as though he needed a nod to go on. He took off his cap and showed me his long hair. As he did so, his glasses slid down over his nose and there was a blind, indifferent friendliness in his eyes, which didn't see me at all. It came to me that this was the first time in months that I'd been able to look at someone close up without strain. It was as if someone else were looking at the marine. At the same time I felt offended that he had picked me to tell his story to. Why was it that people always told *me* their stories? One look at me must have told them I wouldn't like it. But that didn't prevent them from telling me the stupidest stories with perfect calm, as if they took it for granted that I'd listen with the ears of an accomplice.

"Do I still have to act myself out to be seen as I am?" I asked myself when I had left the marine on the pretense of having to make a phone call. "Is it only when I talk and contradict that people can see what I'm like and want to be like? Can't they tell from the way I move, from the way I hold my head and look around?" "Or," I asked myself in the cab on the way to my hotel, "do I still have the same gestures as before? Do I still have to think up a new attitude at every step? Can people see that among many gestures I always have to choose one? And does that make them think I'm ready to accept every possible opinion?"

"Or are they only trying to frighten me?" I thought in the doorway of the hotel, while watching the cab driver hand my suitcase to the hotel porter. "Maybe people can see at a glance that I'm the kind that puts up with anything, that the usual precautions people take when getting acquainted are pointless, that they can be friendly from the start, because we like everything and everybody so much that anything goes and there's nothing to fear."

Without thinking, I tilted my head back as if I had had a nosebleed: the clouds glittered bright; I was afraid that would make the night fall sooner. In the morning I had taken a short train ride; then I had strolled around the square with the marine for a little while, and already it was late afternoon: the shadows were long when the sun came out for a moment just to show that it would soon be dark and everything would mean something different. With a feeling that the foot I was putting forward was too light and the one that stayed behind too heavy, I followed the porter deep into the hotel to the registration desk. I quickly signed my name in the book and waited in the elevator only long enough for someone to be pushed in in a wheel chair; but by the time I got to my room the sun was setting. When I stepped out of the bathroom, it was dusk; and after I hung my coat in the closet, perhaps a little more carefully than usual, it was dark.

"You *beast!*" I said. "I'll beat you to a pulp, I'll beat you to a pulp. Please don't let me find you, you *monster*. It wouldn't be nice for you if I found you."

Someone was thrashing about, they carried him out of the house, I ran out and watched him gasping and choking—"from pollen!"; someone who was holding him slipped and fell, I helped to carry the dead man into the house, then I slowly slipped away; I was barefoot, I stepped on a sharp stone and an intense pain electrified me from the soles of my feet to the top of my head. Some women behind me whispered that he was dead, but very softly and considerately; they didn't even whisper, only their dresses rustled, two toad's eyes looked out of a swamp, a door handle moved slowly up and down—considerately? I stretched my bare legs and they went into a clump of nettles. A lizard darted by at the edge of my field of vision; but it was only the hotel emblem on my door key, which was swinging back and forth in the lock. "I don't want to be alone any more," I said.

I had written a woman in Phoenixville, a small town west of Philadelphia, to say that I might go and see her. Her name was Claire Madison. Three years before, on my previous visit to America, we had made love just once. We hardly knew each other; because of the way I had precipitated matters, I often thought about it.

I looked her up in the phone book and called her. "Where are you?" she asked. "In Philadelphia," I said. "I'm leaving for St. Louis tomorrow with my child," she said. "Would you like to come along?" We arranged that I should go to Phoenixville for lunch next day; we would start out after the child's afternoon nap.

Then she hung up and I remained by the telephone. There was a small electric clock on the bedside table. Its dial cast a somber glow deep into the room. Each minute the number changed with a soft click. I pulled out the clock plug and the room was in total darkness. Clair had been about thirty when we met for the first time. She was a big girl, with wide lips that didn't open but only narrowed slightly when she smiled. Her face was big too, not the kind of face it seemed appropriate to stroke. Altogether it was impossible to caress her. She never talked about herself, and it never occurred to me that there could be anything to say about her. She was always so physically present that there was nothing to be said. So I talked about myself or about things outside the window; there was no other way to show affection. Anything else would have required a skipping of steps that would have put a strain on us both. The last time I went to see her, she called out to me to come in, that the door was open: the open door and the way, when I went in, that she was leaning against the door leading to another room, arranged themselves, as in a dream, into a signal to take her in my arms and thrust my leg between her legs. Recalling the scene, I stood up, sat down again, and closed my eyes so hard that it hurt. And then the prolonged murmurs while she was taking her clothes off! We stood looking to one side, speaking with unnatural voices; then we turned and gazed at each other long and silently with feverish yet empty eyes and caressed each other until our desire made us cough aloud. Bewildered, we would break apart and look up from each other's loins till our eyes met. Then we would have to turn away again, and again one of us would murmur in that unnatural voice, until the other interrupted with mannered caresses. Actually the door she was leaning against was only the door of a large American refrigerator. Suddenly, in the course of our half-hearted caresses, I was inside her. I wanted to murmur her name but couldn't. She was a German instructor at some college. Her father had been stationed in Heidelberg after the war, and instead of sending for her, he had only written her letters telling her to learn German. She had been married for a time. Her child was not by me.

Deep night. My room was on the top floor, too high for the street lamps to shine in; the buildings across the street were office buildings and the cleaning women had gone. Once a glare swept across my walls, when a plane flew over with blinking lights. I phoned a few hotels in Philadelphia that were expensive enough for Judith to stop at: the Sheraton, the Warwick, the Adelphia, the Normandie. Then it crossed my mind that she might be right here at the Barclay, and I called the desk. Yes, she had stayed here, but had checked out two days before. She had left nothing in her room and had paid her bill in cash.

I was furious; then my anger passed and my horror became so great that the objects in the room seemed to flutter like bats' wings. Then the horror passed too, giving way to an enormous feeling of disgust, because I was still my same old helpless self. I called room service and ordered some toast and French red wine and put on all the lights, producing an effect ordinarily seen only in photos advertising hotel rooms. I also turned the light on in the bathroom. After the waiter had wheeled in his cart with its ludicrous still life of toast and wine, I switched on the color TV. I ate and drank, casting an occasional glance at the screen when a woman screamed or when there was a long silence. Once when for some time there had been no sound but the hum of the television set, I looked up and saw a row of deserted German middle-class houses in the background: in the foreground, so close that I could only see his head, a monster whished by. Intermittently, a man in a chef's hat praised the qualities of a five-course dinner in a cellophane bag, that one had only to immerse in boiling water for a few minutes; the chef also showed how to cut the bag open with scissors and then, in close-up, plopped the steaming dishes down on paper plates. Later, still drinking my wine, I switched to another channel and watched an animated cartoon in which a cat blows a wad of bubblegum so big that it bursts and the cat chokes to death. It was the first time I had ever seen anyone die in an animated cartoon.

At that point I had had enough of my room. Leaving the TV running and the lights on, I rode down in the elevator. It being Sunday, the bar was closed, so I went out. In Philadelphia the streets run parallel or at right angles to each other. I went straight ahead, turned into Chestnut Street, which is one of the main thoroughfares, and then again went straight ahead. The streets were all very quiet. I dropped into what looked like a nightclub and caught sight of the marine; he seemed to be drunk, though no liquor was being served. He was leaning against the wall watching the dancers, who were all very young. No longer in uniform, he was wearing a leather jacket; his glasses were in the breast pocket. I nodded to him. He waved but didn't seem to recognize me. I sat down at a table with a dark-colored drink that tasted burned and was called root beer. I couldn't take my eyes off him.

The band had withdrawn, only one of the singers stayed on. He picked up a steel guitar and sat down on a stool by the mike. He began to sing a talking blues. The people, who had stopped dancing, gathered around the singer and listened. His story was about a feeble-minded girl, who had been raped by a farmer she was working for and given birth to a child. "And I was that child!" said the singer, striking a chord, which echoed on while he continued his story. "She had the child while she was going out to the well for water; she wrapped it in her apron and carried it into the house, and the farmer and his wife raised me as their own child. And one day I climbed up a fence and got stuck. The feeble-minded woman, who couldn't even talk, came running and helped the child down. And the child said to the farmer's wife, 'Hey, Ma, why are the idiot girl's hands so soft?' And that idiot girl was my mother!" the singer screamed. Then he took the guitar and played a series of long, tremulous chords.

Suddenly, as the music became more incisive and impatient, the marine came to life. He raised his arms as though to stretch. He was pushing something upward but, arrived at head height, it would go no farther, and, frustrated, his hands clenched into trembling fists. He closed his eyes so tight that his eyeballs began to tremble. Fighting against insuperable resistance, he bent his head to one side, then jerked one shoulder, trying to hit his ear with it. His lips opened, he ground his teeth. Every movement he attempted was blocked by an equal countermovement. His face was twisted and his head bent far back. Over and over, he struggled to lift a weight; each time his arms fought their way to shoulder level, began to shake, lost height, thrashed about for a moment, and steadied themselves with a last muscular exertion; even letting his arms fall seemed to demand a painful effort. He raised one knee, forced his head down, and rubbed his forehead against his knee. The sweat poured from his long sideburns, his gums were bright with saliva, yet I watched him with respect and affection. His ecstasy was not artificial and imitative like the movements of the other people, who had meanwhile resumed their dancing; it had taken him by surprise and he didn't know what to do with it. No longer able to speak or even to stammer, he tried to free himself by acting as if some primeval monster were dying inside him. Then suddenly he was still and there was a knife in his hand.

Someone who had been watching him struck him on the forearm and the knife fell to the floor. Only a few people were looking on as the marine was led away.

I went back to the hotel and read about Green Heinrich, how he began to sketch from nature but looked only for what was grotesque and mysterious in nature. He tried to go nature one better, to make himself interesting as an observer by imagining blasted willow trunks and cliff-ghosts. He invented fantastically grimacing trees and rocks and peopled his landscape with weird ragged figures, because he knew so little about himself that nature as he found it still meant nothing to him. Then a cousin, who had always lived in the country, showed him that all the trees he drew looked alike, and that none looked like a real tree. "These boulders couldn't be piled up like that for a second without collapsing!" His cousin gave him an assignment: to sketch his property. And though his cousin spoke as a proprietor, Heinrich was now obliged for the first time to look at things. Now the simplest objects, even the tiles on the roof, gave him more trouble than he would ever have thought possible. It occurred to me that for a long time my own vision of the world around me had been twisted: when I tried to describe something, I never knew what it looked like; I remembered only its anomalies, and if there weren't any, I make them up. All the people I described were giants with birthmarks and falsetto voices. Most often they were escaped convicts, who sat for hours on tree trunks in the woods, telling their stories to the wind. I was quick to see cripples, blind men, and idiots, but even these I could not have described in detail. I was more interested in ruins than houses. I liked to spend my time in graveyards and always counted the suicides' graves along the wall. I could be with someone for hours and then, if he went away and came back, fail to recognize him; at the most I might remember that he had a pimple or lisped. Only abnormalities and bad habits held my attention; after the first glance I stopped looking at everything else and had to invent things if anyone asked me to tell what I had seen. Since at that time my imagination also knew nothing, I lied, throwing in distinguishing marks as though making out a warrant, and these distinguishing marks would take the place of whole landscapes, situations, and biographies. It was only when I met Judith, and for the first time really experienced something, that I began to see the world with something more than a malignant first glance. I became more patient and stopped collecting distinguishing marks.

I had fallen asleep without turning out the lights and in my dream the sun shone in my face. I was waiting at a crossroads; a car stopped beside me; I went over and moved the windshield wiper to the middle of the windshield. A woman sitting beside the driver leaned out and pulled it down again. She pointed at the sky and I saw the sun was shining. I laughed; the driver, a *Frenchman,* joined in my laughter, and yet, as though my dream had been a nightmare, I woke up with an erection but no excitement. I turned out the lights. Toward morning someone clapped his hands violently. I shouted, "Yes!" and jumped out of bed. It was only a pigeon that had fluttered past my window.

Phoenixville is a small town with a population of about fifteen thousand, some twenty miles from Philadelphia. I settled the price with a cab driver and started after breakfast. On the way we made one stop; I bought a harmonica for the child and some film packs for the Polaroid camera in a discount store, where they only cost half as much as at airports. A present for Claire would only have embarrassed her. I couldn't think of anything that would have been right for her, and I couldn't visualize her with something in her hands; it would have looked incongruous.

Nevertheless, she was carrying a suitcase out to the car when my cab drew up to her house on Greenleaf Street. The car was an Oldsmobile, the trunk was open. The child was toddling awkwardly up and down in front of Claire, carrying a little draw-string bag. The house door was open, a few suitcases were standing beside it, the front lawn was still sparkling with dew.

I got out of the cab and took my bag over to the car. We exchanged greetings and I put my bag in the trunk. Then I brought the other bags over from the doorway and passed them to her. She stowed them away. The child screamed at her to close the trunk. The child was a girl, about two years old; she had been born in New Orleans and her name was Delta Benedictine. Claire closed the trunk and explained, "I can't leave anything open in front of Benedictine. It frightens her. Yesterday she began to scream and wouldn't stop; finally I found out what the trouble was: a button was open on my blouse." She picked up the child, who refused to walk in my presence, and we went inside.

"You've changed," said Claire. "You look more carefree. It doesn't bother you any more to be wearing a dirty shirt. Three years ago you always came to see me in a white shirt, a new one each time, I could still see the creases on the chest. And here you are in the same old coat, it's been darned with nylon thread."

"I've lost interest in buying clothes," I said. "I hardly look at shop windows anymore. In the past I wanted to wear something different every day, now I wear the same thing for months. As for my shirt, there was no laundry service at the hotel yesterday."

"What have you got in your bag?" Claire asked.

"Underwear and books," I said.

"What are you reading now?"

"*Green Heinrich* by Gottfried Keller."

147

She hadn't read it and I said I'd read parts of it to her. "Maybe tonight, before we go to bed," she said.

"Where will that be?" I asked.

"In Donora, south of Pittsburgh," she said. "I know a motel there, it's off the road, it will be quieter for the child. I hope we get that far, it's almost three hundred miles and the Allegheny Mountains are in between. Have you learned to drive in the meantime?"

"No," I said. "Never again will I let anybody examine me. The thought of someone asking me questions and making something depend on my answers had become intolerable to me. In the past, say ten years ago, it would have disgusted me and made me furious, but I'd have let them examine me. Now I won't."

"You keep talking about 'the past' and 'now,'" said Claire.

"It's because I can't wait to be older," I said, and couldn't help laughing.

"How old are you?" Claire asked.

"In three days I'll be thirty," I said.

"In St. Louis," she said.

"Yes," I said. "And I can't wait."

"To get to St. Louis or to be thirty?"

"To be thirty and in St. Louis," I said.

She fed the child while I went into the bathroom and washed my hair. She had packed the dryer, so I sat down on the front lawn with my wet hair. It struck me as quite extraordinary that the sun should be shining that day.

When I came back in, she was undressing the child, and I watched her. She zipped her into a sleeping bag and put her to bed in another room. I heard her drawing the curtains. Then she came out; for lunch we had roast beef and dumplings with beer.

"Do you like Austria any better now?" she asked.

"Yes," I said. "I was glad to be there. I realized that I had gone so far as to imagine that they had different sets of symbols from the rest of the world. But now I saw the same traffic signs, the same bottle shapes, the same screw threads as everywhere else. In all seriousness I was surprised to find hotels, department stores, paved roads, all perfectly available. Maybe I was so surprised because this was the country of my childhood and because as a child I didn't see those things and what I did see wasn't available to me. Little by little, I'm even beginning to see nature, which used to make me nervous and miserable, with new eyes." There I stopped. I had meant to say something else.

After lunch I cleared the table and got myself a bottle of beer out of the refrigerator. Claire explained that she was going to visit friends in St. Louis during the college vacation. "They're lovers," she said. And another reason for going to St. Louis was that a German dramatic group was at the university there, doing some classical plays she had never seen performed.

I wanted to help with the dishes, but since my last visit she had acquired a dishwasher. She showed me how it worked. "A few things still have to be washed by hand," she explained. "Silver, for instance, and pots and pans that are too big for the machine. I haven't got any silver, but I have to use big pots because I often cook for weeks ahead. I keep the stuff in the deep freeze." She showed me the frozen soup in the deep freeze. "I'll be able to eat it when I get back in the fall," she said, and I had a feeling that nothing could possibly go wrong before the fall came and she would thaw out the soup.

When the dishwasher had shut itself off, we put the dishes away. If anyone had asked me, I wouldn't have known, but once I set to work I remembered where everything belonged. I tossed the beer bottles into the garbage disposal, then I turned on the record player without looking to see what record was on it. With a glance at the door behind which the child was sleeping, Claire turned down the volume a little. The record was called *She Wore a Yellow Ribbon* and consisted of some tunes from John Ford's movies played on the jew's-harp. "In Providence I heard a regimental band playing those things," I exclaimed, and repeated the sentence very softly, as though Claire couldn't have understood it when I said it in a loud voice.

She went about barefoot, collecting little things for the trip, needles, medicines the child might need, a fever thermometer, the child's inoculation certificate, a straw hat to shade her from the sun. Then she brewed fennel tea in soda water for the road. It was a pleasure to watch her: all so wonderfully innocent.

She disappeared into one of the rooms, and when she came out of another, I looked up and didn't know her. She was wearing a different dress, but that had nothing to do with it. We went outside and she lay down in a hammock; I sat in a rocking chair and told her about my life during the last three years.

Then we heard the child calling and Claire went in and dressed her, while I sat rocking. I noticed that some articles of the child's clothing were still hanging on the clothesline. Without telling Claire, I stuffed them into the bag she had used for the other odds and ends. I was infected with the serenity of my surroundings. With the child in the back seat, we drove out of Phoenixville.

On the way to Interstate 76, she remembered the clothes on the line, and I pointed to the bag where I had put them. "I also unplugged the record player and the hot water heater," I told her.

Interstate 76 from Philadelphia to Pittsburgh is known as the Pennsylvania Turnpike and is more than three hundred miles long. We entered it from State Route 100, near Downingtown, after the eighth toll station. On the seat beside her Claire had a box full of coins; at each toll station she would toss a few of them out the window into the hopper without coming to a full stop. From there to Donora we passed another fifteen toll stations. In the course of the day Claire tossed more than five dollars into hoppers.

We didn't talk much, and then only to the child, who asked questions about various things in the landscape. The sky was cloudless, the hops and wheat had begun to sprout. Smoke rose from towns tucked away behind the hills. Although every inch of ground looked as if it had just been cultivated, there wasn't a living soul in the fields, which were impersonating unspoiled nature. And nowhere on the road, which seemed new, were there men at work; the asphalt glittered peacefully; the cars drove slowly, no one did more than seventy. Once an air force plane flew over very low, casting so big a shadow I thought it was going to crash. There seemed to be less wind in the distance than in the bushes nearby. A flock of white birds changed direction suddenly and turned black. The air was pure and clear; only rarely was an insect dashed against the windshield. From time to time I saw animals that had been run over; the dogs and cats had been moved to the side of the road, the hedgehogs had been left in the middle. Claire told the child there was water in the big aluminum globes on top of the farmhouses.

I felt like using the camera, though there wasn't much to be seen, and in quick succession took several pictures that were almost all alike. Then I took one of the child standing on the back seat, looking out. Last, I snapped Claire, moving away from her as far as possible because the camera was no good for close-ups. I had used up the last film pack by the time we passed Harrisburg. I lined up the pictures on the windshield and looked back and forth between them and the countryside.

"You've changed too," I said to Claire, surprised that there was something to be said of her, and pointed at one of the photographs. "You look as if you are always thinking of what your next thought will be. You used to go off into absences, half the time you were hardly awake, now you look so businesslike and somehow troubled."

"Somehow?"

"Yes, somehow," I said. "I can't quite put my finger on it. You walk faster, you move more briskly, you're more determined, you talk louder, you make more noise. As if you were trying to distract attention from yourself."

She answered by blowing the horn, but said nothing. After a while the child, who had been listening, ordered us to go on talking.

"I'm more forgetful than before," said Claire. "No, it's not that, it's just that I remember less. Sometimes somebody tells me about something we did together a few days ago, but I just don't want to remember."

"Since I've been in America, I remember more and more," I said when she stopped talking. "I only have to take an escalator and I remember how scared I was the first time I stepped onto an escalator. If I walk into a blind alley, all the forgotten blind alleys I've ever strayed into come back to me. Most of all, I've come to understand since I've been here why the only memory I ever developed was for frightening things. I never had anything with which to compare the things I saw every day. All my impressions were repetitions of impressions that were already known to me. It wasn't just that I didn't get around much, but also that I didn't see many people whose circumstances were different from mine. Since we were poor, nearly all the people I knew were poor. We saw so few things that there was very little to talk about and we had the same conversation almost every day. In those surroundings anyone who was more talkative was a *character* if he was funny and amused people; if he only spun fantasies like me, he was a dreamer; because I had no desire to be a character. In the world I lived in, my dreams were really fantasies, because they had no connection with anything in that world, there was nothing comparable that would have made them possible. As a result, I never became fully conscious of the world around me or of my dreams, and that's why I never remember them. All I remember is moments of terror, because at such moments my world and my dreams, which at other times were unrelated, suddenly became one and the same thing. My world provoked my dream, and my dream made me see the world, which otherwise I had simply ignored in my fantasies. So states of fear were for me ways to knowledge; it was only when I was afraid that I paid attention to my surroundings, looking for a sign to tell me whether things would get better or still worse, and later on I remembered those moments of fear. But that kind of memory was something that happened to me from outside, I never learned to cultivate it. If I had moments of hope in those days, I've forgotten them."

We had been climbing steadily, though there were no big mountains to be seen. The sun was halfway down the sky and now and then a sparkling went up from the hillsides. The child wanted to hear us talking again. Claire told her we'd be talking a good deal later on. I gave her a cup of fennel tea to drink. She held the cup in both hands and gave it back when it was empty. After New Baltimore, there was a tunnel and Claire put the child beside her on the front seat. When we got out of the tunnel she asked me to move the child back again. Now there were dark shadows between the hills and I could see the moon through the back window.

"If we get to Donora before seven," said Claire, "the child can come to dinner with us. There's a restaurant across from the motel. The Yellow Ribbon, it's called."

We stopped at a gas station. While the tank was filling up, Claire took the child to the back to do her business. While waiting, I got a can of soda out of the vending machine. It was late in the day, the machine must have been almost empty, because my can tumbled down from a considerable height and foamed over when I opened it. The red, white, and blue oval AMERICAN sign over the gas station rotated slowly, and the child talked about it when she came back with Claire. As we drove off, the child suddenly let out a yell; we turned around and saw that the lights had gone on in the gas station. "But it wasn't dark yet!" Suddenly it seemed to me that the country we had been driving through was country that one could also arrive in. I began to talk and was relieved to find that I had stopped hearing my own voice.

"I think I'm developing something that looks like an active memory," I said. "Up until now I had only a passive memory. But in this active remembering I don't try to repeat complete experiences; all I want is to prevent the first little hopes I felt in connection with those experiences from relapsing into fantasies. As a child, for instance, I used to bury things, hoping that when I dug them up they'd have turned into treasure. I don't regard this as a childish game any more, I'm no longer ashamed of it as I used to be; today I remember such things on purpose in order to assure myself that if I was unable to change the things around me or see them in a different light, my nature was not to blame, but only momentary dullness or bad humor. I see this even more clearly when I remember how often I pretended to be a magician. What I wanted was not so much to make something out of nothing or change one thing into another as to enchant myself. I twisted a ring or pulled a blanket over me and said it would spirit me away. Of course it was ridiculous when somebody pulled the blanket away and I was still there, but what was more important for memory was the brief moment when I really thought I wasn't there any more. Today I interpret that feeling not as a desire to vanish from the face of the earth, but as joyful anticipation of a future when I would cease to be the person I was at the moment. It's very much the same now when every day I tell myself that I'm one more day older and that it must show. It's got so I really want the time to pass and make me older."

"And die," said Claire.

"I seldom think of my own death," I said.

Before Pittsburgh, where the turnpike continues northwestward, we turned off to the southwest onto Interstate 70, where there were no more toll stations, and reached Donora soon after sunset. In the lobby of the motel a movie was showing on TV; Henry Fonda in the role of a police officer had just found out that his daughter was taking drugs. Next to the TV set a canary was pecking at a cuttlebone in its cage. We took two adjoining rooms.

Crossing the parking place to the car, I saw a narrow little cloud that was still lit up by the sun, which had vanished behind a hill. The hill had been transformed into a flat surface, and above it the cloud shimmered so white that at first I saw a cuttlebone in the sky. All at once I understood how illusions and mistaken identities give rise to metaphors. The quarter of sky where the sun had just gone down was more dazzling than the direct rays had been before. When I looked at the ground, glowworms were hopping up and down, and even in my room I groped for a moment in darkness. "My whole being hearkens in silence": that was how people used to feel in the presence of natural phenomena; but what nature gave me at such moments was a clear sense of myself.

I opened the door to the other room and watched while Claire changed the child's dress for a pair of pants and a sweater. The sight of these human activities comforted me. Then we crossed the highway on the overpass and went to the Yellow Ribbon, in front of which there was a luminous statue of a pioneer woman with a yellow neckerchief. The waitresses also wore yellow neckerchiefs whose ends hung down over their shoulders. The child had milk and corn flakes; now and then Claire gave her a bite of the trout she and I were eating. The sky outside the big windows grew darker, and again the hills brightened. Then the hills grew dark and when I looked out, all I could see was some of myself in the windowpanes. The child became very talkative, her pupils dilated, she left the table and ran out into the middle of the room. Claire said the child was tired; she let her run about for a little while, then picked her up and carried her to the motel after promising to come back as soon as the child was asleep.

After a while she reappeared, smiling. In the meantime I had ordered some wine and filled our glasses. "Benedictine wanted to know why your fingernails are so dirty," said Claire. "She fell asleep right away."

I began to explain my dirty fingernails; then I stopped talking about myself and we talked about America.

"I haven't got an America I can go away to like you," said Claire. "It's as if you'd come over on a time machine, not for the change of place but for a glimpse of the future. Over here we've lost all sense of where we're going. If we draw any comparisons, it's with the past. And we've given up wanting anything, except perhaps to be children again. We're always talking about the first years, our own first years and the first years of our history; not to repudiate them, but with a kind of longing to be little again. You'll see that most of our mental cases don't rave, they just relapse into childhood. You look at them on the street, and suddenly they have the faces of children. They start singing lullabies or reciting historical dates, and they keep it up till their dying day. Most European madmen talk in religious formulas; even when American madmen are talking about food, they have to stop now and then and reel off lists of our nation's victorious battles."

"The first time I was over here," I said, "I was only interested in images; gas stations, yellow taxis, drive-in movies, advertising posters, highways, a Greyhound bus, a bus-stop sign on the highway, the Santa Fe Railway, the desert. There were no people in my consciousness and I felt good about it. Now I'm sick of all these images, I want to be something different but I don't feel good as often, because people are still too new to me." "But you feel good right now?" Claire asked. "Yes," I said.

I saw I'd been talking about myself again and asked if I could take her back to the motel and read her a few pages of *Green Heinrich*. We took the overpass again. The stars had come out and the moon was so bright that the cars had big shadows when they swung around the curve up the road. When they came closer, in the lights of the motel and the restaurant, they lost their shadows and shrank. We looked down for a while, then we crossed the long court, where the stillness increased at every step, to our rooms.

She looked in on the child, then came into my room. She sat down on the bed and leaned back. Now and then a car whished softly by. I sat in a big armchair with my legs over one arm and read how when Heinrich Lee embraced a girl for the first time an icy coldness came over him and he and the girl suddenly felt like enemies. They went home together and Heinrich fed the horse while the girl stood at the open window, undoing her hair and watching him. "The slow movements of our hands in the silence that lay over the yard filled us with a profound and, all in all, happy peace; we would have been glad to go on like that for years; from time to time I bit into a piece of bread before giving it to the horse, whereupon Anna took some bread out of the cupboard and ate it at the window. That made us laugh, and just as dry bread tasted so good after the festive, noisy meal, so the way we were now living together seemed to be the right channel; we had put into it after our little storm, and that was where we should stay." I also read about another girl whom Heinrich loved because the look on her face told him that she longed to be thinking whatever he happened to be thinking.

I saw that Claire had closed her eyes and was almost asleep. We sat silent for a while; then she said, "It's late. All that driving has made me tired." A little dizzily she went to her room.

That night the time passed too slowly, even when I was sleeping. The bed was so big; I kept moving from side to side, and that made the night longer. But here for the first time in months I dreamed of being with a woman and wanting to make love to her. During the last six months with Judith, when the mere sight of each other made us dry in the mouth with hatred, I hadn't even dreamed of touching a woman. I don't mean that the thought disgusted me, I mean that I wasn't even capable of such a thought. Of course, I remembered that these things were possible, but I wasn't tempted to visualize them. I cultivated my condition, and little by little it developed into a frozen detachment that frightened me. Now at least I had dreamed about being with a woman; that filled my long night with excitement and I woke up in a state of impatience. I wanted to tell Claire about my dreams, but then it seemed better to wait until they recurred.

When I heard the child talking in the other room, I dressed and went in. I helped Claire to pack up, we ate breakfast and drove off. We wanted to be in Columbus, Ohio, before noon, and it was more than two hundred miles. That, we reckoned, would take about five hours, because in Ohio we would have to drive through several cities and we could count on being held up at intersections. We planned to eat lunch in Columbus; then the child would take her nap in the car. Our goal for the day was Indianapolis, something under four hundred miles in all.

Again the day was cloudless; the sun, which had just risen, shone into the car through the rear window. I put the straw hat on the child; she was frantic because I hadn't put it on straight and began to scream. No sooner had she calmed down than a car passed us with its trunk partly open because of some sacks inside. She started screaming again, but we managed to make her understand that the trunk had to be open because of the sacks.

After leaving Pennsylvania, we drove a few miles through the northern tip of West Virginia. I remembered a sentence I had once read in an adventure story: "What is a Virginia meadow compared to a Texas priarie?"

We crossed the Ohio River into Ohio. It was hot in the car. The child sat quietly, looking out with interest. There were beads of sweat on her upper lip, though we had opened the windows a little. Then she grew restless and kept standing up and sitting down again. I tried to pass her the bottle of tea but she wouldn't take it. She looked terrified. Claire suggested that maybe I was holding the bottle "in the wrong hand." I shifted it to the other hand. Then she took it and drank with a long sigh. After putting the bottle away, I spoke to her, calling her by her two names. "Better stick to one name," said Claire. "It was a mistake to give her two names. I used to switch back and forth between them, and when I felt especially affectionate, I even made up new ones. It got her all mixed up. She wanted to be called by one name, any change upset her.

"I made a lot of mistakes with the child," said Claire. "I've mentioned one: calling her by different names. But that wasn't all: when I felt especially loving, I would use pet names for familiar objects, and that confused her even more. I finally understood that she attached herself to the first name I called a thing by; any other drove her crazy. Sometimes she'd be playing quietly with something or other, and I'd be watching her. After a while it was more than I could bear to be with her and not talk to her. When I began to talk, it wrenched her out of her continuity and I'd have to comfort her. Another big mistake was not wanting to give her an American upbringing. I didn't want her to act as if the world belonged to her or to regard what belonged to her as the world. I thought an American upbringing encouraged possessiveness and I didn't want that. I never bought her toys; I'd only let her play with things intended for other purposes, such as toothbrushes, shoe-polish cans, and household utensils. She played with them and then when she saw them put to their proper use, she didn't mind. But if somebody else wanted to play with them, she wouldn't stand for it, she was just like other children with their toys. She's getting possessive after all, I thought, and tried to persuade her to share with the other child. But she'd cling to whatever it was, and then I'd take it away, because I still interpreted her behavior as possessiveness. Later on I came to understand that what made her cling to things was fear, and now I feel sure that when children can't part with some object, the trouble isn't possessiveness but *fear*. A panic comes over them when suddenly something that belonged to them a moment ago is somewhere else and the place it occupied is empty, and the reason is that when that happens they don't know where they themselves belong. But I was so blinded by my determination to be rational that instead of seeing the child I saw only her behavior patterns, which I automatically interpreted."

"How is it now?" I asked.

"Sometimes I'm at my wits' end," said Claire. "Especially when she's away from home for any time, she gets upset, because when things keep changing around her she can't get her bearings. I'm glad you've come along, that gives her two fixed points to revolve around."

I was going to say something to the child but stopped myself, because she had just calmed down.

"Once somebody stole a wrist watch from me," I said. "The watch didn't mean anything to me, I'd stopped noticing it, but all the same it was a long time before I could look at the empty place on my wrist without feeling frightened."

There was a row of poles in a field and one of them slanted. Again the child began to scream. We stopped outside a shopping center and Claire took the child for a little stroll. Then she put her on a toy elephant that rocked when you inserted a dime. The rocking seemed to relax her. Then suddenly she clamored to be taken off; apparently she had seen the black dog stains on the elephant's base. She looked at various objects but quickly turned away, as though stricken with horror. Claire tried to point out a buzzard that was circling slowly over the building, but the child struck down her mother's hand. Claire laid her down in the back seat of the car. She made no move to get up, but ordered us to rearrange the photographs on the windshield. Claire went into the shopping center for some orange juice, and I got to work on the photographs. I tried every possible combination; none seemed to suit her, but she wouldn't let me put them away. As I was shifting one of the pictures, the child bellowed with panic, her voice was almost that of a grownup. She must have set her mind on some secret pattern. In each of my helpless attempts I seemed to begin right and then go wrong. When Claire came back, the child was frantic. I halted in my manipulations and instantly she was quiet, though I couldn't make out any particular order in the pictures. Claire filled the bottle with orange juice and gave it to the child to drink. None of us spoke. The child's eyes widened, she blinked more and more infrequently, then she fell asleep. We bought some sandwiches and fruit and drove on.

"All of a sudden I was in the child's place," I said after a time. "The first thing I remember in my life is the scream I let out when I was being bathed in the washbasin and suddenly the stopper was pulled out and the water gurgled away under me."

"Sometimes I forget her completely," said Claire. "That's when I feel most carefree. I don't even notice her, she runs around me like a dog or a cat. Then I notice her again and it comes to me how I love her. And the greater my love is, the greater becomes my fear of death. Sometimes when I've been looking at the child for a long time, I can't distinguish between my love and my fear of death. Once when I felt that way I took a piece of candy out of her mouth, because I thought I saw her choking." Claire spoke calmly, as though surprised at herself. She checked the green signs over the highway to be sure of taking the detour around Columbus. For some time now the road had been almost straight, there had hardly been a curve in the last hour. That made it easier for the child to sleep. Here the hills were smaller, the fields a denser green, and the wheat higher than in Pennsylvania. After Columbus Claire pointed at the rearview mirror and I saw the child was waking up; the hair on her temples was wet, her face was flushed. For a time she lay still with her eyes open; then she saw she was being watched and grinned. She said nothing, just looked quietly around. It was a game, each of us was waiting for someone else to say the first word or make the first move. In the end I lost by shifting my position; the child began to talk.

We turned off the highway, stopped on a back road, and walked a short way into a pasture. The breeze ruffled our hair. I saw that the child's temples were still wet; we bent over her and saw that down there at the child's level the air was almost motionless. Claire picked her up and her hair soon dried. We sat down at the edge of a pond. The grass was as hard as marsh grass, there were little white mushrooms in the cows' footprints. Here and there mounds of mud rose above the surface of the water; frog spawn and bits of cow dung clustered around them. Now and then a dancing gnat sent a ripple over the water; foam gathered around a half-sunken log, the air over the pond was hazy.

We ate our sandwiches; the sun was getting too hot, so we stood up and headed for a clump of trees. The child let me carry her, and I picked my way through oaks and elms. Claire lagged behind and after a while stopped altogether. There must have been a railroad line nearby, because after the child had torn some leaves off the trees, her hands were covered with soot, though the leaves had hardly opened. We came to a clearing beside a brook that was almost hidden by swamp growth. Out of the corner of my eye I saw a big animal; I swung around, but it was only a water rat. It crawled away under the leaves and stopped still; its tail was still sticking out. I bent down, looking for a stone to throw at it, but there weren't any. When I straightened up, I saw we had sunk into the mud a little; water had gathered around our shoes. I took a long step to one side and my leg sank to the knee in the warm mud.

Though I heard nothing, I felt rotten branches cracking under my foot, deep down in the mud.

I stood motionless with my legs wide apart but sank no deeper. The water rat's tail had disappeared. The child clung to me; she was breathing heavily. I called out for Claire, making my voice as calm as I could. "Don't shout!" said the child. I tugged at my leg. Before it was quite free, I jumped back to the trees and my shoe stayed in the mud, I thought the child was screaming with fear, but she was laughing at the way I was hopping. Claire sat leaning against a tree trunk, alseep. I sat down near her; the child found some acorns among the fallen leaves and lined them up beside me. After a while, Claire opened her eyes as though she had only been pretending to be asleep; instantly she saw that I was missing a shoe and that my trousers were coated with mud. As though describing a dream, she told me what had happened to me and I confirmed her story. "Were you afraid?" "Not exactly," I said. "More angry than afraid."

We went back across the pasture. Swallows were flying high overhead; as a rule it's only in big cities that they fly so high. "In America," Claire said, "hardly anybody goes walking. They drive around in cars or they sit outside the house in rocking chairs. If you go walking in the country, people look at you." She pointed to a man in a checkered shirt who was running toward us across the field; he was carrying a big club. When we stood still, he stopped running; then, apparently noticing that we had a child with us, he too stood still, dropped his club, and tossed a cake of cow dung on it. He waited. As we were slowly starting off, he pulled out his penis and urinated in our direction, moving slowly back and forth as in sexual intercourse and splattering his trousers and shoes; in the end, he lost his balance and fell over backward.

Still walking very slowly, we watched him. Claire

said nothing. In the car, before starting the motor, she broke into a soundless laugh. She laughed so hard she had to hold her head in her hands.

Those were the only shoes I had. We stopped at the next shopping center and bought another pair. When we were moving again, I looked at the mud on my trousers; it hadn't dried yet, and that made me irritable and impatient. I kept looking to see if it was dry, and finally transferred my impatience to the country we were driving through. I looked from the mud that refused to dry to the landscape that refused to change, and our motion seemed so futile that I couldn't conceive of our ever getting to Indianapolis. I had a disagreeable feeling that we had come to a stop with the motor running, and at the same time I wished we would really stop. I kept looking to see when the Ohio license plates would give way to Indiana plates, when instead of THE BUCKEYE STATE the plates on the cars we passed would say something else. Then there began to be more and more cars from THE HOOSIER STATE. Once we were in Indiana, the dry mud began to flake off my trousers, but still my impatience grew; I counted the milestones that still separated us from Indianapolis, because they were the only sign of change in the unchanging landscape. My breathing took on the rhythm of the intervals between them and my head began to ache. I was sick of having to put distances behind me when I wanted to be somewhere else, and the pressure of Claire's foot on the accelerator struck me as absurd, even useless. At the same time I wanted her to step on it and was tempted to prod her foot with the heel of my new shoe; my impatience grew so great that I could have murdered someone in my exasperation. Though the sun was setting, the light was as bright as ever, there was no darkening, and later on, as we drove into Indianapolis in the dusk and I glanced at

Claire's profile, the imperturbable, disembodied calm that came over me felt like the calm of a murderer.

I didn't want to see the city. As though it had disappointed me in advance and I already had enough of it, I looked at the floor while Claire was asking for two rooms at the Holiday Inn, right behind the Speedway. In the room I immediately drew the curtain and phoned the hotel in Providence. Someone had called the day before, they had given him my addresses in New York and Philadelphia. "Him?" "No, it was a lady," said the operator. I phoned the Algonquin, then the Barclay in Philadelphia; Judith had called the Barclay and asked if I was still there, but had left no message. I gave them my address in Indianapolis and said I would call again next day and give them my address in St. Louis. I had hardly hung up when the phone rang. It was Claire. There was no connecting door between our rooms, so she had phoned to ask if I was all right and if I wanted to go down to the restaurant for dinner.

I wasn't hungry. I suggested a walk after the child was asleep. She agreed. While hanging up, I heard a bell ring briefly behind the wall as she too rang off. I opened the curtain and looked out but saw nothing in particular. An even rhythm outside the window lulled me and at the same time sharpened my perception. Some distance away there was a cypress on a little hill. Its branches looked almost bare in the evening light. It swayed gently back and forth in a movement that resembled my own breathing. I forgot the cypress, I also forgot myself and stared into space. But then the cypress, still gently swaying, moved closer with every breath and finally penetrated my chest. I stood motionless, the pulse in my temples stopped beating, my heart stopped. I ceased to breathe, my skin died away, and with a sense of will-less well-being I felt that the movement of the cypress was taking over the function of my respiratory center, making me sway with it, and freeing itself from me. At length, feeling that I no longer offered resistance, that I was superfluous, I detached myself from its gentle motion. Then my murderous calm left me and I fell on the bed, weak and pleasantly sluggish. It no longer mattered to me where I was or when I could be somewhere else; the time passed quickly. Already it was night, and already Claire was knocking at my door.

We were sitting in Warren Park in Indianapolis; one of the chambermaids at the Holiday Inn had promised to look in on the child from time to time. It was only then that the full moon rose; the benches and bushes stood white around us, like phantoms. The globe of one of the street lamps was broken, a moth fluttered about inside and caught fire. The moonlight was very bright, but not bright enough to make you think you were bursting. My heart pounded painfully and now and then, when I took a breath, I sighed. Along the paths there were flowers with long stems, their white petals were wide open in the moonlight, totally motionless in a paroxysm of madness, and I no longer had strength enough to set them in motion; from time to time a bud popped. There was a rustling in one of the trash baskets, and then again silence. The grass was gray, as though scorched, the short shadows of the trees looked like burns, and though the air was rather cool, I felt hot inside. Behind the palms and tulip trees glittered the arrow and five-pronged star of the Holiday Inn.

"Since coming to America," I said, "I've been having the same experiences as in childhood. Fears and longings that I thought I'd forgotten have been cropping up again. I have the same feeling as when I was little that the world around me might suddenly burst and turn into something entirely different, a monster's maw, for instance. In the car today I longed to have seven-league boots, so it wouldn't take any time to cover distances. When I was little, I couldn't bear to think there was another place that I couldn't get to in a flash. Today it's the same, except that then the thought sent me into a frenzy whereas now I talk about it, draw comparisons, and learn. Any attempt to interpret these enigmas would strike me as absurd; I speak of them only because it makes me feel less isolated than I did then. I've thrown off my embarrassment, I talk a lot, I laugh a lot, I wish I were fat enough to move a revolving door with my belly, and I'm glad to say that I've almost stopped noticing myself."

"Green Heinrich didn't want to interpret things either," said Claire. "All he wanted was to be as detached as possible; he looked on as one experience interpreted the last, and so on down through the chain of experiences. He let experience pass before his eyes and never got involved; the people he knew just danced by him. He neither challenged them nor withdrew from the dance. He made no attempt to decipher anything; one event would simply follow from another. You're the same way, I think; you just let the world dance past you. As if life were taking place on a stage and there were no need for you to get mixed up in it. As if the world were a big bundle of Christmas presents, all for you. You watch while it's being unpacked; to help would be rude. You just let the world unfold, and if something happens to you, you take it with surprise, you marvel at its enigmatic aspects and compare it with past enigmas." I thought of Judith; I was aghast and so ashamed that I broke out in sweat; I had to stand up and walk about in the moonlight.

"That's true," I said, carefree again, as untouched as if I were playing a game. "When I see something and it enters into my experience, I think, 'Yes, this is it. This is the new experience I needed!' I check it off, so to speak. The moment I begin to get involved in something, I extricate myself by formulating it; instead of going through with the experience, I let it pass me by. 'So that was it,' I think, and wait to see what will come next."

"And yet," said Claire playfully, "Green Heinrich is lovable, even if he does make you want to push his nose into things. Because when he sidesteps an experience, it's not out of cowardice or faintheartedness, but because he's afraid that it's not meant for him, and that if he gets involved he'll only be rebuffed as he was always rebuffed as a child."

"But isn't that cowardice?" I said. Claire stood up and I stepped aside. She smoothed her dress and sat down, and I sat down beside her. Talking so much had broken our resistance. We didn't embrace yet, we didn't even touch each other, but we sensed that our mere closeness to each other was an exchange of affection. I knew she had rebuked me but felt as self-assured as if I had been flattered. I was afraid that Claire had been right, but in the next moment glad she hadn't been. That was often my reaction when someone spoke to me of my character; he had hit the mark, but at the same time what he said was a bare-faced lie. When I went into someone else's character, I didn't lie, but I felt like a show-off. "And now," I said to Claire, "the story of Green Heinrich is at an end."

As though in agreement she took a breath, and as she breathed it was as though her body slowly expanded and touched me. She didn't actually touch me, my imagination had merely anticipated what I was looking forward to so eagerly yet uneasily. I thought of the man who had urinated in front of us, but his image no longer troubled me. I began to tremble for fear of giving myself away. I stood up, eager but still without impatience. I touched Claire's arm, outwardly a signal that we should go back to the motel, and at the same time tried to hold back from her. Before standing up, Claire stretched. Again I stepped up to her and in a brief pantomime helped her up but without touching her. "My neck aches from looking straight ahead all day," Claire said, and it gave me a start to hear her mention a part of her body, as though *she* had now given *her*self away. I walked faster so as not to show my excitement, and Claire followed me slowly, dazzled by the moonlight.

The sound of her steps behind me made me think of an old John Ford picture, *The Iron Horse;* it was about the building of the transcontinental railroad from Missouri to California between 1861 and 1869. Beginning at the opposite ends, two railroad companies were laying tracks toward the middle, the Central Pacific from the west, the Union Pacific from the east. Years before, a man had dreamed of this railroad and gone west with his son to look for a passage through the Rocky Mountains. While he took leave of his neighbor, his little son awkwardly kissed the neighbor's still littler daughter goodbye. The father was killed, but later on, now a grown man, the son found the passage. The neighbor became the president of the Union Pacific. After long years, which were painfully long in the picture as well, for the construction work was shown in great detail, the two lines met at Promontory Point, Utah, and the president drove a golden spike into the last tie. Whereupon the dreamer's son and the president's daughter kissed for the first time since their parting as children. Though I didn't know why, I had felt wretched throughout the picture —shooting pains in my chest, compulsive swallowing, internal soreness, itching, chills—but the moment the spoke was driven in and the two fell into each other's arms, I felt their embrace inside me and I stretched inwardly with a sense of infinite relief: my whole body had hungered for the two of them to come together.

I let Claire catch up with me and side by side we went back to the Holiday Inn. The chambermaid told us the child was sleeping peacefully. I noticed that I was hungry. I ate something or other and, leaning back with her hands in her lap, Claire watched me. She blinked seldom and hesitantly, as though her eyes were closing. I looked back attentively. All at once we saw the time we had made love, and now we understood. The feeling for Claire that came over me was so strong that I had to look away. That OTHER TIME, which I had experienced in Providence when the right number had briefly flashed up on the die, now lay stretched out before me like another world that I had only to enter to be rid at last of my fear-ridden nature and its limitations. But then I took fright; it occurred to me how empty and unbeing, how without life of my own, I should be in that other world; overcome by a feeling of universal bliss, free from fear and tension, I myself, as in the play of the cypress, ceased to exist, and for a moment I was so horrified at that empty world that I experienced the child's boundless dread at suddenly seeing nothing in a place where only a moment before it had seen something. In that moment I lost forever my longing to be rid of myself; the thought of my often childish fears, of my reluctance to become really involved with other people, my spells of obtuseness, filled me with sudden pride, followed by a sense of well-being that seemed almost self-evident. I knew that I would never again want to be rid of all those limitations, and that from then on only one thing would be important: to fit them all into an order and mode of life that would do me justice and enable others to do me justice. And as though all this had merely been a test, I caught myself thinking, "This is it! This is serious!"

I sensed that Claire was still looking at me. "The poor thing!" I said to myself, but the thought was no barrier between us. Often in the past I had been overcome by confusion and disgust at the thought that someone was different from myself, but in these mo-

ments I calmly let the thought think itself out and instead of egotistical disgust I felt a profound pity for
Claire, because she couldn't be in my place and
couldn't experience what I was experiencing—how
tedious it must be for her to be Claire!—and then
again I felt envious because conversely I couldn't be
in her place. But these thoughts no longer took on an
existence of their own, they were only brief entrances
and exits in a long eipsode, rich in vicissitudes, that
revolved around something entirely different. I told
Claire about seeing John Ford's *Iron Horse* and my
feelings at the time.

She had seen the picture at her college film club
and remembered that whenever the Irish workers
were shown laying ties they had sung the same song
at the top of their lungs. "But that picture was a silent!" she exclaimed suddenly. Between the two of us
we remembered that a bar of music had always appeared over the heads of the singing workers. We
went on talking, but not about ourselves; we told stories, more and more of them, neither of us wanted to
let the other have the last word, though not to be in
the bedroom yet was almost unbearable. Finally, while
I with pounding heart was telling a story about a pig
and a coach, Claire grew so grave that I wouldn't have
known her. At one time I might have thought she
was going mad, but that night, taking an almost forgotten pleasure in past solemnities, I experienced this
moment as the moment of a truth that made my own
madness, my fear that someone might go mad in my
presence, forever ridiculous.

We made love almost sleepily, scarcely moving,
then holding our breath. In the middle of the night,
I thought of the child lying in the other room and
felt so sorry for her that I said we ought to go and
take a look at her. "The thought that Benedictine is

alone," I said, "makes me miserably lonely for her. Not because we're together here, but because when I think that there's no one with her I experience her not-yet-consciousness as a state of cruel boredom. I feel I ought to wake the child up, talk to her, and drive away her boredom. I sense that the monotony of her sleeping and dreaming makes her suffer, and I want to lie down beside her, to comfort her and help her through her long loneliness. It's intolerable that someone is born into the world, he can't automatically come to consciousness. Now I understand all those stories about somebody trying to save somebody." I told Claire about the soldier in Philadelphia and how he had been in need of being saved.

We went to the other room and I watched as the child lay sleeping.

While Claire was in the bathroom, I secretly woke her up. She opened her eyes and talked confusedly in her dream. She yawned a long yawn, I looked into her pink mouth, her tongue quivered, she was asleep again. Claire came back, we lay side by side; then she too fell asleep and snored softly, exhausted by the trip. I looked at the darkly shimmering television screen; the arrow and five-pronged star of the Holiday Inn were reflected on it in miniature. While falling asleep, I took a last look at my wrist watch; it was long after midnight and it came to me that I was now thirty years old.

I slept uneasily, I stuck a knife into an overcooked chicken, which instantly fell apart, a fat woman and a thin woman stood side by side, the thin one melted into the fat one, they burst, a governess with a child walked on a knife blade into the open door of a subway car, there were special delivery letters, signs in the sand which a stupid gardener watered like flowers, plants that formed words, secret messages written on gingerbread hearts at a church fair, an AUSTRIAN hotel room with four beds, only one of which was made up. I awoke from my nightmares with an erection, penetrated the sleeping Claire, went limp, and fell asleep again.

"Is it then so surprising that a change of place should contribute so much to making us forget what we don't like to think of as real, as though it were a dream?"

Karl Philipp Moritz, *Anton Reiser*

The
Long Farewell

*A*T noon that day we arrived in St. Louis. In the days that followed I was always with Claire and the child. We stayed at the house of Claire's friends, whom she had called "lovers," in Rock Hill, a suburb to the west of St. Louis, and seldom went out. It was a wooden house, the "lovers" were painting it, and we helped them. I never found out what their real names were, they addressed each other only by pet names and were always thinking up new ones. When I first saw them, I thought about the desire to shrink that Claire had told me about; at the second glance, I forgot all possible generalizations, and from then on I just watched them, curious to see what their mode of life might tell me. The woman was always looking mysterious, the man disappointed and injured, but after I had been with them for a while, I saw that the woman had no secret and that the man was perfectly happy and contented. But every morning I had to find out all over again that their mysterious and disappointed expressions meant nothing at all. The man painted movie posters in St. Louis, the woman helped him with the backgrounds. He also painted episodes in the settlement of the West, landscapes with covered wagons and riverboats, and sold them to the department stores. Their affection for each other was so violent that it kept shifting into irritation. They would feel the irritation coming on and start mollifying each other, which only made them more irritable. In trying to calm down, they wouldn't stop talking and leave each other alone, but would cling together, caressing, embracing, and as their exasperation increased, still trying to mollify each other with pet names—even when they were arguing about something, they always referred to it by pet names. Then, little by little, they relaxed and were able to move apart. Those were the only moments when they had a kind of vacation from each other. They had been living like this for ten years, never letting each other out of their sight.

And they still didn't know how to deal with each other. If one of them had done some chore, it didn't mean that he would do it the next time, but it also didn't mean that the other would do it. Every activity had to be renegotiated whenever it came up; since both wanted to do it, it took them forever to settle on either one of them. Neither had found his role: if something one of them had done, whether it was painting, cooking, saying something, or merely making some motion, met with the other's approval, it didn't mean that he would paint, cook, or say something similar again, or try to repeat his movement; nor did he do the opposite; everything in their dealings with each other had to be started all over again from scratch. But if one of them had done something to displease the other, he didn't simply avoid doing it again; he first tried to show that this particular action was inherent in his way of life.

They were so engrossed in each other that the most trifling objects that had accumulated in the course of their life together became as precious to them as the parts of their own bodies. They hoarded household utensils and furniture, as though it were only in the midst of these objects that they could be sure of remaining themselves. Once when the child broke a glass, we could see how aghast and hurt they were. In silence one of them swept up the pieces, while the other looked on disconsolately. When they spoke of people who had come to see them, it was usually in reference to the damage they had done: one had leaned against the wall and left the imprint of his heel, another had torn the label off a towel, a third had left a fingerprint on a painting that was not yet dry, a fourth had borrowed a book and failed to return it. They would point to the gap in the bookshelf, and then suddenly I saw that their mysterious, injured expressions actually did reflect their states of mind and their attitude toward a hostile outside world. With a sinking feeling I watched them as the pieces of glass dropped in the garbage pail and they exchanged looks of sadness at this new disappointment. They made no explicit complaint; their way of reproaching you was to shut you out by exaggerating their preoccupation with each other.

They were friendly to everyone, and in their lust for new disappointments that would throw them back on each other, they kept taking in guests. The moment you came near an object, they warned you by telling you the part it had played in their life, or, anticipating your movements, they gave you a demonstration of the best way to handle it. One feature of the way they coddled their possessions was that they owned nothing in common; each object belonged strictly to one of them. And each object had the additional protection of having been specially dedicated to one of them. This was true not only of napkin rings, monogrammed towels and sheets, but of every book, phonograph record, and sofa pillow. Every corner of the house belonged to one or the other, never to both in common. Of course, they would make exchanges and trespass on each other's territory, but the very thought that one was using objects dedicated to the other seemed time and again to renew the bond between them. These arrangements provided them with a kind of constitution that enabled them to imitate the legendary El Dorado, that outwardly inaccessible, inwardly self-sufficient state.

They took their daily routine so seriously that it became a ritual. At every step one became a servant to the other. When the painter undertook a department-store painting, his wife did all the preparatory work: she stretched the canvas, lined up the tubes of paint, set out the brushes, and opened the curtains, while the husband paced the floor with folded arms. When the wife undertook to cook a meal, the husband arranged her equipment so efficiently that in cooking she had only to make a few majestic gestures. But once they embarked on their main activity, they disliked being helped. When it came to painting the house, for instance, they only let me set up the ladders or mix the paint; anything more seemed to offend them.

Their ingrown tenderness oppressed me. It seemed to reproach me with being alone and leaving Claire alone. I would have to look at Claire to remind myself how inconceivable it would be to see her otherwise than alone. We were often together; even when we weren't, we didn't become strangers, but we made no claims on each other. For me a different relationship was no longer possible, and as for Claire, she didn't even seem to suspect the existence of any such possibility. She regarded the lovers' life as a strain, as the kind of thing that could never happen to her. Watching the two of them, we felt free, and I saw that she often smiled.

Our calm merged into desire and our desire into calm. We hardly noticed what was going on; as in a dream, one movement led to the next. We seldom touched one another and never kissed; our way of caressing was to lie side by side, breathing in and breathing out. I expressed my tenderness by talking a lot, Claire hers by listening to me and saying something from time to time.

I also talked a good deal to the child; every day I took her picture and studied the pictures to see if she had changed. Of course, they all made fun of me, but I no longer minded; lining up the photographs, I showed them that merely because her picture was being taken, she assumed different attitudes from day to day. I also thought my daily photography would provide the child with pictures to remember by later on, and I imagined that the pictures would give me a place in the child's memories. With the same purpose in mind, I took her out; once we went to St. Louis on the bus and stood for a long time on the bank of the Mississippi; perhaps the smell of the water would help her memory. When we were together and the child kept asking me the names of things, I realized how concerned I had always been with myself, to the exclusion of almost everything else, because I often didn't know what the things we saw were. For the first time it occurred to me that I had no words for some of the most common movements about me. Gradually I learned to observe certain happenings from beginning to end, instead of just gaping and saying "Aha!" In particular, I seldom knew what to call sounds; sometimes even the shorthand of the comic strips failed me, and when I had no answer, the child took fright and began to scream. If I spoke to her while she was playing, she seldom reacted; she was too busy with her own world; but if I said a word that was new to her, she perked up. Once in the late afternoon it grew cold; I couldn't persuade the child to let me put her jacket on, but when I said that without it she would get *goose flesh,* she listened and let me put the jacket on.

To my surprise, Benedictine took little notice of nature; to her the artificial signs and objects of civilization had become nature. She was much more likely to ask questions about television antennas, the stripes on the pedestrian crosswalks, and police sirens than about forests and fields. The presence of traffic lights and electric signs seemed to soothe her and at the same time to make her more lively. She took letters and numbers for granted and felt no need to decipher them; they stood for themselves. And then I noticed that I too grew bored after a while when there was nothing but nature around me and I couldn't discover anything to read in it.

When the child saw a representation of nature, one of the painter's pictures, for example, she never thought of asking whether there really was such a scene, and if so where, because the copy had replaced the original forever. I remembered that, unlike her, I myself as a child had always wanted to know where the object represented actually was. In our house, for instance, there was an oil painting of a glacier land-scape with a mountain hut at the lower edge. I had always been convinced that this landscape and this hut existed in nature; I even thought I knew where the painter must have stood, and when someone told me the picture was pure imagination I couldn't believe it. For a long time I could hardly breathe when it came to me that the picture was alone and that I could find nothing to go with it. It was very much the same when I learned to read: I couldn't see how it was possible to describe something that didn't exist. The village described in my primer was a real village, not my own of course, but another not far away. I even knew which village. And because the first books I read on my own were told in the first person, I was horrified when for the first time I opened a book in which there was no "I" narrator. These forms of perception had so powerful an influence on my other experience that now in retrospect it seemed to me that the shock of discovering they were not valid had been a turning point of my life. I felt almost jealous of this child, who from the first looked on symbols and representa-tions as having an existence of their own.

The painter was also unable, as I discovered, to conceive of sketching anything that did not exist: his landscapes had to be exact imitations of real landscapes, the people in them had to have really lived, and they had to have done what they were doing in the pictures. Accordingly, he painted only historical moments in historical landscapes, the first wagon to cross the Mississippi bridge at St. Louis or Abraham Lincoln being shot at the theater; at the most, he would embellish a little on the reality: to paint in any other way struck him as fraudulent. "That's why I don't like to paint the battle of the Little Bighorn," he explained. "The Indians didn't leave a single American survivor, and there were no eye-witness accounts." It crossed my mind that none of the pictures I had seen so far in America had been fantasies; they had all represented something, for the most part scenes in American history.

I asked the painter if he would paint different subjects if he were working not for a specific clientele but for himself. He said that he couldn't conceive of a picture standing for itself, and his wife went on, "We all of us here learned to see in terms of historical pictures. A landscape had meaning only if something historical had happened in it. A giant oak tree in itself wasn't a picture: it became a picture only in association with something else, for instance, if the Mormons had camped under it on their way to the Great Salt Lake. Everything we've seen since we were children had stories connected with it, and all those stories were heroic. So what we see in the landscape isn't nature, but the deeds of the men who took possession of America, and at the same time a call to be worthy of such deeds. We were brought up to look at nature with a moral awe. Every view of a canyon might just as well have a sentence from the Constitution under it." "We've often said that there's nothing left to love about this country," said the husband. "And still we can't help seeing the Constitution in our landscape.

Every bird becomes a national bird, every flower a national emblem." "Whenever I see a Cherokee rose," said the wife, "I'm moved in spite of myself. Not because I was born in Georgia, but because the Cherokee rose is the Georgia state flower." Claire spoke up: "And you're just as moved by your own possessions, not because you spent so much for them, but because they're symbols of your life together." The lovers laughed, and, infected by their laughter, the child broke into a perplexed guffaw. "In time," said the lovers, "even our household utensils will become symbols of the United States in our dreams. Then we'll at last be able to dream the same thing."

During this conversation we were sitting on the top deck of the riverboat *Mark Twain,* waiting for it to put out into the Mississippi. The tourists around us, all Americans, were also waiting. They didn't talk much. Holding beer cans, Coca-Cola bottles, and bags of popcorn, they looked at the cables that were just being removed from the bollards on the pier, then at the ship's two tall black smokestacks, then again at the cables. The ship backed into the current and came to a stop, rocking gently; steam hissed from the safety valves and thick black smoke poured from the smokestacks, darkening the sky. Then the steam whistle blew a signal that none of us, not even Claire, was able to describe to the child, who had instantly hidden her head down among our legs: it was as though a whole nation had set its lips to a giant flute—a long-drawn-out screech so bestial and brutal, but at the same time, what with the billowing clouds of black smoke and the vastness of the Mississippi, so proud, so grandiose, that, embarrassed and yet bodily shaken, I could only look off to one side. So overpowering was that signal that, splintered by fear, I lived a dream of America that up until then I had only heard about. It was a moment of expertly organized resurrection, in which the things around me ceased to be unrelated, and people and landscape, the living and the dead, took their places in a single painful and theatrical revelation of history. Theatrically flowed the Mississippi, theatrically the tourists moved from deck to deck, while an old man's deep, far-carrying voice told the story of the great riverboats over the loudspeaker: the new era of travel and commerce they had initiated, steamboat races, black slaves loading firewood by the light of the moon, boiler explosions; and finally, how the railroads had taken the place of the riverboats. Sick as I was of loudspeaker voices on tours, I could have listened to that dramatic voice forever.

In those days, for the first time, my enjoyment of life was sustained, rather than feverish and spasmodic; I sat there, we ate and drank, and I was at peace with myself. I was no more active than before; if anything. I grew lazier; I scarcely moved, I paid no attention to myself, but neither did I concentrate on others as I had done before; my observations just *happened,* they flowed effortlessly from my life-feeling. When the others danced, I only watched; I was entirely with them, but felt no need to join in. Why in the past had I let myself be blackmailed by other modes of life? I had never been happy while dancing; you started, you stopped, you had to wait till it was time to start again. What was beautiful in life was a simple movement that just happened in the course of your daily comings and goings, a gesture of farewell made at exactly the right place and time, a facial expression that dispensed with an explicit answer, yet expressed sympathy and consideration, and even the graceful gesture with which you told the waiter to keep the change; such movements made me feel happy, almost weightless, as others probably felt while dancing.

I drank a good deal but didn't get drunk. I neglected my appearance but moved with self-assurance. When we went out, we sat at a long table and ate festively, and it was the child, sitting between us with her smudged face, that made our banquet joyful and complete. Sometimes she told us afterward, in complete sentences, what we had done: "We were at the restaurant, we ate and drank, we talked and laughed." But even as she described these actions in complete sentences, yet left everything unsaid, I was once again taken aback and overcome with pity; so different were our reactions to the same experience that it seemed to me as if she hadn't been there at all: true and sensible as they were, her words, precisely because they were said in a reasonable tone, gave an impression of muddled, solitary babbling. I remembered how for many years I myself had learned the names for experiences (if only negatively by being told what was forbidden), but had no possibility of conceiving the actual content of any experience, let alone putting my conception into practice. The boarding schools I grew up in were almost completely cut off from the outside world, and yet, precisely because so many things were forbidden, I became acquainted with many more possibilities of experience than I could have in a normal environment in the outside world. And my imagination babbled until I was half crazy. Nevertheless—and this thought made me wretched again—because the prohibitions formed a *system,* they enabled me later on, when experience was open to me, to experience them *systematically,* to classify my experiences, to know which experiences were still lacking, not to mistake one for another, in short, to avoid going mad. It also helped me to fight off the thought of suicide, though on the other hand it increased my fear that others, who hadn't my system to sustain them, might commit suicide.

I had stopped talking to myself; I looked forward to the day as I had formerly to the night; my fingernails and hair grew faster.

But I still had nightmares; I would wake with a

start and lie there for a long while unaware that I was awake. My nightmares woke me "like a postilion's horn from the remotest depths of my own heart" (*Green Heinrich*). Once I dreamed that my mouth was open; I woke up and it was closed tight.

It was in St. Louis that I told Claire about Judith. My fears for her had left me, and now at last, as if after trying several times in vain to unscrew a screw I suddenly knew that my next try would succeed, I was able to speak without difficulty. "I was afraid I'd murder her," I said. "I'm still afraid. Once we clutched at each other's throats on the street; then I went into the house and automatically washed my hands. Another time we met after a separation; at first we were friends again, but after a few minutes, after a few questions, I felt as if a toilet with hardly any water in the tank had been flushed inside me. We were still living together, but our relations were so wretched that when we went to the beach together, for instance, each of us rubbed sun lotion on his own back. We held up best while walking along side by side. But in spite of everything, we hardly ever left each other alone; at the most, one of us would go out on the balcony after a scene, but in a little while he'd come back. We still worried about each other. Once after I had hit her in the dark, I came back a few minutes later, put my arms around her, and asked her if she was still alive.

"When I try to explain to myself how it all happened, the events lose their body and become mere signs and symptoms. Then it seems to me that I'm being unfair to Judith, because the game of causes I'm playing is rigged and all events have lost their reality by having been interpreted in advance. Our feelings of hatred were so real that, even though we tried at first to explain them, our explanations struck us both as ridiculous, as an insult to our misery. Once I told Judith that the religious fanaticism that made her convert every bit of information about the environment, in fact everything she saw in print, into universal wisdom, and try to change her whole mode of life accordingly—her air pollution mania, her diet fads—was due to her faulty education; for lack of sound information, she tended to make a magical idol out of every trifle. At the end of my harangue, I bit my lips and was forced to agree when Judith said that my way of interpreting things was itself a form of idolatry, with which I tried to distract attention from myself. At first, when I noticed the changes in Judith only occasionally and hadn't begun to take them seriously, the explanations just poured out of me; to tell the truth, I was proud of them and Judith understood them; only one thing surprised me—they had no effect on her behavior. Then I saw that she was beginning to hate my explanations and was sick of listening to them, not because she thought they were wrong but because they were explanations. 'You're stupid,' she said, and suddenly I felt stupid. This feeling of stupidity grew in me, I cajoled myself with it, it actually made me feel good. At that point we definitely became enemies; I stopped explaining and only scolded; it was obvious that we wouldn't be able to stand it much longer and that we wanted to hurt each other physically. Now and then, though I was almost choking with rage, I was cheered by the thought that I had become as vicious as other people; because up until then what had horrified me more than anything else was that people who had been my friends until then should suddenly get vicious. 'How is it possible!" I would say. Now it had happened to me, I couldn't help it, we had both turned into monsters.

"We didn't separate, because neither of us was willing to give up. When we reproached each other, the important thing was not to be right. More important—and this is what we were always on the lookout for—was that after being reproached the other should put himself in the wrong. The one who had done the reproaching would observe the other's movements, waiting for him to convict himself. The worst of it was that we no longer accused each other, but silently brought about situations in which the other would feel guilty of his own accord. We had stopped scolding, we only wanted to shame each other. One of us, for instance, would wash dishes that the other had just finished washing, clear the table the moment the other had finished eating, secretly do some chore that was normally done by the other, or move some object the other had put in the wrong place. Judith would lug heavy things from room to room and take out the garbage before I had time to help her. 'It's been done,' she would say. We never rested, we were too frantically busy looking for something more we could do, trying to get the jump on each other. Our conflicts were never settled by discussion but by the duel of activities that started up after our arguments. And the outcome of our duels was decided not by what we did but by how we did it. A halting rhythm, a superfluous motion, a moment's hesitation between one activity and the next would instantly put the guilty party in the wrong. The winner was the one who without stopping to think hit on the quickest way of doing what he had chosen to do. We would flit past and around each other, our choreography became more and more studied and graceful, and when, as sometimes happened, both of us had executed our movements perfectly, we treated each other for a time as equals.

"Like our lovers here," I said, "we began attributing the objects around us to each other. Not out of affection, no, out of hostility; we transferred our hostility to our possessions. For instance, we'd make remarks like, 'Your chair squeaks,' or 'Someone's been taking bites out of your apples,' though obviously we weren't telling each other anything new.

"Sometimes we'd discuss our behavior. That frightened us and made us both feel ridiculous. When we were away from each other, it all seemed unreal. But by then we were defenseless against our nerves. We tried to think about other things, but it was no longer possible.

"There were moments of accidental reconciliation: some encumbrance would bring our paths together and before we knew it we had our arms around each other. Or she would bend over me to take something off the table, and suddenly, without even wanting to, I had pulled her down to me. For a while we would hold each other close, feeling emptier all the while; then finally, in exasperation, we'd break apart. Those reconciliations were as accidental as your child's whims: once when the car was going around a curve, she was thrown slightly off balance and that made her feel like lying down. And she did lie down, but she got right up again because she wasn't tired. It was the same with us: we had no real need to be reconciled.

"With it all, I felt more and more free, and I thought she felt the same way. I was relieved to see that the old intimacies, which had often taken the form of alliance against others, were no longer possible, that we no longer felt the need to tease each other, that we had stopped excluding other people from our conversations by speaking the secret language of married couples and dropping allusions that no one else could understand. We hardly spoke to each other, yet I felt that I was being perfectly frank and open. When we were not alone, but playing roles—the role of hosts at a restaurant, of travelers at the airport, of movie-goers or guests—when other people treated us as the embodiments of these roles, we got along, because then we too saw ourselves as actors and were almost proud of having slipped into our roles so easily. At such times, of course, we were careful not to come too close to each other, at the most we would give each other a little poke in passing. After an incredibly beastly scene, when all we could do was stand there pale and trembling, a feeling of tenderness for Judith would come over me. That happened more and more often as time went on, and my feeling of tenderness was stronger than my love had been. Then I would busy myself with something else and little by little my hysteria would dissolve into soothing pain.

"I could have gone on living like that. It was a deliciously sweet alienation: in moments of hatred I thought of Judith as a *thing*, then, when I relaxed, as a *being*. I thought Judith felt the same way, but then I saw that she had merely grown indifferent. She started when I spoke to her. She played games requiring several players all by herself. She told me she was gratifying herself; but I didn't tell her that I too had begun to masturbate. The thought that we were lying in different rooms and possibly masturbating at the same time struck me as ridiculous, yet made me feel wretched. But I couldn't help her; hatred and meanness had squeezed me dry and I could only lie there benumbed. I even stopped dreaming of being with a woman. I couldn't imagine a woman when I was masturbating: I had to keep my eyes open and look at a nude photograph.

"By then we rarely exchanged pinpricks. Judith would often avert her face, but she no longer burst into tears. She spent her money as soon as she got it, she bought all sorts of things, a polar bear rug, a hand-wind phonograph, a flute that caught her fancy only because there was a spider web in the mouthpiece. For our meals she stopped buying anything but delicacies. Sometimes she came home empty-handed, furious with the stupid salesgirls because nothing had looked exactly as she had imagined. I lost patience, but I still worried about her. When she leaned out the window, I stood behind her, as though I too wanted to look out. I kept seeing her stumbling and bumping into walls. Once when I looked at a bookcase she had made years before, it gave me a real fright to see that the bookcase was still intact and still standing in its old place, and at that moment I suddenly realized that I had already given up Judith for lost. Her face became more and more thoughtful, but I couldn't bear to see that thoughtful look any more. Now you know why I'm here."

Immediately after our arrival I had phoned the hotel in Philadelphia and given my address and telephone number in St. Louis. Then, while speaking of Judith, I gradually forgot her and the thought that she might be nearby passed out of my mind. It seemed to me that I had shaken the whole thing off. One evening we were sitting on the veranda; the child was already in bed and was talking aloud to herself; we listened to her and occasionally said something to each other in an undertone; the lovers were sitting on a love seat with a shawl over their shoulders; Claire was reading *Green Heinrich*, and I was watching her, when the phone rang in the house. The woman went in; I stopped my rocking chair, I already knew it was for me. The woman came to the door, looked in my direction, and pointed silently at the phone. I was already half out of my chair. I tiptoed into the house as though I were doing something wrong. In hardly more than a whisper I said my name, but there was no answer. I repeated my name; it didn't occur to me to ask who it was. I heard nothing, only once the sound of a truck going by very fast, then a bell that made me think instantly of a gas pump. I said nothing more and quietly hung up. And I didn't ask the woman who had asked for me.

Two days later I received a printed birthday card. Between the words "Happy" and "Birthday" the word "last" had been inserted by hand; though it resembled Judith's, the writing was quite strange; but then she had always written with a fountain pen, never with a ballpoint. On the other side, next to the address, an indistinct Polaroid photograph of a revolver had been pasted. One cartridge protruded from the cylinder. It dawned on me only gradually that the card was meant as a threat; then I knew that Judith wanted to kill me. I didn't actually believe she would do it, but the mere intention made me almost proud of myself. Now, at least, I thought, nothing else could happen to me; the threat was a kind of insurance against other dangers and accidents. Nothing more can happen to me now," I thought and went so far as to convert all my traveler's checks into cash.

It also became clear to me that Judith had followed me in my travels with this purpose in mind. We had several times threatened to kill each other, not because we wanted to see each other dead, but because we wanted to obliterate and destroy each other. It would have been a kind of sadistic murder, in which one tortured and humiliated the victim in order to make him feel at long last how insignificant he was. But how terrified either of us would have been if the other suddenly demanded to be murdered! To have written and mailed this card was typical of Judith's way of striking poses even in despair: her face in profile, she was sitting beside a half-drawn curtain in the twilight of a hotel room; she was twisting her rings and the revolver lay in her lap. Once in a half dream I had lived my own death: some people were standing in front of me; now and then they would stand up on their tiptoes; little by little, each one found his place and stopped moving; a few more people arrived, and stopped a little farther away; far in the background a child came running, jiggled for a moment, then stood still, and I was dead. Just as since that time I had never thought of my own death but at the most had felt uneasy now and again, so now my image of Judith beside the half-drawn curtain was for me a farewell image, and I knew that from then on we no longer belonged together. I no longer even dreamed of her and my own murderous feelings were forgotten. Sometimes I felt watched, but I didn't look around. Formerly, when we hadn't seen each other for some time, we would occasionally write: "I'm curious about you." I was no longer curious.

We often went to the movies; the painter was given free tickets to the pictures he had done posters for. Most of them made me long to be somewhere else; it was a relief when they were over. There were things that strained my eyes and mind; the rhythm of the images hemmed me in and gave me a pain in the chest. I lost myself only once, when Claire had taken the child to the amusement park at the 1904 World's Fair ground and I went to see John Ford's *Young Mr. Lincoln*; then I dreamed as I watched. Looking at the images of the past, scenes from the early life of Abraham Lincoln, I dreamed of my own future; the people on the screen prefigured the people I would meet. The longer I watched, the more eager I became to meet only people like those in the picture; then I would never again have to pretend; like them I would be fully present in body and mind, an equal moving among equals, carried along by their motion, yet free to be myself while respecting the freedom of others. As a child I had tried to imitate everything, gestures, attitudes, even handwritings, but now I took these figures who had made the best of themselves as *examples*: I didn't want to become like them, I wanted to make the best of myself. Only a short while before, I might have tried to imitate their backwoods accent, their manner of speaking as if their only purpose was to remind each other gently of something, or the inimitably warm smile—never put on for his own benefit but always selflessly addressed to others—of the young Henry Fonda, who more than thirty years before had played the role of the young lawyer Abraham Lincoln. Now I was done with the longings of affectation, and in looking up at the screen it was as though I were only greeting old friends.

Abraham Lincoln had taken the case of two brothers, strangers to the region, who were accused of murdering a deputy sheriff. J. Palmer Cass, the other deputy sheriff, claimed to have seen the elder brother stab the man in the moonlight, whereupon the younger brother took the blame on himself. Sitting in her covered wagon, their mother had witnessed the fight, but she refused to say which of her sons was the murderer. Some drunks tried to lynch the brothers, but Lincoln stopped them by softly reminding them of themselves, of what they were, what they could be, and what they had forgotten. This scene—Lincoln on the wooden steps of the jailhouse, with his hand on the mob's battering ram—embodied every possibility of human behavior. In the end not only the drunks, but also the actors playing the drunks, were listening intently to Lincoln, and when he had finished they dispersed, changed forever. All around me in the theater I felt the audience breathing differently and coming to life again. Later on at the trial, Lincoln proved that Cass could not have been the murderer because there had been a new moon that night. From then on he addressed him not as J. Palmer Cass but as John P. Cass and proceeded to charge this John P. Cass with the murder of his fellow deputy, who had only been hurt in his brawl with the two brothers. Leaning out of the covered wagon as the family prepared to continue their journey westward, the mother handed Abraham Lincoln a pouch containing his fee. "Take it, it's all I have!" And Lincoln took it! "Thank you, ma'am!" Then he left the settlers and went up on a hill alone. At one point in the picture, he and an old trapper were riding through the spring landscape on a donkey. Lincoln was wearing a top hat, his feet were almost dragging on the ground, and he was playing a jew's-harp. "What kind of an instrument is that?" the trapper asked. "A jew's-harp," said Lincoln. "Funny people making that kind of music," said the trapper. "But it sounds real purty." The one strumming the jew's-harp, the other wagging his head in time, they were long seen riding through the countryside.

"I'm going to visit John Ford," I said to Claire when we called for them at the fairground. "I'm going to ask him about his memories of the picture, and whether he still sees Henry Fonda, who's doing soap operas on TV now. I'm going to tell him that I learned about America from that picture, that it taught me to understand history by seeing people in nature, and that it made me happy. I'm going to ask him to tell me what he used to be like and how America has changed since he stopped making pictures."

After that we strolled awhile, the child ran on ahead, the street lamps glittered in the setting sun as if they had already been lit. I felt like throwing something away and tossed a piece of chewing gum through the bars of an animal's cage. We passed some people coming away from the roller coaster all bleary-eyed, so then we all sat down in one of the cars, and while we were riding the sun sank behind the big billboards, but shimmered through a little; we saw it again when our car was at the top of a grade; the next time it had set behind the Missouri plains.

As night fell, we were standing in the garden; deep in thought, we were almost motionless, at the most shifting our weight from one foot to the other now and then. From time to time, one of us took a sip of wine from a glass that seemed forgotten the moment he picked it up. We were so drained of sensation that sometimes we were afraid of dropping our glasses. The birds had stopped singing and were only hopping about in the bushes. A few doors away some people got out of their car and went into their house. On the street no one was moving; now and then a faint breeze sent a ripple over the fallen magnolia blossoms that the first wind after sunset had blown out onto the sidewalks from under the bushes. In the window of a house nearby I saw a play of collors that changed every few seconds: the color TV had been switched on in a dark room. A window was open on the ground floor of our house; the light was on; all I could see was the brightly lighted back wall and Claire, who was putting the child to bed, passing in front of it, once with the naked child in her arms, then from the other direction alone with a bottle of tea; then the wall was bare except for faint shadows of Claire bending over the child somewhere in the room, and in the end there was only the bare wall, which, as the darkness deepened round about, shone more and more brightly, with an even, deep-yellow light, which the wall seemed to generate rather than reflect. "You'll only find that kind of yellow light in the Western paintings of the last century," said the painter. "That light doesn't come from somewhere else, the sky for instance, it's given off by the ground itself. In Catlin's or Remington's paintings the sky is always pale, smoky, and colorless, you never see the sun, but a strangely deep yellow shines from the ground and lights up the faces from below. In all those pictures yellow is the dominant color: wagon wheels, powder smoke rising from rifles, the teeth of dying horses, railroad tracks—everything shimmers yellow from within; it makes every single object stand out as in a coat of arms. Nowadays you see imitations of that yellow wherever you go: the signs on parking lots, the markings on highways, the arches of the McDonald's restaurants, traffic lights, U.S.A. T shirts." "The yellow arrow of the Holiday Inn," I said. The painter and his wife showed me the palms of their hands. The woman's—she painted only the skies—could hardly be seen, but the man's hands shone yellow in colorless darkness. "It's a color that makes you remember," the man said. "And the longer you look at it, the further back you remember, till you reach a point where you can't go any further. At that point you can only stand there and dream." "In the years of gold," said the woman suddenly. The light in the room went out; whichever way I looked, there was a blinding afterimage. Claire came out of the house, munching a piece of bread left over from the child's supper. Then we sat on the veranda and the lovers played old records, reminding each other of things they had done when the records were new. *I Want to Hold Hold Your Hand*: "We were in that Mexican restaurant outside Los Angeles, drinking out of iced beer mugs." *Satisfaction*: "Remember the way the air mattresses skittered across the sand in the storm?" *Summer in the City*: "That was when we got our last money from home." *Wild Thing*: "We lived like gypsies in those days!" *The House of the Rising Sun . . .* They were getting more and more excited, and suddenly Claire put in, "You've got hymns enough for a lifetime. You'll never have to mind anything that happens to you. Whatever it is will be a great experience when you come to look back on it." I said that memory hadn't transfigured the events of my own life but only made them more repugnant. "A long hike only gets longer, a slap in the face stings twice as much. I can hardly bear to think of the things I've lived through."

"My father was a drinker," I said in a tone that made it sound like a variation on "My father was a gambling man" in "The House of the Rising Sun." "Lying in bed at night, I'd hear him pouring liquor into his glass: whenever the memory of that glug-glug comes back to me, I want to cut off his head with a flail; all I wanted then was to fall alseep. The feelings aroused by my memories have never been pleasant ones; it's only when I hear other people reminiscing that I sometimes feel free from my own memory and long for a past. Once, for instance, I overheard a woman saying, 'That was when I was putting up all those vegetables . . .' It almost made me cry. And I once heard another woman, whom I never really looked at because I never saw her except in her butcher shop, with chains of slippery sausages over her arms, saying, 'When my children had whooping cough and I had to take them on plane rides . . .' I envied her memory and hankered after the days when I myself had whooping cough, and whenever I read about people taking plane rides I feel as if I'd missed something that can never be retrieved. And then things that I ordinarily detest take on a weird sort of attraction for me."

"But when you talk about Green Heinrich," said Claire, "you seem to think you can retrieve his adventures. You think that with the help of a man who lived in other times you can repeat those times and pile up experiences, until at the very end of the story you're perfect and complete."

"I know it's no longer possible to live by easy stages like Green Heinrich," I answered. "When I read about him, I feel pretty much as he did when, 'lying in a quiet forest glade, he passionately relived the pastoral delights of a past century'; in reading his story, I too relive the ideas of another age, when people still believed that a man can be remade by easy stages and that the world is open to each one of us. To tell you the truth, it has seemed to me in the last few days that the world really is open to me and that every time I open my eyes I experience something new. And as long as this pleasure, even if it does belong to the last century, is within my reach, I mean to take it seriously and examine it."

"Until you run out of money," said Claire. I was thinking the same thing at the moment and I showed her the packet of dollars I had obtained in exchange for my traveler's checks. The lovers smiled at our conversation; we stopped talking and listened to the records and the stories the lovers told each other about them, occasionally disagreeing about details, until the night grew brighter and the dew started falling. Then, when the lovers thought the dew might be bad for their records, we all went to bed.

The following afternoon, as Claire, the child, and I were about to leave the lovers and go to see *Don Carlos,* the first performance of the German theater group, a special delivery package came for me. It was a small, neatly wrapped box, addressed in block letters that looked as if they had been written with the left hand. I went behind the house, cut it open with the garden shears, and carefully removed the wrapping paper. Around the box was a wire; its ends covered by a red seal. When I broke open the seal, my hand contracted; I touched the wire again, and again my hand contracted. I realized that I was getting mild electric shocks. I put on a pair of rubber gloves that had been put down in the fork of a tree, slipped the wire off the box, and saw it was connected with something inside. When I tugged at it, the cover fell off but nothing else happened. Inside the box there was a small battery, to which the ends of the wire were attached. I knew that Judith was clever enough to make something much more dangerous, but I couldn't laugh. Suddenly I *heard* the tiny little blow she had struck me as a high, soft whimper, and almost turned toward it. Now I was hurting myself. What was the matter? What was all this about? Why was I unhappy? Wasn't it all over? I didn't want to think about it just then, but I knew I would have to leave soon. The grass around me grew very bright, then darkened; again lizards were darting about in the corners of my eyes, the objects around me twined themselves into hieroglyphics, I ducked to avoid an insect, but it was only a motorcycle droning in the distance. There was a frightened rustling in the bushes. I threw the box in the incinerator and went back to Claire, who was already sitting in the car. When I reached for the door handle, I noticed that I still had the rubber gloves on. "Aren't they a lovely yellow?" I said while taking them off. Claire wasn't curious. As I slammed the door, my fingers contracted again around the metal.

The theater was a colonial-style building. Inside, mural paintings gave the illusion of other, adjoining rooms; in the vestibule, you picked up your foot to climb steps that were only painted, stepped on painted bases of columns, reached out to feel a relief whose elevations receded when you touched them. The theater itself was rather small, but around it and above it there were many loges where already I could see the glint of opera glasses in the darkness. Before the performance began, two men stepped in front of the curtain: the dean of the university welcomed the dramaturge of the German theater group. Something about the dramaturge caught my attention; I looked again and recognized a friend, a man I had enjoyed talking to in former days. When they withdrew, out came a costumed group, representing the German community of St. Louis. First in choral song, then in a series of tableaux, they told the story of how their ancestors had come to America and settled. Before emigrating, they had lived in the petty principalities of pre-1848 Germany. Both in work and in pleasure, they had hampered each other's movements, and the restrictions imposed by the craft guilds had prevented them from using their tools; in the American tableaux, the group broke apart, individuals were born, and, as a sign that they were now free to do what work they chose, they exchanged tools. And now there was room also for pleasure. In the last tableau they danced, the men waved beribboned hats over their heads and raised their knees to chest height; only one stood still with legs outspread and hands on hips; the women pivoted on tiptoe, each stretching out one hand to her partner while the other hand gracefully held up the hem of her skirt; only the partner of the man who was standing still looked him straight in the eye, brazenly holding up the hem of her skirt in both hands. All stood motionless in front of the curtain, swaying a little from time to time; the sweat poured from the men's hair, the women trembled on their tiptoes. Then suddenly they let out a cry of joy, a peculiarly American hoot, and began to dance in earnest. Again they waved their hats. Below them in the orchestra three musicians popped up; two with thick veins in their necks were playing violins, while the third, who had a thoughtful look, ponderously stroked a bull fiddle. At the last stroke of their bows, the musicians sank into the chairs, the dancers bowed and ran dancing and jostling into the wings, and the curtain opened on the slow entrance of Don Carlos and a monk.

Afterward I said to the dramaturge, "Like everybody else, I first looked to see if the curtain would fold back evenly on both sides—because the dancers had been moving so mechanically. And it upset me that when the two actors came in they didn't put their feet down at the same time. They entered as though stepping into a no man's land. And then their acting was anxious and hurried, as if they had no right to be playing here. The stage wasn't a mere stage, it was foreign territory."

"That's why they kept stumbling," said the dramaturge. "They sensed that their movements weren't right. All of a sudden while crossing the stage they'd decided to change their walk, as if they thought the audience must be getting sick of the way they were walking. Instead of striding, they'd begin to hop. Or they'd muff their lines because they thought it was time to sing something. They knew the rhythm of the audience was different from what they were used to, but they weren't able to fall into this audience's rhythm."

"And they kept regrouping," I said, "because when they were grouped in the usual way, the audience didn't listen."

"Over here," said Claire, "we're used to seeing historical figures in stationary tableaux. Instead of letting them play their parts, we pose them, and always with their officially known gestures. We'd think it was silly if we saw them doing anything else but their traditional deeds. For us they haven't any biography, they're trademarks for what they did or what was done in their day, we're not interested in their lives. We remember them as they appear in monuments and postage stamps. In parades they're not represented by living men but by silent puppets. Only the movies show something of their lives, but even then they usually appear as marginal figures. The one exception is Abraham Lincoln; his story really interests us, because it's potentially our own. Even so, we could hardly conceive of seeing him in a stage play, making laborious entrances and exits like King Philip. One reason why we don't think of our Presidents as heroes is that they were elected by us and we never had to approach them with fear and trembling. Our heroes are our early settlers and pioneers, men in their own right, who had adventures."

"Don Carlos," said the dramaturge, "is a European adventure story. Schiller isn't portraying historical figures but himself; under their names, he acts out the adventures into which they themselves put so little charm and dignity. He shows us how much more faithful *he* would have been to himself and his role. In Schiller's Europe only princes could be historical figures, and only historical figures could play roles and have adventures. In writing for princes, Schiller provided examples to show them how they should behave in their adventures."

Claire's lips narrowed slightly and she smiled. "The American audience's heroes are pioneers. That's why they regard only physical action as adventure. They don't want to see roles, they want action; as they see it, a role isn't an adventure, because in our country everyone can play a role. When they see a hand on a sword hilt and nothing happens but talk and more talk, they lose patience. All they want in character portrayal is a hint or two, but they want to see actions carried through from start to finish. They're disappointed when the shot at Marquis Posa is fired offstage. When Don Carlos finally draws his sword, they want to get up and cheer. An adventure! But since we are unable to act out such adventures, much less the adventures of the pioneers, and since we're not interested in your historical figures, we tend in our own theater to imitate ourselves, seen for the most part as people who no longer have adventures but only dream of having them."

"But why, if there are no adventures in your own plays, does *Don Carlos* make the people restless?" the dramaturge asked.

Claire said, "Because that hand on the sword hilt promises something that can't happen on the stage." She pointed to a print on the wall of the French café where she had taken us after the performance; it showed Sheriff Garrett shooting Billy the Kid. Night. A large room with a fireplace and a chest of drawers. The two men stood facing each other with leveled revolvers; in his other hand Billy the Kid held a knife; no flame came from his gun, but the broad flame from the sheriff's gun had almost reached him. The full moon shone in through the barred window; in the moonlight three dogs could be seen running between the two men. The sheriff wore gleaming black boots, Billy the Kid was barefoot.

"Where's Judith?" the dramaturge asked me while taking a pill from his pocket medical kit. "I saw her

206

in Washington. She came backstage and asked if she could join the troupe. I was delighted; one of our actresses wants to go back to Europe anyway. We arranged to meet in St. Louis. We were going to rehearse here, and then the day after tomorrow in Kansas City she was going to play Princess Eboli. Today I received a telegram saying she's not coming."

"Where was it sent from?" Claire asked.

"Some place I never heard of," said the dramaturge. "It's called Rock Hill."

Rock Hill was the suburb of St. Louis where I had been living the last few days.

"I don't know where Judith is," I said. "We've separated."

The dramaturge took another small pill, which, he explained, had to be taken along with the first to counteract its side effects, and asked if I had done any more work on my play.

"It's hard for me," I said, "to write roles. When I characterize somebody, it seems to me that I'm degrading him. Everything that's individual about him becomes a tic. I feel that I can't be as fair to other people as I am to myself. When I make somebody talk on the stage, he clams up on me after the first few sentences; I've reduced him to a concept. I think maybe I'd do better to write stories."

"What concept?"

"You must know people," I said, "why try to reduce everything they see, even the most extraordinary things, to a concept, to do away with it by formulating it, so they won't have to experience it any more. They have words for everything. And then, because there aren't really any words for what they're trying to say, what they say is usually an invitation to laugh, a joke, even if they haven't formulated it with this in mind. That's how it is in my play. As soon as somebody says something, if only with a gesture, the character is reduced to a concept and I can't do anything more with him. I've been wondering whether I oughtn't to bring in someone else in every scene, a servant figure to interpret the new situation for the others, a kind of counterfigure to the usual wise observer who comments on the story and keeps the threads together. Because everything this servant says in his comments—and he comments on everything—turns out to be wrong. What he predicts never happens, all his explanations are absurd. He turns up as a deus ex machina where none is needed. Two characters need only look in different directions and he barges in to reconcile them."

"What's the play called?" the dramaturge asked.

"Hans Moser and His World," I said.

I explained to Claire that Hans Moser was an Austrian actor who played only servant parts but who in the course of the action showed everyone his place. "He played very carefully, very seriously, because he always took the action to heart, but sometimes, after engineering some intrigue, you'd see a shy smile on his face. In his movies we couldn't wait for him to come on."

I had talked a good deal and now I recovered my perception of what was going on around me. On the next table there was a cellophane cigar wrapper in the ash tray. The cigar must have been very long! I laughed. Claire gave me a quick glance and we wanted to be closer together. The woman behind the bar tapped the buttons of the cash register with the top of a ballpoint pen; the drawer jumped out and hit her in the stomach! The dramaturge looked sleepy, his eyeballs were yellow, I'd have liked to put my arm around him but didn't want to frighten him. "She liked having that drawer slam into her," he said. I was going to disagree with him, but then I noticed that he was only pondering a theatrical situation.

We drank a good deal. Claire treated us to rye and drank more than the two of us together. In the street we zigzagged, there were hardly any cars, we kept pointing things out to each other. In a side street the dramaturge went up to two black prostitutes. He'd look around at us now and then; he was standing a few feet away from the women and talking to them; when they said something, he'd bend over as though straining to hear. That gesture of inclining his ear without moving closer to them suddenly showed me how much he had aged, and that made him seem more lovable than ever before. With two fingers he plucked lightly at one girl's wig; she slapped his hand and said something in an angry voice. He came back to us and told us what she had said: "Don't touch me! This is my country! Don't touch me in my country!" For a moment he rubbed his chest, a gesture I had never seen him make. That gesture seemed to be his only answer to his helplessness.

"I'm completely cut off from life," he said later in the bar of his hotel. "It exists for me only in comparisons with my inner states. I haven't seen a fish being scaled for years, but last night when I woke up in a state of anxiety, I saw glittering scales all around me. I haven't been exposed to nature for ages, but when I reach out my hand for my glass, I feel like the body of a spider that's just been killed and is slowly, as though still alive, sinking to the ground on its thread. I've stopped noticing the commonplace acts of life, like putting my hat on, riding on escalators, or eating a soft-boiled egg; but later they come back to me as metaphors for my situation." He left the room, came back after a while and told us he had vomited. His lips were still wet from the water he had drunk afterward. He lined up a few pills of various colors in front of him and swallowed them in a strictly determined order. "At first I felt as if I'd stuck my finger into a water faucet and the air in it had exploded," he said. He bowed to Claire and asked my permission to dance with her. I watched them: Claire moved lazily in one place, while he, in a variety of steps, moved back and forth in front of her; through the low-ceilinged bar droned the gloomy music of the Creedence Clearwater Revival: "Run through the Jungle."

We took him up to his room. "I'm leaving town tomorrow," I said. When I stepped out of the hotel with Claire, the night was so bottomlessly dark that I reeled. Clinging to each other, we went to the car. In the stillness I heard a ghostly din; from the Mississippi, I think. We went into a building site; I sat on a crate, drew Claire down to me, and penetrated her right away; something seemed to crunch. We couldn't hear each other any more, I hurt, I was bleeding, the pain eased, and a tune ran through my head, the same words over and over: "Peppermint steak on Sunday."

In the car on the way back to Rock Hill, I said to Claire, "I feel as if I were half asleep: I woke up gradually and in waking my dream images became slower and slower; then they stopped and turned into beautiful, quiet half-sleep images. I'm no longer afraid as I was in my dream, I let the images soothe me."

As we were passing a street lamp after getting out of the car, the shadow of a great night bird flew soundlessly across the brightly lit street. "Once on a boat ride through the Louisiana bayous a night owl flew into my face," said Claire. "That was when I was pregnant."

Next day she drove me to the airport. She stood on the terrace with the child as I was walking across the tarmac to the gleaming yellow Braniff Airlines plane that would take me to Tucson, Arizona. All three of us waved until we couldn't see each other any more.

After a stop in Denver, Colorado, I arrived in Tucson with a feeling of breathless exaltation. The city is in the middle of the desert, a hot wind blows all day; sand clouds raced across the runway, and on both sides of it there was cactus with white and yellow flowers. While waiting for my suitcase, I put my watch back an hour. In doing so, I made a gesture that was somehow ambiguous; I looked around as if I had been caught doing something forbidden; all I saw was pieces of luggage on the conveyors, which were circling as slowly as the hands on the clock. I calmed down; now my breath was coming evenly again. What was I doing in Tucson? The clerk at the travel agency had put down Tucson on my tourist ticket because he thought from looking at me that I suffered from the cold. "In Tucson it's already summer," he said. What was I doing in the summer? It had already become inconceivable to me on the plane that I could be curious about anything in Tucson. I'd seen pictures of everything the place could possibly offer. And now, at the edge of the airfield, the first thing I saw was the agaves from the label of the tequila bottle in Providence! A hot flush came over me as if I were to blame. For this or something else. Though the building was airconditioned I sweated, not at the thought of going out into the heat, but because I couldn't even conceive of going out into the heat. My thinking cramp again! The sun shone darkly through the big tinted panes, the travelers were in a solar eclipse. Disgruntled, I strolled back and forth, looking around for my suitcase, which finally turned up alone on the Braniff Airlines conveyor. I got myself a can of Coke out of a vending machine and sat down with it in a niche where you could watch movies on a small screen without paying. People passed by the niche; now and then one of them stopped and looked in, more at the spectators than at the picture. Aside from me, there was a Mexican with his feet beside him on his seat and his knees drawn up so high that to look past them at the screen he had to lean his head on one shoulder. On one knee lay his hat, it had a wide yellow band; one of the Mexican's hands was resting on the hat. The movie was publicity for an orange plantation near Tucson. Where was his other hand? I looked at the Mexican again and saw it was lying motionless under my coat, which I had put down beside me. I stood up and took a last glance at a basket brimful of oranges, one of which was toppling. At the same time I slowly picked up my coat and, again in the corners of my eyes, saw . . . the Mexican's motionless fist; between index finger and middle finger, between middle finger and ring finger there were razor blades. The man himself seemed to have fallen asleep. I tiptoed out of the niche.

On another airplane's conveyor another single piece of luggage was circling. I had already passed it when something caught my attention. I went over to it: it was Judith's brown doeskin bag. A sheaf of baggage checks from various airlines was attached to the handle. The bag had come from Kansas City on a Frontier Airlines plane. I let it circle around once again, then I picked it up and tugged at the baggage checks, but they were on elastic bands that stretched so much that I stumbled. I put the bag back on the conveyor, again it turned, I followed it, picked it up again, put it back. I took my suitcase off the Braniff Airlines conveyor and stood around with it for a while. Somebody whispered in a doorway behind me; a woman gasped for fright. A short eerie sound came out of a throat, then someone was suffocating. White moths were darting about in the marsh grass. I heard nothing; all at once my ears hung heavy from my head, as they had when I woke up in the gray of dawn beside my grandmother who had just died. I looked toward the exit, someone was sighing or wheezing: yes, the glass doors that must have just opened for someone were closing automatically with a wheeze; I breathed again. Outside: a man wearing a hat with a wide light-colored band was going toward a car; he was holding his hat tight, and the wind was so strong that it kept turning up the brim. Inside: a woman came out of the ladies' toilet. She was heavily made up and was wearing a pants suit with sharp creases, beside which I could see the previous creases! An Indian woman: an Indian woman entered the hall, the doors closed behind her, she turned around to a child who was approaching the doors from outside. She motioned the child to step on the rubber mat in front of the doors. The child hopped up and down on the mat, but wasn't heavy enough, the doors stayed closed. The Indian woman went out through the doors and came in again with the child. And so, little by little, everything calmed down.

That first day in Tucson I didn't leave the hotel. I took a long bath and dragged out the process of dressing as long as possible; day turned to night while I was buttoning my shirt, pulling up zippers, and lacing my shoes. In St. Louis I had become so unused to being alone that now I didn't know what to do with myself. Alone, I felt superfluous. It was ridiculous to be so alone. I was so bored with myself that I could have hit my head against the wall. It wasn't company I wanted, I only wanted to be rid of myself. The slightest contact with myself was disagreeable; I kept my arms as far away from me as possible. The moment I felt my body heat in a chair, I moved to another. After a while I had the impression that I had warmed all the chairs, so I just stood. It shook me to think that I had ever masturbated. I went about with my legs far apart, so as not to hear the rubbing of my trouser legs. Don't touch anything! Don't see anything! Can't somebody knock at the door! A horrible thought: to turn on the TV and hear voices, see images! I went to the mirror and made faces at myself. I wanted to stick my finger down my throat and vomit until there was nothing left of me. To hurt myself, maim myself! I paced the floor, forward and backward. Or open a book and read some loathsome sentence! Or look out the window and be confronted again with SNACK BAR, TEXACO, ICE CREAM! Shut everything up, cast everything in cement! I lay down on the bed and piled all the pillows on my head. I bit the back of my hand and thrashed around with my feet.

"The time drags so."

That sentence from a story by Adalbert Stifter ran through my head. I sat up and sneezed. It seemed to me that in sneezing I had leaped over a long stretch of time. Then I wished something would happen to me as soon as possible.

That night I dreamed a good deal. But my dreams were so violent that I remembered only the pain of dreaming them. An Indian waiter brought me my breakfast. In front of him I counted the money I had left—it was a lot more than half—and wondered what I could do with it. The Indian stopped on the way out when he saw me counting, but I went right on. His face was inflamed, there were little black dots on his forehead. A few days before, the Indian told me, the wind had been so strong that the grains of sand had made his face bleed. He lived outside the city with his parents, near the San Xavier del Bac mission, and had to walk several blocks to the bus line. "My parents have never left the reservation," said the Indian waiter. He had difficulty in speaking; his teeth were covered with saliva. He told me that although the hotel swimming pool was in a sheltered patio, the sand had to be cleaned out of it every other day.

At noon I took a cab to the airport to make sure that Judith's doeskin bag wasn't still circling around on the conveyor. I went to the checkroom too, but didn't inquire; I only looked at the shelves from a distance. I rode back to town and paced. I kept turning around because I didn't know which way to go. I waited at red lights; they turned green and still I waited, till they turned red again. I also waited at bus stops and let the bus drive on. I went to a phone booth and stood in a pile of sand that had blown in. I picked up the phone and was about to put a coin in the slot. Then I thought I'd buy something, but left the department store before I had even looked at anything. I went to all sorts of places but lost interest as soon as I was there. I was hungry, but the moment I saw the menu outside a restaurant my hunger was gone. Finally I went to a cafeteria. You walked in through an open door hung with glass beads, there were no formalities, you just plunked something edible on your tray and picked up your utensils and paper napkin in passing: this, I felt, was the right place for me. And when I went to the cash desk and the woman didn't look at me but only counted the plates on my tray, I was at peace with the world again. Forgotten the dining ceremonies which had been becoming a need for me. And not looking at the cashier but only at the check she had put down on my tray, I blindly passed her the money. Then I sat down at a table and without a care in the world ate a chicken leg with french fries and catchup.

San Xavier del Bac is one of the oldest missions in America. It is south of Tucson, at the edge of an Indian reservation. I had no idea what to do with myself alone and for the first time in my life felt a desire to see sights. It was very bright outside, the hubcaps on the cars were dazzling. I bought a pair of sunglasses and, informed by a poster that this was straw hat week, a straw hat that one could tie under the chin to keep it on in the wind. On Broadway, an Armed Forces Day parade was passing. It was the third Saturday in May, crowds of people were sitting on the curbstones with their legs stretched out, children were licking ice cream cones and running around with American flags, they were all wearing T shirts with legends appropriate to the day: AMERICA—LOVE IT OR LEAVE IT; OPTIMIST INTERNATIONAL. Girls in crinolines were walking along beside the parade, selling bumper stickers with similar slogans. Some veterans of the First World War were driven by in a coach, the Second World War veterans followed on foot, among them an Indian, a member of one of the Indian commando teams that had led the way in the Normandy landing. Then came a group of horsemen who were supposed to look like Civil War cavalry; it was hot and there was so much cheering and laughing all around that the horses' hoofbeats were almost inaudible. The horsemen carried big flags that flapped violently in the wind and made the horses shy from time to time. Then they would cross the freshly painted double line in the middle of the street; when their riders checked them and they crossed back again, they left white hoofprints on the asphalt. On a parallel street I finally found a cab to take me to San Xavier.

There, after all the noise, it was so still that I thought I was dreaming and rubbed my eyes. Every few feet, I looked around. My double would jump out from behind one of the corrugated-iron shacks and chase me away! One false step would be the end of me, I was an interloper; now he had come back to take his rightful place. I'd topple out of myself and I wouldn't exist any more. Instead of a chimney, one of the shacks had a black stovepipe sticking out the window, and soot was billowing from it; a dog crawled around a corner on its belly. I was an imposter, I had set myself up in someone's place. Where was I to go? I was superfluous; I had crept into something, and now I stood there, unmasked. It wasn't too late; I could still save myself, *with a leap*. But I stood stock still with clenched fists, hiding behind my straw hat. This feeling of being the wrong man was so brief that a moment later I laughed it off as a whim. Then I remembered how as a child I had longed for a double, someone exactly like myself; and I took it as a good sign that since then the whole idea of a double, of someone just like me, had come to horrify and disgust me. The thought of somebody else with my movements was

216

obscene. The very outline of my own shadow struck me as indecent. Another body like mine, a caricature of myself? No! Then I ran a few steps.

On the other hand, I had no desire to meet anyone else. I was satisfied to be moving and to look into the Indians' shacks. No one spoke to me. I stepped into the doorway of a shack; the old woman who was sitting there with a corncob in her lap and a pipe in her mouth only smiled. Despite the heat, a fire was burning on the hearth; there was a stack of tin plates in a dishpan, and water from a faucet was running over them soundlessly. It helped me to look at such things, it crowded out my double feeling of myself. As I went on, a dust mop came out of a door, then disappeared; in the window of the next house, a blond wig was shaken, then put aside. I observed all this with the awe I had once experienced while looking at the saints and holy vessels in church. And in this strange feeling of piety I saw one more indication that it was possible for me to lose myself in objects, but not in people! Had nothing changed in me? I stamped my foot. Childishness! Perplexed but comforted, I arrived at the mission.

In the church, I removed my sunglasses and straw hat. It was late afternoon, the Rosary was being said. In moments of silence, I could hear the sand beating against the chruch door. A few women were standing in a row in front of their prie-dieu. When I looked up at the altar, I saw, in memory, a swallow flying around it. Once more I lost myself in everything I looked at. Religion had long been repellent to me, yet I longed to relate to something. It was unbearable to be alone and isolated. It must be possible for two human beings to belong to each other, to establish a relationship that is not personal, fortuitous, and ephemeral, not based on a fraudulent and continually extorted love, but on a necessary, impersonal bond. Why had I never managed to be as unreflectingly loving to Judith as I was now while looking at this church dome or at the drops of wax on the stone floor? It was ghastly to have such feelings and not to be able to get out of myself! To stand there in dull-witted piety, wholly immersed in objects and movements.

As I stepped out of the church, a sprinkler on the lawn splashed a few drops of water in my face. I went to the cemetery and sat down on the base of a big Spanish tomb. My eyes burned and I covered my face with my hands. I felt as if my brain were pushing against my forehead. At that moment, the evening bells began to ring, and I looked up. A white-breasted bird flew out of the window of the church and gleamed in the sky. At every stroke of the bells the steeples seemed to recede a little, and then move back into place. I had seen all that before! Covertly, with my hand to one side, I looked at the image, and at the same time listened to a memory. The memory was there, but every time I came near it, my brain shrunk back. The church and myself were giving me the creeps. Enough; I turned away.

The traffic lights were slung on wires; they were shaking so violently that when they were green you couldn't tell which direction was meant. Metal spikes stuck out from the black-painted telegraph poles and whistled in the wind. I tied a handkerchief over my face to protect it from the wind. Then I walked north, in the direction of Tucson, as fast as I could.

An Indian beggar stopped me. I gave him a dollar bill. He followed me and grabbed me by the shoulder. I broke into a run, he ran after me. When I stopped, he grinned and passed me by. I took a cab and got out in a Mexican neighborhood at the edge of the town. The houses were wooden and two-storied. Some had overhanging balconies. There were children on one of the balconies; they trotted along with me as far as they could go. A bell rang; a locomotive emerged almost silently from between two houses and stopped in the middle of the street. The sun had so overheated the metal levers that the engineer was wearing thick gloves. Again I saw the image as though listening to it at the same time. I knew the street I was standing on would begin to tilt; the image would be far below me, and I would fall into it head first. A child ran past the locomotive and disappeared between the houses like someone out of another dream. I turned off into a side street.

It wasn't getting dark and the air was still as hot as at noon. Down the street buses passed in the setting sun; I could see the passengers' shadows on the dusty windowpanes. I stepped into a bar, and just as I was ordering a Coke I noticed that I still had my handkerchief on my face. I shook the sand out of my shoes and trouser cuffs under the table. Even the records in the jukebox had been scratched by the sand. I put in a coin but didn't press any of the buttons. On the street, people with flags were still drifting home from the parade. I sat there, looking at the clock after every swallow. A child came in, so blond that it wrung my heart.

I looked at the slice of lemon on the rim of my glass and lost myself. All at once it was night. Irresolutely I went out into the street, crossed over, crossed back again. In among the houses it was pitch-dark, but lifting my head I could see the smoke trail of a jet in the sunlight. Behind me fat began to sizzle. A car came up slowly from behind me with the sound of fat starting to sizzle. But I forgot the car when some teenagers with the blond child in tow came up to me and asked me for money for a bus ticket. They stood around me and asked what country I was from. From Austria, I told them. They laughed and said the word after me. Except for the blond child, they were Mexicans; one of them was wearing light-colored gym shoes with imitation spurs. He stroked my cheek, I stepped back, bumping into another who was standing behind me. I reached into my pocket for a coin, my hand was held fast, and I saw a knife against my belly. It had a short blade that hardly protruded from the boy's fist.

The blond child stood a little to one side, hopping from foot to foot and shadow-boxing in my direction. One of the Mexicans tripped him and he fell on his knees. I grinned in embarrassment. There were some soldiers across the street, but I was ashamed to cry out. My hat was knocked off. Deftly moving hands turned my pockets inside out without touching me; the blond child crawled around on the ground, picking up what fell out. Someone slapped me; then they all ran to the car behind me. Its doors were already open, they jumped in, and it started up. The doors were slammed one by one; on the windshield I read HERTZ. I had seen Judith at the wheel; her face was pale, her eyes concentrated on the steering gear. A match was dangling from her parted lips; it fell when the car started moving.

I took a few steps, this way and that. Ridiculous! Pockets were hanging out all over me. I stuffed them in, pulled them out again, as if that would prove something. Then I noticed that my inside pockets had also been pulled out. I looked down; the white lining of my breast pocket looked up at me. My train ticket from New York to Philadelphia was lying on the sidewalk. *"A wooden sidewalk!"* I thought. Then I said it aloud. I put my hat back on, turned my pockets back in, and withdrew; *withdrew.*

I couldn't find my way back to the hotel. It occurred to me that I sometimes put money in my shirt pocket. Sure enough, I found a ten-dollar bill and took a cab. I couldn't help laughing when I got to my room: the door was locked and this time there were no scratch marks on the lock. I lay down on the bed. At last! I was beginning to feel pretty good. Lucky I'd put my plane ticket in my overcoat pocket; I'd even tucked some money into it, more than a hundred dollars, small bills that I had received as change. I had always paid with big bills, so as not to reach into my pocket more than once; and now my magnificence had paid off. My spirits rose and rose. I looked through all my clothes for money. Bills crackled in every shirt I touched; I even found a quarter in one of the trouser cuffs. I piled the money on the table and lost myself in the sight of it as I had that afternoon in the water running silently from the faucet. The window curtain swayed gently in the outflow of the air conditioning. There was a radiator too! With five coils. They were not parallel! When I looked again, I realized that I had forgotten about perspective.

I called up my mother in Austria. There it was early next morning. She said there had just been thunder and lightning. A storm in the early morning! She had already been outside and taken in the washing. She had been very active lately; that made her forget about time. The Social-Democratic president had been reelected; at an election rally, the opposition candidate had denied that he was a National Socialist, let alone a Jew. I had the impression that my mother was telling jokes. I asked her for my brother's address; for the last few years he had been working in a lumber cap in northern Oregon. What did I want it for? "I've got to go see him," I said. I wrote down the address: the name of the town was Estacada. I'd have my ticket changed and fly there next day.

I went down to the patio and settled under a palm tree by the swimming pool. There was no wind; now and then the bartender behind me shook a drink; from time to time the soft-drink machines rumbled and the cans inside clanked, when the cooling motor shut off. There was no one in the water; in the indirect lighting, it stirred gently, as though in memory of the fallen wind. Above the patio the stars twinkled so brightly that I couldn't help blinking, and the air was so clear that I saw not only the lighted crescent, but the dark part of the moon as well. So far, I thought, I had hardly met anyone in America who was immersed in anything. One look was enough; then you turned to something else. Anyone who stopped to look a little longer assumed the pose of a connoisseur. The same with the villages, they were never immersed in the landscape, they were always plunked on top of it; they stood out from their surroundings and seemed to have been put there by accident. Only insensible drunks, drug addicts, and the unemployed stared at anything in this country. Was I drunk? I pushed my glass so close to the rounded edge of the table that in the end it tipped all by itself and fell into the swimming pool.

I could hear that when the traffic lights changed outside only a few cars started up. A man behind me at the bar was talking into his empty glass to his girl; now and then he would rub his teeth against the rim of the glass. I couldn't stand it any more. Again I withdrew.

Back in my room, I finished reading *Green Heinrich*. When he found himself unable to draw a certain plaster figurine, he realized that he had never really concerned himself with people. He went home to his mother, who had been supporting him up until then, and found her with quivering cheeks, dying. For years after that he was morose, weary of life, as though pumped dry. He revived only when the woman who had loved him because she envied him for his thoughts came back from America. At that point his story became a fairy tale, and when I came to the passage: "Happy and content, we ate together in the dining room of the *Golden Star*," I had to look away for fear of bursting into tears. Then I cried all the same, rather hysterically, but it made me forget time.

I lay in the darkness; all at once, when I was almost asleep, I felt sad because my money had been stolen. It wasn't a sorrow or regret, only a senseless physical pain that I couldn't talk myself out of: something had been torn out of me; there was a hollow place inside me that would have to heal. I didn't want to think any more. In my dream, tomatoes were being washed in an enormous bowl; someone fell into it and vanished under the tomatoes. I looked at the bowl (it was on a stage) to see if he would come up again. "If anything more happens to me," I said to myself aloud in my dream, "I'll crack up."

When I arrived in Oregon late next morning, it was raining. Though hitchhiking was forbidden, I stood outside the airport in Portland with my straw hat on my head, trying to thumb a ride to Estacada. I had come via Salt Lake City on a Hughes Airwest plane. Time and again during the trip, I had felt that I was someone else's double, moving in a vacuum. I had read once that people make senseless chewing motions after a bad fright; my trip to Oregon was like that, I thought.

A vegetable truck hauling California lettuce to the mountains finally picked me up. There was no windshield wiper on my side and I couldn't see much. That was all right with me, I had a headache. Once in a while I'd forget the pain, then I'd take a breath and remember it again. The driver was wearing a checkered shirt with a buttoned undershirt under it. He must have had a tune running through his head the whole time, because he kept drumming on the wheel with his fingers. But he didn't sing; the only sound out of him was a whistle as the road climbed and the rain turned to snow. At first the snow fell off the windows, then it began to stick.

Estacada is a town of eleven hundred, at an altitude of over three thousand feet. The main source of livelihood is lumbering. I caught myself looking for first aid, police, fire department signs. At the intersection of two state highways just outside the town, the driver pointed out the motor inn, and there I took a room for the night. The price was five dollars. I slept until late in the afternoon; then I rolled off the bed. When I began to feel cold on the floor, I put on my coat and walked up and down in front of the television set. The images were blurred, because Estacada is surrounded by mountains. I went down to the lobby and asked the way to the unmarried loggers' quarters. The snow plows weren't running so late in the year and I walked through deep snow. There were hardly any trees in the town, only here and there they had left a symbolic fir tree, which gave you a start when the snow came tumbling down and the branches swished upward. The curtains of all the houses were drawn; steam rose from the ventilators of the snack bars and from the sewer gratings, around which the snow had melted. The door of the drugstore was open; inside, someone with bandaged thumbs was drinking coffee.

The light bulb over the entrance to Gregor's barracks had burned out, maybe from a short circuit caused by the melting snow. I stamped the snow off my shoes, but no one came out. The door wasn't locked; I went in, it was almost dark, the only light came from a street lamp outside. I saw a piece of paper on the floor. Thinking it was a message for me, I picked it up and turned on the light. It was a Western Union telegram that I had sent my brother from Salt Lake City.

On the table there was a deck of ornate German playing cards; beside them lay a small alarm clock that seemed to have fallen over from ringing. On one chair, two long, mud-caked shoelaces; on the other, a pair of pajama pants, hand-me-downs from me; on top of them a handkerchief with 248, my clothing number at boarding school, embroidered on it; that handkerchief must have been fifteen years old.

The clothes closet was open; a string had been attached to the inside of the door and at the other end to the stovepipe; socks and underdrawers were hanging on it. I touched them; they were dry and felt hard. On the cold stove lay a saucer with a lump of rancid butter in it; in the butter there was a thumbprint. In the closet, a few wire hangers, the kind the dry cleaners give you; and on the hangers unironed shirts, torn at the seams and armpits.

The bed was unmade; on the sheets gray spots, crushed moths, and in a fold still another moth; under the bed, empty beer cans.

On the windowsill, a box of soap flakes; beside it, marks of cat's paws.

On the wall, a calendar from Austria with a color photograph of a woman in a peasant hat against a field of daffodils; under the photograph, a print of the general store in our home village.

That photograph on the calendar—

So little happened in our childhood and there was so little to see that we looked forward every year to the picture on the new calendar. In the fall, we waited eagerly for the insurance agent who came to collect our annual premium and in return left the insurance company's calendar for next year, with a new picture on it.

Was my brother in America still sending for the new calendar with the new picture?

That thought was so intolerable that it was quickly crowded out by a feeling that came as a relief. I put the telegram on the table, cautiously following up with my other hand for fear of breaking something.

On my way out I saw, beside a wash basin, a pair of low-cut shoes; inside them a pair of cotton socks that seemed to have grown into them. They were very pointed shoes, a style that had been fashionable ten years before. Children were running around in a slaughtering yard; a butcher's apprentice picked a child up and held him over a dead pig. Slipping now and then in the snow, I went up the main street of Estacada. I didn't look back.

It was so still that I stopped more and more often. Steam rose from the neon PIZZERIA and GAS signs. Far away in the village I made out the screen of a drive-in movie; on it I saw only light and shade, there was no sound to be heard. I dropped into an amusement arcade, but I had no desire to play games. Nevertheless

I went from one pinball machine to another, absently pushing the balls around. I knew then that I had come to loathe all games; I couldn't conceive of ever again manipulating dice. No, never again. I was tired. I sat down on a stool next to a drunk, who was leaning against the wall, asleep. His whole face was sweating, his shirt was open, the sweat collected in the hollow of his collarbone and overflowed now and then. He opened his eyes and had to blink before they focused, a scalped rabbit; I left.

At the motel I went to the bathroom to wash my hands. The hot water faucet was hot to the touch. Had someone just been running water? I stepped back and turned the faucet. First air came out, then a boiling liquid gushed into the basin; a few drops splashed onto my pants and instantly made little holes with black edges. Perfect! I nodded as though in approval. I saw that the threads of both faucets had been scratched. Carefully I opened the cold water faucet and let the acid run out. While washing my hands, I noticed that the cellophane wrapper had been removed from one of the glasses—an invitation to use it. I stared at the glasses: objects from another world, another star.

During the night I left my room door open. Once I thought I heard someone moving outside the window, but it was only a moth caught between the curtain and the windowpane. For the first time in ages I dreamed nothing at all.

I woke up as though in a strange element. Early in the morning I went to the sawmill where my brother worked. The air was hazy, the melting snow gurgled under the sewer gratings. I moved in a strange element, as though in someone else's thoughts. Again I had to run, I couldn't walk any more. I looked for an image as I usually looked for words, to bring me back to myself. Charred tree trunks, gashed hillsides, burned trash bins; in a field somewhere else, straw crackled in the noonday heat. I didn't want any more imaginings connected with myself. But then suddenly I heard myself as a ventriloquist, my belly took over my part and told me things I didn't want to know. A girl with a milk bottle came toward me; she was so thin that my astonishment pulled me together.

The sawmill was in a hollow beside the Clackamas River. From a distance I recognized my brother among the men who were stripping the bark off a fir tree beside a throbbing drying kiln. He was standing on the tree, thrusting a crowbar between bark and trunk. I had stopped on a hummock and was looking down at him. He was wearing gloves and a woolen cap. Occasionally, as he put pressure on the crowbar, his right foot slipped off the peeled tree trunk. A second worker had thrust another crowbar under the bark; the two of them pulled at the loose bark from either side until only long fibers clung to the tree. They cut the fibers with axes and threw the bark on a waste pile.

Gregor went off to one side. I thought he had seen me and took a step forward. He stopped in a clump of bushes and looked around, but without raising his head. Beside the bushes there was still snow on the ground. He let his pants down and squatted. I looked on as the feces emerged from between his bare buttocks and dropped slowly into the snow. He kept his squatting position long after he had finished. Then he stood up, pulled up his underdrawers and trousers with one motion, and, beating his hands together, went back to the tree trunk. As if that were all I had come to see, I turned around and ran all the way to the motel.

There was mail for me: a picture postcard with an aerial view of Twin Rocks, a town on the Pacific coast some seventy-five miles west of Estacada. The shore road by-passed the town in a long arc, two black rocks jutted out of the sea, the water foamed around them. In spite of the height from which the picture had been taken, the lines on the road could be distinguished clearly. At one point, where there was a loop in the road, as though for a bus stop or a lookout, a cross had been made with a fountain pen, so forcefully that the imprint could be seen on the other side of the card. "So she's got herself another fountain pen," I said to the lady at the reception desk, who was busy sorting out the coins I had paid my bill with. She looked up and had to start counting all over again. She was counting with one hand, holding the other flat on the desk to let her nail polish dry; through the ruffles around her neck I saw a long red scar, which only a moment ago I had seen as a makeup smear. I didn't ask her how she had come by it; I didn't want to get her mixed up again.

With my last money I took a taxi to the coast. It was a dark day, made for traveling; the sky brightened only during occasional showers. I had the camera in my lap; there were plenty of sights, above and below, to the right and left, but I was too sad to take pictures.

Off and on I fell asleep; when I woke up, there was a river valley where I had just seen a bare mountaintop; at my next waking we were driving through dark evergreen woods and I had to lean out the window to see the sky. "Don't open the window," said the driver, "it throws the heating off." It was unbearable to be awake with my eyes closed; whatever I had seen last pressed in on me and took my breath away; it didn't move back into place until I opened my eyes. A shower was coming down again and I couldn't see through the windows; I must have fallen asleep, because a moment later the windows were clean and dry, the sun was shining feebly, and an enormous gray mountain wall rose up in front of the windshield. I straightened up and shook myself, the wall widened and reached out to the horizon; it was the Pacific Ocean. The driver turned on the radio; it only crackled. A few minutes later we stopped in Twin Rocks;

there were sea gulls on the roof of the one gas station.

Out! "There are hardly more than a hundred people in this town." But such sentences were no longer of any use. I wanted to put down my suitcase but I carried it farther and farther. Here the sky was very bright; when the sun shone through the clouds, the chrome fittings on the cars sparkled. Once I stood still, but didn't put my suitcase down. I saw a child in a window; he was watching me and, lost in a dream, imitating my expression. I went on; swallows were flying about, so fast that I hardly saw anything but motion; like bats in the twilight.

> *Sitting on the joiner's bench*
> *waiting for our mother.*
> *Then the black ram comes along,*
> *butts and knocks us over;*
> *then the white bat comes along,*
> *picks us up again.*

The ocean was reflected in the windowpanes of the last houses. Actually: burned-out trash bins! Outside a shop a red and white cylinder was revolving: barbershop and beauty parlor. A woman was sitting inside; her head was under the dryer, hidden down to the eyes; squatting on her heels in front of her, the hairdresser was lacquering the woman's toenails, which were gnarled and crooked, with calluses on the joints. Those were Judith's toes! Her early years as a salesgirl had ruined her feet. Then I saw her brown doeskin bag on a chair; it was open; no doubt she had opened it to take out the dressing gown she had over her shoulders. It was brocade and glowed darkly in the setting sun. "She's brought her dressing gown to America!" I thought aloud. While the hairdresser was lacquering her fingernails, I observed Judith: two toes of one foot were twined around the big toe of her other foot. Dreams; wake up in the morning and spit out a night worm. I couldn't take my eyes off her. Judith moved in her chair, with an angry jerk as though anticipating something. In an inexplicable memory, a cork being pulled out of a bottle squeaked obsessively. The hairdresser looked up, half blind from the fingers she had been holding so close to her face; I quickly removed myself from her field of vision.

Fish skeletons between the bars of sewer gratings; sponges in the cracks between the logs of log cabins; people stepping out of houses, looking up at the sky, and going back in; here the pioneers' monuments were barrels of lard and soft soap outside the supermarket, with inscriptions relating to the founding of the town. A drunk with bare skin showing under his open fly veered from his path and strode stiffly toward me. I made room for him; he staggered over the spot where I had just been standing and fell on his face in a puddle.

The sodium street lights went on, though it was still light; one of the tubes flickered. I had a hair in my mouth and couldn't get rid of it. Besides, I liked it, it gave me something to do while walking. Now and then I broke into a run. I followed the shore road past the last houses until I saw two black rocks in the sea. Then I crossed the street and sat down on my suitcase in the loop that had been marked with a cross on the picture postcard. The sun had just set, a wind had come up. The place was both a viewing point and a bus stop. Hardly any cars passed. I looked down at the rocky beach, which was far below. Pieces of wood tossing about in the foaming water. There was a railing at the edge of the lookout. A woman was standing there with an idiot child, who kept climbing on the railing and shouting down at the ocean. The woman held him fast and finally lifted him down. A bus marked BAY CITY stopped; they got in and I was left alone.

I looked out at the Pacific. Though the water still glittered in the sun, it was deep-dark. I tried to repeat my first impression of it, the towering mountain wall;

but it kept on being flat water until I had brain cramp.

My first impression of Judith: why couldn't I bring it back? I tried: a sweet affection that lifted me up and made me as light as a feather. Couldn't we have kept that feeling for each other? I had forgotten it; we were no longer able to look at each other without grimacing.

I looked at the sea again: it was so empty that I felt it had eaten me up. Wisps of fog drifted across the beach. The symmetrical parts of my body gaped apart with exhaustion; the empty spaces between them made me sick to my stomach. Filthy, bedraggled, frazzled. I had been enjoying all the poses of alienation available to me for too long; I had distanced myself from people by turning them into "beings": *that being*, I had said of Judith, *that monster: that, that, that*. I crouched, letting my arms dangle between my legs. A helicopter flew low across the road, blinking at the asphalt.

It grew very still. From far away I heard a plane; its hum was so soft that listening made my head ache.

I looked around and saw Judith with her bag coming out from between the last houses of Twin Rocks. On the other side of the road she stopped, looked to right and left, then crossed. She had a scarf on her head, maybe her hair wasn't dry yet. Behind her it was almost dark. She was pointing the revolver at me. "She takes me seriously," I thought. "By God, she takes me seriously." She cocked the revolver. The sound was so soft that I heard it only in my imagination and refused to believe it. Though burned to ashes, I was still in one piece, but at the slightest move I would fall apart. So that was it! That was what I thought I had been born for! Disappointed, I stood up from my suitcase and went toward her. With rigid, graven faces we approached one another; suddenly she looked away and screamed like a child having a tantrum, so ferociously that her breath gave out. I held my breath, waiting for her to go on screaming; she was sure to start in again, twice as loud; but she didn't, she only gulped, as though gagging, and I took the gun out of her hand.

We stood side by side, shifting from foot to foot, helpless and sullen. I threw the revolver into the ocean, it fell on a rock and went off, there was a hissing in the water, Judith pressed her lips into her teeth with her fist.

We walked up and down; when one moved, the other stood still. Night fell. A brightly lighted bus pulled into the stop, a Greyhound. The few passengers had pillows behind their heads. The driver motioned to us. I asked him which way he was going, and he said, "South." We got in. Next morning we were in California.

John Ford, then seventy-six, lived in a colonial-style house in Bel Air, not far from Los Angeles. He hadn't made a picture in six years. He spent most of his time sitting on the terrace of his house, talking with old friends. The terrace looks out over a valley of orange and cypress trees. For visitors there is a row of wicker chairs; in front of them, footstools covered with Indian blankets. People sitting in those chairs tend to tell stories.

John Ford was white-haired; his wrinkled face was strewn with white beard stubble. Over one eye he wore a black patch; the other gazed gloomily into space; now and then he plucked at his chin or ear lobes. He had on a navy-blue jacket, baggy khaki trousers, and light-colored canvas shoes with big rubber heels. When he spoke, he kept his hands in his pockets, even when sitting; he made no gestures. When he finished a story, he turned his face toward Judith and me, until he could see us out of his eye. He had a large head, the look on his face was severe, he never smiled; in his presence you grew grave, even if you had to laugh at his stories. From time to time he stood up and poured California red wine into Judith's glass;

he let me help myself to brandy. Later on, his wife, Mary Frances, came out; like him she came of a family of Irish immigrants who had settled in Maine. She too sat down and listened to him. We looked out into the light from the shaded terrace; storm clouds were coming up on all sides.

"In our village in Ireland," John Ford told us, "there was a general store. I remember going there as a kid, they always gave me candy for change. They kept the candy in a bucket for that express purpose. I was there a few weeks ago, first time in more than fifty years. I went to the store for cigars. And what do you know? The storekeeper reached into the bucket and gave me candy for change."

John Ford repeated a good deal of what I had heard about America from Claire and other people during my trip; his ideas were not new, but he backed them up with stories. Sometimes, when you asked a general question, his mind would jump from the general to the particular and he'd talk about incidents in his life and people he'd known. He never judged these people, he simply told us what they had said and done. He never mentioned their names unless they were his friends. "It's unbearable to be enemies with anyone," he said. "Suddenly a man becomes nameless, a blob; a shadow falls on his face, it gets blurred and distorted, we can only dart hurried looks at it, from below, like a mouse. Having an enemy makes us loathe ourselves. Yet we've always had enemies."

"Why do you say 'we' instead of 'I'?" Judith asked.

"We Americans always say 'we' even when we're talking about our private affairs," said John Ford. "Maybe it's because we see everything we do as part of a common effort. 'I' stories are possible only when one stands for all. We don't take our egos as seriously as you Europeans. Over there you'll even hear a salesgirl, selling things that don't belong to her, say,

'*I've* just run out of this or that,' or '*I* also have a Cossack-style shirt.' I heard those things with my own ears when I was over there," said John Ford. "On the other hand, you imitate each other and hide behind each other; even a servant girl answering the phone puts on the voice of the lady of the house. You always say 'I,' but that doesn't prevent you from feeling flattered when you're mistaken for somebody else. And at the same time you all want to be unmistakably unique. That's why you're always *sulking* and taking offense, because every one of you takes himself for something special. Here in America nobody sulks and nobody crawls into his own shell. We don't long to be alone; when a man's alone, he's contemptible; all he can do is poke around in himself, and when he hasn't anybody but himself to talk with, he dries up after the first word."

"Do you dream a lot?" Judith asked.

"We hardly dream at all any more," said John Ford. "And when we do have a dream, we forget it. We talk about everything, so there's nothing left to dream about."

"Tell us about yourself," said Judith.

"Whenever I hear people talking about me," said John Ford, "I have a feeling that it's too soon. My own experiences aren't far enough back. I'd rather talk about what other people have experienced before me. That's why I've always preferred to make pictures about things that happened before my time. I don't feel much nostalgia for my own past; what makes me nostalgic is things I never got around to doing and places where I've never been. Once when I was a boy I was beaten up by a gang of Italian kids—though the whole lot of us were Catholics! One of them, a fat kid, was especially vicious; he didn't even move his hands, he just spat at me and kicked me. An hour later I saw this kid coming down the street by himself; he was as fat as a pig and he had flat feet. All at once I thought he looked unbearably lonely, I only wanted to be nice to him and comfort him. And we actually did get to be friends!" He thought awhile. Then he said, "I was still in short pants."

He looked down into the valley; the last rays of sun were shining through the leaves of the orange trees. "When I see the leaves moving like that and the sun shining through, I have a feeling that they've been moving that way since the world began," he said. "It gives me a feeling of eternity, and I forget that there's such a thing as history. You people call it a medieval feeling. It's as if the whole world were still in a state of nature."

"But those orange trees were planted," said Judith. "They're not nature."

"When the sun shines through and plays in the leaves, I forget that," said John Ford. "I also forget myself and my existence. Then I wish that nothing would ever change, that the leaves would go on moving forever, that the oranges would never be picked and everything would stay just the way it is."

"Then I suppose you'd like people to go on living as they have always lived?" Judith asked.

John Ford gave her a gloomy look. "Yes," he said. "We would. Up to a century ago the people who thought about progress were the people who had the power to bring it about. Until recently new ideas originated with the powerful; with princes, industrialists, public *benefactors*. Today the men with power have ceased to be benefactors of mankind; at best they do things that benefit certain individuals. Today all the new ideas come from the poor and powerless. The men with the power to change anything have stopped thinking. So no change is possible."

"Is that what you want?" Judith asked.

"No, I don't want it," said John Ford. "But that's what runs through my head when I look down there."

An Indian housekeeper came out, leaning on a cane, and spread a blanket over his knees. "She's played in some of my pictures," said John Ford. "She'd have liked to be an actress, but she can't talk; she's mute. So she took up the tightrope. Then she had a fall, and now she's back with me.

"She was happy on the tightrope," he said. "All of a sudden it was as if she could talk. She still walks as if she were on a tightrope.

"There are postures that make you feel like yourself," said John Ford. " 'Yes,' you think, 'this is really me.' Unfortunately you're usually alone when that happens. Then you try it with people around and you're not yourself any more, you fall into a pose. That's no good. It's ridiculous. It's your thoughts you want people to get a glimpse of, not your idiosyncrasies. One day you tell the truth, and you're startled. You're so happy you can't bear it; you try to tell the truth again, and then of course you lie. I still lie," said John Ford. "Two seconds ago I knew what I wanted, but now I've lost it. I'm happy only when I know exactly what I want. Then I'm so happy I feel as if there were no teeth in my mouth."

He took us to his study and showed us a pile of movie scripts; writers were still sending them to him. "There are some good stories in there," he said. "Simple and clear. The kind of stories we need." His wife was standing behind us in the doorway; he turned toward her and she smiled. The housekeeper brought him coffee in a tin cup. He drank with his head high, his free hand propped on his hip; clumps of white hair protruded from his ears. His wife came closer and pointed to the photographs on the wall: in one of them John Ford was directing a picture; he was sitting in a director's swivel chair with a beekeeper's mask on his face; a few people, likewise in beekeeper's masks, were sitting and standing around him; at his feet lay a dog with his ears folded back. In another photograph he had just finished a picture, he was kneeling on one knee, holding the tripod of a movie camera; the whole cast was with him, their heads inclined in his direction;

one actor had his hand on the camera, as though caressing it. "That was the day we finished *The Iron Horse*," said John Ford. "We had one young actress who was always crying. When she stopped, we'd wipe away her tears. That reminded her of her sorrow and she'd start crying again."

He looked out the window and we followed his eye; we saw a hill covered with grass and flowering shrubs; a path twined around the hill to the top. "In America there are no paths, only roads," said John Ford. "I laid out that path because I like to walk in the fresh air." His bed was covered with a Navy blanket; on the wall hung a picture of Mother Cabrini, the first American saint; he wanted to make a picture about her someday.

There was a harmonium in the room. His wife sat down at it and played "Greensleeves." The Indian woman brought in a tray piled with hot buttered corn bread. We ate and looked out the window. "We'll have corn bread coming out of our ears," said John Ford suddenly. "Let's go for a walk."

He gave Judith his arm and we climbed the hill. The path was covered with light-colored dust. A few raindrops fell, and where they landed, the dust coagulated into little balls. John Ford told stories; when one of us lagged behind, he stopped, because he didn't want to turn around when he talked. He talked about his pictures and kept insisting that the stories were true. "Nothing is made up," he said. "It all really happened.

On the hilltop we sat in the grass and looked down into the valley. He lit a cigar with a big kitchen match. "I always want to be with people," said John Ford. "When I'm with people, I always want to be the last to leave, because I don't want any of them to run me down when I'm gone. Besides, I want to be there to make sure nobody runs down anybody else who's left. That's been my principle in making my pictures."

Lightning fell on the hills across the valley. Now and then a gust of wind cut light and dark shadows in the tall grass around us. The leaves on the tree fluttered as though dead. For a time there was no wind at all. Then a bush behind us rustled, though all the other bushes were still. The rustling stopped. A moment later a treetop down by the house was lit up for a moment. For a long while all was quiet, motionless. Then suddenly a murmur ran through the grass at our feet. I blinked, and when I opened my eyes the world around me had darkened and everything in it was close to the ground. The air was oppressive. A big yellow spider that had just been sitting on a leaf popped and fell at our feet. John Ford wiped his fingers in the grass, and turned his signet ring as though to conjure up something. I felt a tickling on the back of my hand. I looked and saw a butterfly that was just folding its wings; at the same time, Judith lowered her eyelashes. To see all this, I had only to take one less breath. We heard the rain falling on the orange trees in the valley. "One night last week," said John Ford, "we were driving through the desert down in Arizona. There was so much dew we had to use the windshield wiper." *Down in Arizona:* at those words I began to remember. John Ford was sitting stooped over, his eye almost closed. Expecting a story, we leaned forward a little; I realized that I was imitating the gesture of a character in one of his pictures who without shifting his position cranes his long neck over a dying man to see if he's still alive.

"Now tell me your story," said John Ford.

And Judith told him how we had come to America, how she had followed me, how she had robbed me and wanted to kill me, and how at last we were ready to part in peace.

When she had done telling our story, a silent laugh spread over John Ford's face.

"Ach Gott!" he said.

He grew grave and turned to Judith.

"Is all that true?" he asked in English. "None of it's made up?"

"No," said Judith, "it all happened."

A Sorrow Beyond Dreams

A Life Story

❧ ❧

TRANSLATED BY RALPH MANHEIM

He not busy being born is busy dying.

Bob Dylan

Dusk was falling quickly. It was just after
7 p.m., and the month was October.

Patricia Highsmith, *A Dog's Ransom*

$\mathcal{T}$HE Sunday edition of the *Kärntner Volks-zeitung* carried the following item under "Local News": "In the village of A. (G. township), a house-wife, aged 51, committed suicide on Friday night by taking an overdose of sleeping pills."

My mother has been dead for almost seven weeks; I had better get to work before the need to write about her, which I felt so strongly at her funeral, dies away and I fall back into the dull speechlessness with which I reacted to the news of her suicide. Yes, get to work: for, intensely as I sometimes feel the need to write about my mother, this need is so vague that if I didn't work at it I would, in my present state of mind, just sit at my typewriter pounding out the same letters over and over again. This sort of kinetic therapy alone would do me no good; it would only make me passive and apathetic. I might just as well take a trip—if I were traveling, my mindless dozing and lounging around wouldn't get on my nerves so much.

During the last few weeks I have been more irritable than usual; disorder, cold, and silence drive me to distraction; I can't see a bread crumb or a bit of fluff on the floor without bending down to pick it up. Thinking about this suicide, I become so insensible that I am sometimes startled to find that an object I have been holding hasn't fallen out of my hand. Yet

I long for such moments, because they shake me out of my apathy and clear my head. My sense of horror makes me feel better: at last my boredom is gone; an unresisting body, no more exhausting distances, a painless passage of time.

The worst thing right now would be sympathy, expressed in a word or even a glance. I would turn away or cut the sympathizer short, because I need the feeling that what I am going through is incomprehensible and incommunicable; only then does the horror seem meaningful and real. If anyone talks to me about it, the boredom comes back, and everything is unreal again. Nevertheless, for no reason at all, I sometimes tell people about my mother's suicide, but if they dare to mention it I am furious. What I really want them to do is change the subject and tease me about something.

In his latest movie someone asks James Bond whether his enemy, whom he has just thrown over a stair rail, is *dead*. His answer—"Let's hope so!"— made me laugh with relief. Jokes about dying and being dead don't bother me at all; on the contrary, they make me feel good.

Actually, my moments of horror are brief, and what I feel is not so much horror as unreality; seconds later, the world closes in again, and if someone is with me I try to be especially attentive, as though I had just been rude.

Now that I've begun to write, these states seem to have dwindled and passed, probably because I try to describe them as accurately as possible. In decribing them, I begin to remember them as belonging to a concluded period of my life, and the effort of remembering and formulating keeps me so busy that the short daydreams of the last few weeks have stopped. I look back on them as intermittent "states": suddenly my day-to-day world—which, after all, consists only of images repeated ad nauseam over a period of years and decades since they were new—fell apart, and my mind became so empty that it ached.

That is over now; I no longer fall into these states. When I write, I necessarily write about the past, about something which, at least while I am writing, is behind me. As usual when engaged in literary work, I am alienated from myself and transformed into an object, a remembering and formulating machine. I am writing the story of my mother, first of all because I think I know more about her and how she came to her death than any outside investigator who might, with the help of a religious, psychological, or sociological guide to the interpretation of dreams, arrive at a facile explanation of this interesting case of suicide; but second in my own interest, because having something to do brings me back to life; and lastly because, like an outside investigator, though in a different way, I would like to represent this VOLUNTARY DEATH as an exemplary case.

Of course, all these justifications are arbitrary and could just as well be replaced by others that would be equally arbitrary. In any case, I experienced moments of extreme speechlessness and needed to formulate them—the motive that has led men to write from time immemorial.

In my mother's pocketbook, when I arrived for the funeral, I found a post-office receipt for a registered letter bearing the number 432. On Friday afternoon, before going home and taking the sleeping pills, she had mailed a registered letter containing a copy of her will to my address in Frankfurt. (But why also SPECIAL DELIVERY?) On Monday I went to the same post office to telephone. That was two and a half days after her death. On the desk in front of the post-office clerk, I saw the yellow roll of registration stickers; nine more registered letters had been mailed over the weekend; the next number was 442, and this image was so

similar to the number I had in my head that at first
glance I became confused and thought for a moment
nothing had happened. The desire to tell someone
about it cheered me up. It was such a bright day;
the snow; we were eating soup with liver dumplings;
"it began with . . ."; if I started like this, it would all
seem to be made up, I would not be extorting personal sympathy from my listener or reader, I would
merely be telling him a rather fantastic story.

* * *

Well then, it began with my mother being born more
than fifty years ago in the same village where she died.
At that time all the land that was good for anything
in the region belonged either to the church or to noble
landowners; part of it was leased to the population,
which consisted mostly of artisans and small peasants.
The general indigence was such that few peasants
owned their land. For practical purposes, the conditions were the same as before 1848; serfdom had been
abolished in a merely formal sense. My grandfather
—he is still living, aged eighty-six—was a carpenter;
in addition, he and his wife worked a few acres of
rented farm and pasture land. He was of Slovenian
descent and illegitimate. Most of the children born to
small peasants in those days were illegitimate, because, years after attaining sexual maturity, few small
peasants were in possession of living quarters or the
means to support a household. His mother was the
daughter of a rather well-to-do peasant, who, however, never regarded his hired man, my grandfather's
father, as anything more than the "baby-maker."
Nevertheless, my grandfather's mother inherited
money enough to buy a small farm.

And so it came about that my grandfather was the
first of his line—generations of hired men with blanks
in their baptismal certificates, who had been born and
who died in other people's houses and left little or no

inheritance because their one and only possession, their Sunday suit, had been lowered into the grave with them—to grow up in surroundings where he could really feel at home and who was not merely tolerated in return for his daily toil.

Recently the financial section of one of our newspapers carried an apologia for the economic principles of the Western world. Property, it said, was MATERIALIZED FREEDOM. This may in his time have been true of my grandfather, the first in a long line of peasants fettered by poverty to own anything at all, let alone a house and a piece of land. The consciousness of owning something had so liberating an effect that after generations of will-lessness a will could now make its appearance: the will to become still freer. And that meant only one thing—justifiably so for my grandfather in his situation—to enlarge his property, for the farm he started out with was so small that nearly all his labors went into holding on to it. The ambitious smallholder's only hope lay in saving.

So my grandfather saved, until the inflation of the twenties ate up all his savings. Then he began to save again, not only by setting aside unneeded money but also and above all by compressing his own needs and demanding the same frugality of his children as well; his wife, being a woman, had never so much as dreamed that any other way of life was possible.

He continued to save toward the day when his children would need SETTLEMENTS for marriage or to set themselves up in a trade. The idea that any of his savings might be spent before then on their EDUCATION couldn't possibly have entered his head, especially where his daughters were concerned. And even in his sons the centuries-old dread of becoming a homeless pauper was so deeply ingrained that one of them, who more by accident than by design had obtained a scholarship to the Gymnasium, found those unfamiliar surroundings unbearable after only a few days. He walked the thirty miles from the provincial capital at night, arriving home on a Saturday, which was house-cleaning day; without a word he started sweeping the yard: the noise he made with his broom in the early dawn told the whole story. He became a proficient and contented carpenter.

He and his older brother were killed early in the Second World War. In the meantime, my grandfather had gone on saving and once again lost his savings in the Depression of the thirties. His saving meant that he neither drank nor smoked, and played cards only on Sunday; but even the money he won in his Sunday card games—and he played so carefully that he almost always won—went into savings; at the most, he would slip his children a bit of small change. After the war, he started saving again; today he receives a government pension and is still at it.

The surviving son, a master carpenter with twenty workers in his employ, has no need to save. He invests, which means that he *can* drink and gamble; in fact, it's expected of him. Unlike his father, who all his life has been speechless and in every way self-denying, he has at least developed speech of a kind, though he uses it only in the town council, where he represents a small and obscure political party with visions of a grandiose future rooted in a grandiose past.

For a woman to be born into such surroundings was in itself deadly. But perhaps there was one comfort: no need to worry about the future. The fortune-tellers at our church fairs took a serious interest only in the palms of the young men; a girl's future was a joke.

No possibilities, it was all settled in advance: a bit of flirtation, a few giggles, brief bewilderment, then the alien, resigned look of a woman starting to keep house again, the first children, a bit of togetherness after the kitchen work, from the start not listened to, and in turn listening less and less, inner monologues, trouble with her legs, varicose veins, mute except for mumbling in her sleep, cancer of the womb, and finally, with death, destiny fulfilled. The girls in our town used to play a game based on the stations in a woman's life: Tired/Exhausted/Sick/Dying/Dead.

My mother was the next to last of five children. She was a good pupil; her teachers gave her the best possible marks and especially praised her neat handwriting. And then her school years were over. Learning had been a mere child's game; once your compulsory education was completed and you began to grow up, there was no need of it. After that a girl stayed home, getting used to the staying at home that would be her future.

No fears, except for an animal fear in the dark and in storms; no changes, except for the change between heat and cold, wet and dry, comfort and discomfort.

The passage of time was marked by church festivals, slaps in the face for secret visits to the dance hall, fits of envy directed against her brothers, and the pleasure of singing in the choir. Everything else that happened in the world was a mystery; no newspapers were read except the Sunday bulletin of the diocese, and then only the serial.

Sundays: boiled beef with horseradish sauce, the card game, the women humbly sitting there, a family photograph showing the first radio.

My mother was high-spirited; in the photographs she propped her hands on her hips or put her arm over her younger brother's shoulder. She was always laughing and seemed incapable of doing anything else.

Rain—sun; outside—inside: feminine feelings were very much dependent on the weather, because "outside" was seldom allowed to mean anything but the yard and "inside" was invariably the house, without a room of one's own.

The climate in that region is extremely variable: cold winters and sultry summers, but at sunset or even in the shade of a tree you shivered. Rain and more rain; from early September on, whole days of damp fog outside the tiny windows (they are hardly any larger today); drops of water on the clotheslines; toads jumping across your path in the dark; gnats, bugs, and moths even in the daytime; worms and wood lice under every log in the woodshed. You couldn't help becoming dependent on those things; there was nothing else. Seldom: desireless and somehow happy; usually: desireless and a little unhappy.

No possibility of comparison with a different way of life: richer? less hemmed in?

It began with my mother suddenly wanting something. She wanted to learn, because in learning her lessons as a child she had felt something of herself. Just as when we say, "I feel like myself." For the first time, a desire, and she didn't keep it to herself; she spoke of it time and time again, and in the end it became an obsession with her. My mother told me she had "begged" my grandfather to let her learn something. But it was out of the question, disposed of with a wave of the hand, unthinkable.

Still, our people had a traditional respect for accomplished facts: a pregnancy, a war, the state, ritual, and death. When at the age of fifteen or sixteen my mother ran away from home to learn cooking at some Hôtel du Lac, my grandfather let her have her own way, *because she was already gone;* and besides, there wasn't much to be learned about cooking.

No other course was open to her; scullery maid, chambermaid, assistant cook, head cook. "People will always eat." In the photographs, a flushed face, glowing cheeks, arm in arm with bashful, serious-looking girl friends; she was the life of the party; self-assured gaiety ("Nothing can happen to me"); exuberant, sociable, nothing to hide.

City life: short skirts ("knee huggers"), high-heeled shoes, permanent wave, earrings, unclouded joy of life. Even a stay abroad! Chambermaid in the

Black Forest, flocks of ADMIRERS, kept at a DISTANCE! Dates, dancing, entertainment, fun; hidden fear of sex ("They weren't my type"). Work, pleasure; heavyhearted, lighthearted; Hitler had a nice voice on the radio. The homesickness of those who can't afford anything; back at the Hôtel du Lac ("I'm doing the bookkeeping now"); glowing references ("Fräulein . . . has shown aptitude and willingness to learn. So conscientious, frank, and cheerful that we find it hard . . . She is leaving our establishment of her own free will"). Boat rides, all-night dances, never tired.

On April 10, 1938, the Yes to Germany! "The Führer arrived at 4:15 p.m., after a triumphal passage thrugh the streets of Klagenfurt to the strains of the Badenweiler March. The rejoicing of the masses seemed to know no bounds. The thousands of swastika flags in the spas and summer resorts were reflected in the already ice-free waters of the Wörthersee. The airplanes of the old Reich and our native planes vied with one another in the clouds overhead."

The newspapers advertised plebiscite badges and silk or paper flags. After football games the teams marched off with a regulation *"Sieg Heil!"* The letter A was replaced by the letter D on the bumpers of motor vehicles. On the radio: 6:15, call to arms; 6:35, motto of the day; 6:40, gymnastics; 8–12 p.m., Radio Königsberg: Richard Wagner concert followed by entertainment and dance music.

"How to mark your ballot on April 10: make a *bold* cross in the *larger* circle under the word YES."

Thieves just out of jail were locked up again when they claimed that the objects found in their possession had been bought in department stores that MEANWHILE HAD GONE OUT OF EXISTENCE because they had belonged to Jews.

Demonstrations, torchlight parades, mass meetings. Buildings decorated with the new national emblem SALUTED; forests and mountains peaks DECKED THEM-

SELVES OUT; the historic events were represented to the rural population as a drama of nature.

"We were kind of excited," my mother told me. For the first time, people did things together. Even the daily grind took on a festive mood, "until late into the night." For once, everything that was strange and incomprehensible in the world took on meaning and became part of a larger context; even disagreeable, mechanical work was festive and meaningful. Your automatic movements took on an athletic quality, because you saw innumerable others making the same movements. A new life, in which you felt protected, yet free.

The rhythm became an existential ritual. "Public need before private greed, the community comes first." You were at home wherever you went; no more homesickness. Addresses on the back of photographs; you bought your first date book (or was it a present?) —all at once you had so many friends and there was so much going on that it became possible to FORGET something. She had always wanted to be proud of something, and now, because what she was doing was somehow important, she actually was proud, not of anything in particular, but in general—a state of mind, a newly attained awareness of being alive—and she was determined never to give up that vague pride.

She still had no interest in politics: what was happening before her eyes was something entirely different from politics—a masquerade, a newsreel festival, a secular church fair. "Politics" was something colorless and abstract, not a carnival, not a dance, not a band in local costume, in short, nothing VISIBLE. Pomp and ceremony on all sides. And what was "politics"? A meaningless word, because, from your schoolbooks on, everything connected with politics had been dished out in catchwords unrelated to any tangible reality and even such images as were used were devoid of human content: oppression as chains or boot heel, freedom as mountaintop, the economic system as a reassuringly smoking factory chimney or as a pipe enjoyed after the day's work, the social system as a descending ladder: "Emperor–King–Nobleman–Burgher–Peasant–Weaver/Carpenter–Beggar–Gravedigger"; a game, incidentally, that could be played properly only in the prolific families of peasants, carpenters, and weavers.

* * *

That period helped my mother to come out of her shell and become independent. She acquired a presence and lost her last fear of human contact: her hat awry, because a young fellow was pressing his head against hers, while she merely laughed into the camera with an expression of self-satisfaction. (The fiction that photographs can "tell us" anything—but isn't all formulation, even of things that have really happened, more or less a fiction? *Less,* if we content ourselves with a mere record of events; *more,* if we try to formulate in depth? And the more fiction we put into a narrative, the more likely it is to interest others, because people identify more readily with formulations than with recorded facts. Does this explain the need for poetry? "Breathless on the riverbank" is one of Thomas Bernhard's formulations.)

* * *

The war—victory communiqués introduced by portentous music, pouring from the "people's radio sets," which gleamed mysteriously in dimly lit "holy corners" —further enhanced people's sense of self, because it "increased the uncertainty of all circumstances" (Clausewitz) and made the day-to-day happenings that had formerly been taken for granted seem excitingly fortuitous. For my mother the war was not a childhood nightmare that would color her whole emotional development as it did mine; more than anything else, it was contact with a fabulous world, hitherto known to her only from travel folders. A new feeling for distances, for how things had been BACK IN PEACETIME, and most of all for other individuals, who up until then had been confined to the shadowy roles of casual friends, dance partners, and fellow workers. And also for the first time, a family feeling: "Dear Brother . . . I am looking at the map to see where you might be now . . . Your sister . . ."

And in the same light of her first love: a German party member, in civilian life a savings-bank clerk, now an army paymaster, which gave him a rather special standing. She was soon in a family way. He was married, and she loved him dearly; anything he said was all right with her. She introduced him to her parents, went hiking with him, kept him company in his soldier's loneliness.

"He was so attentive to me, and I wasn't afraid of him the way I had been with other men."

He did the deciding and she trailed along. Once he gave her a present—perfume. He also lent her a radio for her room and later took it away again. "At that time" he still read books, and together they read one entitled *By the Fireside*. On the way down from a mountain pasture on one of their hikes, they had started to run. My mother broke wind and my father reproved her; a little later he too let a fart escape him and followed it with a slight cough, hem-hem. In telling me of this incident years later, she bent double and giggled maliciously, though at the same time her conscience troubled her because she was belittling her only love. She herself thought it comical that she had once loved someone, especially a man like him. He was smaller than she, many years older, and almost bald; she walked beside him in low-heeled shoes, always at pains to adapt her step to his, her hand repeatedly slipping off his inhospitable arm; an ill-matched, ludicrous couple. And yet, twenty years later, she still longed to feel for someone what she had then felt for that savings-bank wraith. But there never was AN-OTHER: everything in her life had conspired to inculcate a kind of love that remains fixated on a particular irreplaceable object.

It was after graduating from the Gymnasium that I first saw my father: on his way to the rendezvous, he chanced to come toward me in the street; he was wearing sandals, a piece of paper was folded over his sunburned nose, and he was leading a collie on a leash. Then, in a small café in her home village, he met his former love; my mother was excited, my father embarrassed; standing by the jukebox at the other end of the café, I picked out Elvis Presley's "Devil in Disguise." My mother's husband had got wind of all this, but he had merely sent his youngest son to the café as an indication that he was in the know. After buying himself an ice-cream cone, the child stood next to his mother and the stranger, asking her from time to time, always in the same words, if she was going home soon. My father put sunglasses over his regular glasses, said something now and then to the dog, and finally announced that he "might as well" pay up. "No, no, it's on me," he said, when my mother also took her purse out of her handbag. On the trip we took together, the two of us wrote her a postcard. In every hotel we went to, he let it be known that I was his son, for fear we'd be taken for homosexuals (Article 175). Life had disappointed him, he had become more and more lonely. "Now that I know people, I've come to appreciate animals," he said, not quite in earnest of course.

* * *

Shortly before I was born, my mother married a German army sergeant, who had been COURTING her for some time and didn't mind her having a child by someone else. "It's this one or none!" he had decided the first time he laid eyes on her, and bet his buddies that he would get her or, conversely, that she would take him. She found him repulsive, but everyone harped on her duty (to give the child a father); for the first time in her life she let herself be intimidated and laughed rather less. Besides, it impressed her that someone should have taken a shine to her.

"Anyway, I figured he'd be killed in the war," she told me. "But then all of a sudden I started worrying about him."

In any case, she was now entitled to a family allotment. With the child she went to Berlin to stay with her husband's parents. They tolerated her. When the first bombs fell) she went back home—the old story. She began to laugh again, sometimes so loudly that everyone cringed.

She forgot her husband, squeezed her child so hard that it cried, and kept to herself in this house where, after the death of her brothers, those who remained looked uncomprehendingly through one another. Was there, then, nothing more? Had that been all? Masses for the dead, childhood diseases, drawn curtains, correspondence with old acquaintances of carefree days, making herself useful in the kitchen and in the fields, running out now and then to move the child into the shade; then, even here in the country, air-raid sirens, the population scrambling into the cave shelters, the first bomb crater, later used for children's games and as a garbage dump.

The days were haunted, and once again the outside world, which years of daily contact had wrested from the nightmares of childhood and made familiar, became an impalpable ghost.

My mother looked on in wide-eyed astonishment. Fear didn't get the better of her; but sometimes, infected by the general fright, she would burst into a sudden laugh, partly because she was ashamed that her body had suddenly made itself so churlishly independent. In her childhood and even more so in her young girlhood, "Aren't you ashamed?" or "You ought to be ashamed!" had rung in her ears like a litany. In this rural, Catholic environment, any suggestion that a woman might have a life of her own was an impertinence: disapproving looks, until shame, at first acted out in fun, became real and frightened away the most elementary feelings. Even in joy, a "woman's blush," because joy was something to be ashamed of; in sadness, she turned red rather than pale and instead of bursting into tears broke out in sweat.

In the city my mother had thought she had found a way of life that more or less suited her, that at least made her feel good. Now she came to realize that by excluding every other alternative, other people's way of life had set itself up as the one and only *hope of salvation*. When, in speaking of herself, she went beyond a statement of fact, she was silenced by a glance.

A bit of gaiety, a dance step while working, the humming of a song hit, were foolishness, and soon she herself thought so, because no one reacted and she was left alone with her gaiety. In part, the others lived their own lives as an example; they ate so little as an example, were silent in each other's presence as an example, and went to confession only to remind the stay-at-homes of their sins.

And so she was starved. Her little attempts to explain herself were futile mutterings. She felt free—but there was nothing she could do about it. The others, to be sure, were children; but it was oppressive to be looked at so reproachfully, especially by children.

When the war was over, my mother remembered her husband and, though no one had asked for her, went to Berlin. Her husband, who had also forgotten that he had once courted her on a bet, was living with a girl friend in Berlin; after all, there had been a war on.

But she had her child with her, and without enthusiasm they both took the path of duty.

They lived in a sublet room in Berlin-Pankow. The husband worked as a streetcar motorman and drank, worked as a streetcar conductor and drank, worked as a baker and drank. Taking with her her second child, who had been born in the meantime, his wife went to see his employer and begged him to give her husband one more chance, the old story.

In this life of misery, my mother lost her country-round cheeks and achieved a certain chic. She carried her head high and acquired a graceful walk. Whatever she put on was becoming to her. She had no need of fox furs. When her husband sobered up and clung to her and told her he loved her, she gave him a merciful, pitying smile. By then, she had no illusions about anything.

They went out a good deal, an attractive couple. When he was drunk, he got FRESH and she had to be SEVERE with him. Then he would beat her because she had nothing to say to him, when it was he who brought home the bacon.

Without his knowledge, she gave herself an abortion with a knitting needle.

For a time he lived with his parents; then they sent him back to her. Childhood memories: the fresh bread that he sometimes brought home; the black, fatty loaves of pumpernickel around which the dismal room blossomed into life; my mother's words of praise.

In general, these memories are inhabited more by things than by people: a dancing top in a deserted street amid ruins, oat flakes in a sugar spoon, gray mucus in a tin spittoon with a Russian trademark; of people, only separated parts: hair, cheeks, knotted scars on fingers; from her childhood days my mother had a swollen scar on her index finger; I held on to it when I walked beside her.

* * *

And so she was nothing and never would be anything; it was so obvious that there was no need of a forecast. She already said "in my day," though she was not yet thirty. Until then, she hadn't resigned herself, but now life became so hard that for the first time she had to listen to reason. She listened to reason, but understood nothing.

She had already begun to work something out and even, as far as possible, to live accordingly. She said to herself: "Be sensible"—the reason reflex—and "All right, I'll behave."

And so she budgeted herself and also learned to budget people and objects, though on that score there was little to be learned: the people in her life—her husband, whom she couldn't talk to, and her children, whom she couldn't yet talk to—hardly counted, and objects were available only in minimal quantities. Consequently, she became petty and niggardly: Sunday shoes were not to be worn on weekdays, street clothes were to be hung up as soon as you got home, her shopping bag wasn't a toy, the warm bread was for the next day. (Later on, my confirmation watch was locked up right after my confirmation.)

Because she was helpless, she disciplined herself, which went against her grain and made her touchy. She hid her touchiness behind an anxious, exaggerated dignity, but at the slightest provocation a defenseless, panic-stricken look shone through. She was easily humiliated.

Like her father, she thought the time had come to deny herself everything, but then with a shamefaced laugh she would ask the children to let her lick their candy.

The neighbors liked her and admired her for her Austrian sociability and gaiety; they thought her FRANK and SIMPLE, not coquettish and affected like city people; there was no fault to be found with her.

She also got on well with the Russians, because she

could make herself understood in Slovenian. With them she talked and talked, saying everything she was able to say in the words common to both languages; that unburdened her.

But she never had any desire for an affair. Her heart had grown heavy too soon: the shame that had always been preached at her and finally become a part of her. An affair, to her mind, could only mean someone "wanting something" of her, and that put her off; she, after all, didn't want anything of anybody. The men she later liked to be with were GENTLEMEN: their company gave her a pleasant feeling that took the place of affection. As long as there was someone to talk with, she felt relaxed and almost happy. She let no one come too close; she could have been approached only with the delicacy which in former days had enabled her to feel that she belonged to herself—but that was long ago; she remembered it only in her dreams.

She became sexless; everything went into the trivia of daily life.

She wasn't lonely; at most, she sensed that she was only a half. But there was no one to supply the other half. "We rounded each other out so well," she said, thinking back on her days with the savings-bank clerk; that was her ideal of eternal love.

* * *

The postwar period; the big city—in this city, city life was no longer possible. You took shortcuts, up hill and down dale through the rubble, to get there sooner, but even so you found yourself at the end of a long line, jostled by fellow citizens who had ceased to be anything more than elbows and eyes looking into space. A short, unhappy laugh; like the rest of them, you looked away from yourself, into space; like the rest of them, you gave yourself away, showed that you needed something; still, you tried to assert yourself;

pathetic, because that made you just like the people around you: something pushing and pushed, shoving and shoved, cursing and cursed at. In her new situation, her mouth, which up until then had been open at least occasionally—in youthful amazement (or in feminine acting-as-if), in rural fright, at the end of a daydream that lightened her heavy heart—was kept closed with exaggerated firmness, as a sign of adaptation to a universal determination which, because there was so little to be *personally* determined about, could never be more than a pretense.

A masklike face—not rigid as a mask but with a masklike immobility—a disguised voice, which for fear of attracting attention not only spoke the foreign dialect but mimicked the foreign turns of phrase—"Mud in your eye!"—"Keep your paws off that!"—"You're sure shoveling it in today!"—a copied posture, with a bend at the hips and one foot thrust forward . . . all this in order to become, not a different person, but a TYPE: to change from a prewar type to a postwar type, from a country bumpkin to a city person, adequately described in the words: TALL, SLIM, DARK-HAIRED.

In thus becoming a type, she felt freed from her own history, because now she saw herself through the eyes of a stranger making an erotic appraisal.

And so an emotional life that never had a chance of achieving bourgeois composure acquired a superficial stability by clumsily imitating the bourgeois system of emotional relations, prevalent especially among women, the system in which "So-and-so is my type but I'm not his," or "I'm his but he's not mine," or in which "We're made for each other" or "can't stand the sight of each other"—in which clichés are taken as binding rules and any *individual* reaction, which takes some account of an actual person, becomes a deviation. For instance, my mother would say of my father; "Actually, he wasn't my type." And so this typology became a guide to life; it gave you a pleasantly objective feeling about yourself; you stopped worrying about your origins, your possibly dandruff-ridden, sweaty-footed individuality, or the daily renewed problem of how to go on living; being a type relieved the human molecule of his humiliating loneliness and isolation; he lost himself, yet now and then he was somebody, if only briefly.

Once you became a type, you floated through the streets, buoyed up by all the things you could pass with indifference, repelled by everything which, in forcing you to stop, brought you back bothersomely to yourself: the lines outside the shops, a high bridge across the Spree, a shop window with baby carriages in it. (She had given herself another secret abortion.) Always on the move to get away from yourself and keep your peace of mind. Motto: "Today I won't think of anything; today I'll enjoy myself."

At times it worked and everything personal was swallowed up by the typical. Then even sadness was only a passing phase, a suspension of good cheer: "Forsaken, forsaken,/Like a pebble in the street,/That's how forsaken I am"; with the foolproof melancholy of this phony folk song, she contributed her share to the general merriment; the next item on the program might, for instance, be the ribald tone of a male voice getting ready to tell a joke. And then, with a sense of release, you could join in the laughter.

At home, of course, she was alone with the FOUR WALLS; some of the bounce was still there, a hummed tune, a dance step while taking off her shoes, a brief desire to jump out of her skin. And then she was dragging herself around the room again, from husband to child, from child to husband, from one thing to another.

Her calculations always went wrong; the little bourgeois recipes for salvation had stopped working, because in actual fact her living conditions—the one-room apartment, the constant worry about where the next meal was coming from, the fact that communication with her LIFE COMPANION was confined almost exclusively to gestures, involuntary mimicry, and embarrassed sexual intercourse—were actually prebourgeois. It was only by leaving the house that she could get anything at all out of life. Outside: the victor type; inside: the weaker half, the eternal loser! What a life!

Whenever she told me about it later on—and *telling* about it was a need with her—she would shake with disgust and misery, but too feebly to shake them *off;* her shudders only revived her horror.

From my childhood: ridiculous sobs in the toilet, nose blowing, inflamed eyes. She was; she became; she became nothing.

*   *   *

(Of course what is written here about a particular person is rather general; but only such generalizations, in explicit disregard of my mother as a possibly unique protagonist in a possibly unique story, can be of interest to anyone but myself. Merely to relate the vicissitudes of a life that came to a sudden end would be pure presumption.

(The dangers of all these abstractions and formulations is of course that they tend to become independent. When that happens, the individual that gave rise to them is forgotten—like images in a dream, phrases and sentences enter into a chain reaction, and the result is a literary ritual in which an individual life ceases to be anything more than a pretext.

(These two dangers—the danger of merely telling what happened and the danger of a human individual becoming painlessly submerged in poetic sentences—have slowed down my writing, because in every sentence I am afraid of losing my balance. This is true of every literary effort, but especially in this case, where the facts are so overwhelming that there is hardly anything to think out.

(Consequently, I first took the facts as my starting point and looked for ways of formulating them. But I soon noticed that in looking for formulations I was moving away from the facts. I then adopted a new approach—starting not with the facts but with the already available formulations, the linguistic deposit of man's social experience. From my mother's life, I sifted out the elements that were already foreseen in these formulas, for only with the help of a ready-made public language was it possible to single out from among all the irrelevant facts of this life the few that cried out to be made public.

(Accordingly, I compare, sentence by sentence, the stock of formulas applicable to the biolgraphy of a woman with my mother's particular life; the actual work of writing follows from the agreements and contradictions between them. The essential is to avoid mere quotations; even when sentences look quoted, they must never allow one to forget that they deal with someone who to my mind at least is distinct. Only then, only if a sentence is firmly and circumspectly centered on my personal or, if you will, private subject, do I feel that I can use it.

(Another specific feature of this story is that I do not, as is usually the case, let every sentence carry me further away from the inner life of my characters, so as finally, in a liberated and serene holiday mood, to look at them from outside as isolated insects. Rather, I try with unbending earnestness to penetrate my character. And because I cannot fully capture her in any sentence, I keep having to start from scratch and never arrive at the usual sharp and clear bird's-eye view.

(Ordinarily, I start with myself and my own headaches; in the course of my writing, I detach myself from them more and more, and then in the end I ship myself and my headaches off to market as a comodity—but in this case, since I am only a *writer* and can't take the role of the *person written about,* such detachment is impossible. I can only move myself into the distance; my mother can never become for me, as I can for myself, a wingèd art object flying serenely through the air. She refuses to be isolated and remains unfathomable; my sentences crash in the darkness and lie scattered on the paper.

(In stories we often read that something or other is "unnamable" or "indescribable"; ordinarily this strikes me as a cheap excuse. This story, however, is really about the nameless, about speechless moments of terror. It is about moments when the mind boggles with horror, states of fear so brief that speech always comes too late; about dream happenings so gruesome that the mind perceives them physically as worms. The blood curdles, the breath catches, "a cold chill crept up my back, my hair stood on end"—states experienced while listening to a ghost story, while turning on a water faucet that you can quickly turn off again, on the street in the evening with a beer bottle in one hand; in short, it is a record of states, not a well-rounded story with an anticipated, hence comforting, end.

(At best, I am able to capture my mother's story for brief moments in dreams, because then her feelings become so palpable that I experience them as doubles and am identical with them; but these are precisely the moments I have already mentioned, in which extreme need to communicate coincides with extreme speechlessness. That is why I affect the usual biographical pattern and write: "At that time . . . later," "Because . . . although," "was . . . became . . . became nothing," hoping in this way to dominate the horror. That, perhaps, is the comical part of my story.)

* * *

In the early summer of 1948, my mother left the eastern sector of Germany with her husband and two children, carrying the little girl, who was just a year old, in a shopping bag. They had no papers. They crossed two borders illegally, both in the gray of dawn; once a Russian border guard shouted "Halt," and my mother's answer in Slovenian served as a password; those days became fixed in the boy's mind as a triad of gray dawn, whispers, and danger. Happy excitement on the train ride through Austria, and then she was back in the house where she was born, where two small rooms were turned over to her and her family. Her husband was employed as foreman by her carpenter brother; she herself was reincorporated into the household.

In the city she had not been proud of having children; here she was, and often showed herself with them. She no longer took any nonsense from anyone. In the old days her only reaction had been a bit of back talk; now she laughed. She could laugh anyone to silence. Her husband, in particular, got laughed at so vigorously whenever he started discussing his numerous projects that he soon faltered and looked vacantly out the window. True, he would start in again the next day. (That period lives for me in the sound of my mother laughing at people!) She also interrupted the children with her laughter when they wanted something; it was ridiculous to express desires in earnest. In the meantime, she brought her third child into the world.

She took to the native dialect again, though of course only in fun: she was a woman who had been ABROAD. Almost all her old girl friends had by then returned to their native village; they had made only brief excursions to the city or across the borders.

In this life, confined almost entirely to housekeeping and making ends meet, you didn't confide in your friends; at the most, friendship meant familiarity. It was plain from the start that all had the same troubles —the only difference was that some took them more lightly than others, a matter of temperament.

In this section of the population, people without troubles were an oddity—freaks. Drunks didn't get talkative, only more taciturn; they might bellow or brawl for a while, but then they sank back into themselves, until at closing time they would start sobbing for no known reason and hug or thrash whoever was nearest to them.

No one had anything to say about himself, even in church, at Easter confession, when at least once a year there was an opportunity to reveal something of one-self, there was only a mumbling of catchwords out of the catechism, and the word "I" seemed stranger to the speaker himself than a chunk out of the moon. If in talking about himself anyone went beyond relating some droll incident, he was said to be "peculiar." Personal life, it if had ever developed a character of its own, was depersonalized except for dream tatters swallowed up by the rites of religion, custom, and good manners; little remained of the human individual, and indeed, the word "individual" was known only in pejorative combinations.

The sorrowful Rosary; the glorious Rosary; the harvest festival; the plebiscite celebration; ladies' choice; the drinking of brotherhood; April Fools' pranks; wakes; kisses on New Year's Eve: in these rituals all private sorrow, ambition, hunger for com-munication, sense of the unique, wanderlust, sexual drive, and in general all reactions to a lopsided world in which the roles were reversed, were projected out-ward, so that no one was a problem to himself.

All spontaneity—taking a walk on a weekday, fall-ing in love a second time, or, if you were a woman, going to the tavern by yourself for a schnapps—was frowned upon; in a pinch you could ask someone to dance or join in a song "spontaneously," but that was all. Cheated out of your own biography and feelings, you became "skittish"; you shied away from people, stopped talking, or, more seriously touched, went from house to house screaming.

The above-mentioned rites then functioned as a consolation. This consolation didn't address itself to you as a person; it simply swallowed you up, so that in the end you as an individual were content to be nothing, or at least nothing much.

You lost interest in personal matters and stopped inquiring about them. All questions became empty phrases, and the answers were so stereotyped that there was no need to involve *people* in them; *objects* sufficed; the cool grave, the sweet heart of Jesus, the sweet Lady of Sorrows, became fetishes for the death wish that sweetened your daily afflictions; in the midst of these consoling fetishes, you ceased to exist. And because your days were spent in unchanging association with the same things, they became sacred to you; not leisure but work was sweet. Besides, there was nothing else.

You no longer had eyes for anything. "Curiosity" ceased to be a human characteristic and became a womanish vice.

But my mother was curious by nature and had no consoling fetishes. Instead of losing herself in her work, she took it in her stride; consequently she was discontented. The *Weltschmerz* of the Catholic religion was alien to her; she believed only in happiness in this world, and that was a matter of luck; she herself had had bad luck.

She'd show them, though.

But how?

How she would have loved to be really frivolous! And then she actually did something frivolous: "I've been frivolous today, I've bought myself a blouse." All the same—and that was a good deal in those surroundings—she took to smoking and even smoked in public.

Many of the local women were secret drinkers; their thick, twisted lips repelled her: that wasn't the way to show them. At the most she would get tipsy, and then she would drink to lifelong friendship with everyone in sight, and soon she was on friendly terms with all the younger notables. Even in this little village there was a kind of "society," consisting of the few who were somewhat better off than the rest, and she was welcome in their gatherings. Once, disguised as a Roman matron, she won first prize at a masked ball. At least in its merrymaking, country society thought of itself as classless—as long as you were NEAT, CLEAN, and JOLLY.

* * *

At home she was "Mother"; even her husband addressed her as "Mother" more often than by her first name. That was all right with her; for one thing, it corresponded to her feeling about her husband: she had never regarded him as anything resembling a sweetheart.

Now it was she who saved. Her saving, to be sure, could not, like her father's, mean setting money aside. It was pure *scrimping;* your curtailed your needs to the point where they became vices, and then you curtailed them some more.

But even in this wretchedly narrow sphere, she comforted herself with the thought that she was at least imitating the *pattern* of middle-class life: ludicrous as it might seem, it was still possible to classify purchases as necessary, merely useful, and luxurious.

Only food was necessary; winter fuel was useful; everything else was a luxury.

If only once a week, she derived a pleasurable feeling of pride from the fact that a little something was left over for luxury. "We're still better off than the rest of them."

She indulged in the following luxuries: a seat in the ninth row at the movies, followed by a glass of wine and soda water; a one- or two-schilling bar of Bensdorp chocolate to give the children the next morning; once a year, a bottle of homemade eggnog; on occasional winter Sundays she would whip up the cream she had saved during the week by keeping the milk pot between the two panes of the double windows overnight. "What a feast!" I would write if it were my own story; but it was only the slavish aping of an unattainable life style, a child's game of earthly paradise.

Christmas: necessities were packaged as presents. We surprised each other with such necessities as underwear, stockings, and handkerchiefs, and the beneficiary said he had WISHED for just that! We pretended that just about everything that was given to us, except food, was a present; I was sincerely grateful for the most indispensable school materials and spread them out beside my bed like presents.

* * *

A budgeted life, determined by the hourly wages she toted up for her husband, always hoping to discover a forgotten half hour; dread of rainy spells, when the wages were next to nothing, which he passed in their little room talking to her or looking resentfully out the window.

In the winter, when there was no building, her husband spent his unemployment benefits on drink. She went from tavern to tavern looking for him; with gleeful malice, he would show her what was left. She ducked to avoid his blows. She stopped talking to him. The children, repelled and frightened by her silence, clung to their contrite father. Witch! The children looked at her with hostility; she was so stern and unbending. They slept with pounding hearts when their parents were out and pulled the blanket over their heads when toward morning the husband pushed the wife into the room. At every step she stopped until he pushed her. Both were obstinately mute. Then finally she opened her mouth and said what he had been waiting to hear: "You beast! You beast!" whereupon he was able to beat her in earnest. To every blow she responded with a short, crushing laugh.

They seldom looked at each other except in these moments of open hatred; then they looked deep and unflinchingly into each other's eyes, he from below, she from above. The children under the blanket heard only the shoving and breathing, and occasionally the rattling of dishes in the cupboard. Next morning they made their own breakfast while husband and wife lay in bed, he dead to the world, she with her eyes closed, pretending to be asleep. (Undoubtedly, this kind of account seems copied, borrowed from accounts of other incidents; an old story interchangeable with other old stories; unrelated to the time when it took place; in short, it smacks of the nineteenth century. But just that seems necessary, for, at least in that part of the world and under the given economic conditions, such anachronistic, interchangeable nineteenth-century happenings were still the rule. And even today the Town Hall bulletin board is taken up almost entirely by notices to the effect that So-and-so and So-and-so are forbidden to enter the taverns.)

* * *

She never ran away. She had learned her place. "I'm only waiting for the children to grow up." A third abortion, this time followed by a severe hemorrhage. Shortly before she was forty, she became pregnant again. An abortion was no longer possible; the child was born.

The word "poverty" was a fine, somehow noble word. It evoked an image out of old schoolbooks: poor but clean. Cleanliness made the poor socially acceptable.

271

Social progress meant teaching people to be clean; once the indigent had been cleaned up, "poverty" became a title of honor. Even in the eyes of the poor, the squalor of destitution applied only to the filthy riffraff of foreign countries.

"The tenant's visiting card is his windowpane."

And so the have-nots obediently bought soap with the money provided for that purpose by the progressive authorities. As paupers, they had shocked the official mind with repulsive, but for that very reason palpable, images; now, as a reclaimed and cleansed "poorer class," their life became so unimaginably abstract that they could be forgotten. Squalid misery can be described in concrete terms; poverty can only be intimated in symbols.

Moreover, the graphic accounts of squalor were concerned only with its physically disgusting aspect; they *produced* disgust by the relish they took in it, so that disgust, instead of being translated into action, merely became a reminder of the anal, shit-eating phase.

In certain households, for instance, there was only one bowl; at night it was used as a chamberpot and by day for kneading bread dough. Undoubtedly the bowl was washed out with boiling water in between, so there was little harm done; the dual use of the bowl became disgusting only when it was *described:* "They relieve themselves in the same bowl they eat out of."—"Ugh!" Words convey this sort of passive, complacent disgust much better than the sight of the phenomena they refer to. (A memory of my own: shuddering while describing spots of egg yolk on a dressing gown.) Hence my distaste for descriptions of misery; for in hygienic, but equally miserable, poverty, there is nothing to describe.

Accordingly, when the word "poverty" comes up, I always think: "once upon a time"; and, for the most part, one hears it in the mouth of persons who have gone through it in the past, a word connected with childhood; not "I was poor" but "I was the child of poor parents" (Maurice Chevalier): a quaint note to season memoirs with. But at the thought of my mother's living conditions, I am unable to embroider on my memory. From the first, she was under pressure to keep up the forms: in country schools, the subject most stressed for girls was called "the outward form and appearance of written work"; in later life, this found its continuation in a woman's obligation to keep up the appearance of a united family; not cheerful poverty but formally perfect squalor; and gradually, in its daily effort to keep up appearances, her face lost its soul.

Maybe we would have felt better in formless squalor; we might have achieved a degree of proletarian class-consciousness. But in that part of the world there was no proletariat, at most, beggars and tramps; no one fought or even talked back; the totally destitute were merely embarrassed; poverty was indeed a disgrace.

* * *

Nevertheless, my mother, who had not learned to take all this for granted, was humiliated by the eternal stringency. In symbolic terms: she was no longer a NATIVE WHO HAD NEVER SEEN A WHITE MAN; she was capable of imagining a life that was something more than lifelong housework. If someone had given her the slightest hint, she would have got the right idea.

If, would have.

What actually happened: a nature play with a human prop that was systematically dehumanized. Pleading with her brother not to dismiss her husband for drunknness; pleading with the local radio spotter not to report her unregistered radio; pleading with the bank for a building loan, protesting that she was a good citizen and would prove worthy of it; from office to office for a certificate of indigence, which had to be renewed each year if her son, who was now at the university, was to obtain a scholarship; applications for sick relief, family allowances, reduction of church taxes—most of which depended on the benevolent judgment of the authorities, but even if you had a legal right to something, you had to prove it over and over again in such detail that when the "Approved" stamp finally came, you received it with gratitude, as a favor.

* * *

No machines in the house; everything was still done by hand. Objects out of a past century, now generally transfigured with nostalgia: not only the coffee mill, which you had actually come to love as a toy—also the GOOD OLD ironing board, the COZY hearth, the often-mended cooking pots, the DANGEROUS poker, the STURDY wheelbarrow, the ENTERPRISING weed cutter, the SHINING BRIGHT knives, which over the years had been ground to a vanishing narrowness by BURLY scissors grinders, the FIENDISH thimble, the STUPID darning egg, the CLUMSY OLD flatiron, which provided variety by having to be put back on the stove every so often, and finally the PRIZE PIECE, the foot-and-hand-operated Singer sewing machine. But the golden haze is all in the manner of listing.

Another way of listing would be equally idyllic; your aching back; your hands scalded in the wash boiler, then frozen red while hanging up the clothes (how the frozen washing crackled as you folded it up!); an occasional nosebleed when you straightened up after hours of bending over; being in such a hurry to get through with the day's work that you went marketing with the telltale blood spot on the back of your skirt; the eternal moaning about little aches and pains, because after all you were only a woman. Women among themselves: not "How are you feeling?" but "Are you feeling better?"

All that is known. It proves nothing; its demonstrative value is destroyed by the habit of thinking in terms of advantages and disadvantages, the most evil of all ways of looking at life. "Everything has its advantages and disadvantages." Once that is said, the unbearable becomes bearable—a mere disadvantage, and what after all is a disadvantage but a necessary adjunct of every advantage?

An advantage, as a rule, was merely the absence of a disadvantage: *no* noise, *no* responsibility, *not* working for strangers, *not* having to leave your home and children every day. The disadvantages that were absent made up for those that were present.

So it wasn't really so bad; you could do it with one hand tied behind your back. Except that no end was in sight.

Today was yesterday, yesterday was always. Another day behind you, another week gone, and Happy New Year. What will we have to eat tomorrow? Has the mailman come? What have you been doing around the house all day?

Setting the table, clearing the table: "Has everybody been served?" Open the curtains, draw the curtains; turn the light on, turn the light out; "Why do you always leave the light on in the bathroom?"; folding, unfolding; emptying, filling; plugging in, unplugging. "Well, that does it for today."

The first electrical appliance: an iron, a marvel she had "always longed for." Embarrassment, as though she had been unworthy of it: "What have I done to deserve it? From now on I'll always look forward to ironing! Maybe I'll have a little more time for myself."

The mixer, the electric stove, the refrigerator, the

washing machine: more and more time for herself.
But she only stood there stiff with terror, dizzy after
her long years as the good household fairy. But she
had also had to husband her feelings so much that she
expressed them only in slips of the tongue, and then
did her best to gloss them over. The animal spirits that
had once filled her whole body now showed themselves
only seldom; one finger of her heavy, listless hand
would quiver, and instantly this hand would be covered by the other.

* * *

But my mother had not been crushed for good. She
began to assert herself. No longer obliged to work her
fingers to the bone, she gradually became herself
again. She got over her skittishness. She showed people the face with which she felt more or less at ease.

She read newspapers, but preferred books with stories she could compare with her own life. She
read the books I was reading, first Fallada, Knut
Hamsun, Dostoevsky, Maxim Gorky, then Thomas
Wolfe and William Faulkner. What she said about
books could not have been put into print; she merely
told me what had particularly caught her attention.
"I'm not like that," she sometimes said, as though
the author had written about *her*. To her, every book
was an account of her own life, and in reading she
came to life; for the first time, she came out of her
shell; she learned to talk about *herself;* and with each
book she had more ideas on the subject. Little by
little, I learned something about her.

* * *

Up until then she had got on her own nerves, her
own presence had made her uncomfortable; now she

lost herself in reading and conversation, and emerged with a new feeling about herself. "It's making me young again."

True, books to her were only stories out of the past, never dreams of the future; in them she found everything she had missed and would never make good. Early in life she had dismissed all thought of a future. Thus, her second spring was merely a transfiguration of her past experience.

Literature didn't teach her to start thinking of herself but showed her it was too late for that. She COULD HAVE made something of herself. Now, at the most, she gave SOME thought to herself, and now and then after shopping she would treat herself to a cup of coffee at the tavern and worry a LITTLE LESS about what people might think.

She became indulgent toward her husband; when he started talking, she let him finish; she no longer stopped him after the first sentence with a nod so violent that it made him swallow his words. She felt sorry for him; often her pity left her defenseless when he wasn't suffering at all and she merely thought of him in connection with some object which to her mind stood for her own past despair: a washbasin with cracked enamel, a tiny electric hot plate, blackened by boiled-over milk.

When a member of the family was absent, she surrounded him with images of loneliness; if he wasn't at home with her, he was sure to be alone. Cold, hunger, unfriendly people: and it was all her fault. She included her despised husband in these guilt feelings and worried about him when he had to manage without her; even during her frequent stays at the hospital, once on suspicion of cancer, her conscience tormented her: her poor husband at home wasn't getting anything hot to eat.

Her sympathy for him when he was absent prevented her from ever feeling lonely; only a brief moment of forsakenness when she had him on her hands again; the irrepressible distaste inspired by his wobbly knees and the drooping seat of his trousers. "If only I had a man I could look up to"; it was no good having to despise someone all the time.

This visible disgust in her very first gesture, attenuated over the years into a patient, polite looking-up from whatever she happened to be doing, only crushed him the more. She had always thought him WEAK-KNEED. He often made the mistake of asking her why she couldn't bear him. Invariably she answered: "What makes you think that?" He persisted: was he really so repulsive? She comforted him, and all the while her loathing grew. They were growing old together; the thought didn't move her, but on the surface it made life easier, because he got out of the habit of beating her and bullying her.

Exhausted by the daily labors that got him nowhere, he became sickly and gentle. He woke from his maunderings into a real loneliness, to which she could respond only in his absence.

They hadn't grown apart; they had never been really together. A sentence from a letter: "My husband has calmed down." And she lived more calmly beside him, drawing satisfaction from the thought that she had always been and always would be a mystery to him.

* * *

She began to take an interest in politics; she no longer voted like her husband, for his employer's and her brother's party. Now she voted Socialist; and after a while her husband, who felt an increasing need to lean on her, did so too. But she never believed that politics could be of any help to her personally. She cast her ballot as a gift, never expecting anything in

return. "The Socialists do more for the workers"—
but she didn't feel herself to be a worker.

The preoccupations that meant more and more to
her, as housekeeping took up less of her time, had no
place in what she knew of the Socialist system. She
remained alone with her sexual disgust, repressed till
it found an outlet only in dreams, with the fog-
dampened bedclothes and the low ceiling over her
head. The things that really mattered to her were not
political. Of course there was a flaw in her reasoning
—but what was it? And what politician could explain it to her? And in what words?

Politicians lived in another world. When you asked
them a question, they didn't answer; they merely
stated their positions. "You can't talk about most
things anyway." Politics was concerned only with the
things that could be talked about; you had to handle
the rest for yourself, or leave it to God. And besides, if a politician were to take an interest in you
personally, you'd bolt. That would be getting too in-
timate.

* * *

She was gradually becoming an individual.

* * *

Away from the house, she took on an air of dignity;
sitting beside me as I drove the secondhand car I had
bought her, she looked unsmilingly straight ahead. At
home she no longer bellowed when she sneezed, and
she didn't laugh as loudly as before.

(At her funeral, her youngest son was to remember
how on his way home in those days he had heard her,
while still a long way off, screaming with laughter.)

When shopping, she dispensed token greetings to
the right and left; she went to the hairdresser's more

often and had her nails manicured. This was no longer the assumed dignity with which she had run the gauntlet in the days of postwar misery—today no one could destroy her composure with a glance.

But sometimes at home, while her husband, his back turned to her, his shirttails hanging out, his hands thrust deep into his pockets, silent except for an occasional suppressed cough, gazed down into the valley and her youngest son sat snotnosed on the kitchen sofa reading a Mickey Mouse comic book, she would sit at the table in her new, erect posture, angrily rapping her knuckles on the table edge, and then suddenly raise her hand to her cheek. At this her husband, as often as not, would leave the house, stand outside the door for a while clearing his throat, and come in again. She sat there with her hand on her cheek until her son asked for a slice of bread with something on it. To stand up she had to prop herself on both hands.

Another son wrecked the car and was thrown in jail for driving without a license. Like his father, he drank, and again she went from tavern to tavern. What a brood! He paid no attention to her reproofs, she always said the same thing, she lacked the vocabulary that might have had some effect on him. "Aren't you ashamed?"—"I know," he said.—"You could at least get yourself a room somewhere else." —"I know." He went on living at home, duplicated her husband, and even damaged the next car. She packed his bag and put it outside the house; he left the country. She dreamed the worst about him, wrote him a letter signed "Your unhappy mother," and he came right back. And so on. She felt that she was to blame. She took it hard.

And then the always identical objects all about her, in always the same places! She tried to be untidy, but her daily puttings-away had become too automatic. If only she could die! But she was afraid of death. Besides, she was too curious. "I've always had to be strong; I'd much rather have been weak."

She had no hobbies; she didn't collect anything or swap anything. She had stopped doing crossword puzzles. She had given up pasting photographs in albums; she just put them away somewhere.

She took no part in public life; once a year she gave blood and wore the blood donor's badge on her coat. One day she was introduced on the radio as the hundred thousandth donor of the year and rewarded with a gift basket.

Now and then she went bowling at the new automatic bowling alley. She giggled with her mouth closed when the tenpins all toppled over and the bell rang.

Once, on the Heart's Desire radio program, relatives in East Berlin sent the whole family greetings, followed by Handel's Hallelujah Chorus.

She dreaded the winter, when they all spent their days in one room; no one came to see her; when she heard a sound and looked up, it was always her husband again: "Oh, it's you."

She began having bad headaches. She couldn't keep pills down; at first suppositories helped, but not for long. Her head throbbed so that she could only touch it, ever so gently, with her fingertips. Each week the doctor gave her an injection that eased the pain for a while. But soon the injections became ineffectual. The doctor told her to keep her head warm, and she went about with a scarf on her head. She took sleeping pills but usually woke up soon after midnight; then she would cover her face with her pillow. She lay awake trembling until it was light, and the trembling lasted all day. The pain made her see ghosts.

In the meantime her husband had been sent to a sanatorium with tuberculosis; he wrote affectionate letters, he begged her to let him lie beside her again. Her answers were friendly.

The doctor didn't know what was wrong with her; the usual female trouble? change of life?

She was so weak that often when she reached out for something, she missed her aim; her hands hung down limp at her sides. After washing the lunch dishes, she lay down awhile on the kitchen sofa; it was too cold in the bedroom. Sometimes her headache was so bad that she didn't recognize anyone. Nothing interested her. When her head was throbbing, we had to raise our voices to talk to her. She lost all sense of balance and orientation, bumped into the corners of things, and fell down stairs. It hurt her to laugh, she only grimaced now and then. The doctor said it was probably a strangulated nerve. She hardly spoke above a whisper, she was even too miserable to complain. She let her head droop, first on one side, then on the other, but the pain followed her.

"I'm not human anymore."

* * *

Once, when staying with her, summer before last, I found her lying on her bed with so wretched a look on her face that I didn't dare go near her. A picture of animal misery, as in a zoo. It was a torment to see how shamelessly she had turned herself inside out; everything about her was dislocated, split, open, inflamed, a tangle of entrails. And she looked at me from far away as if I were her BROKEN HEART, as Karl Rossmann was for the humiliated stoker in Kafka's novel. BROKEN HEART. Frightened and exasperated, I left the room.

Only since then have I been fully aware of my mother. Before that, I kept forgetting her, at the most feeling an occasional pang when I thought about the idiocy of her life. Now she imposed herself on me, took on body and reality, and her condition was so palpable that at some moments it became a part of me.

The people in the neighborhood also began to see her with other eyes; as though she had been chosen to bring their own lives home to them. They still asked why and wherefore, but only on the surface; they understood her without asking.

* * *

She became insensible, she couldn't remember anything or recognize even the most familiar objects. More and more often, when her youngest son came home from school, he found a note on the table saying she had gone out, he should make himself some sandwiches or go next door to eat. These notes, torn from an account book, piled up in the drawer.

She was no longer able to play the housewife. Her whole body was sore when she woke up in the morning. She dropped everything she picked up, and would gladly have followed it in its fall.

Doors got in her way; the mold seemed to rain from the walls as she passed.

She watched television but couldn't follow. She moved her hands this way and that to keep from falling asleep.

Sometimes in her walks she forgot herself. She sat at the edge of the woods, as far as possible from the houses, or beside the brook below an abandoned sawmill. Looking at the grain fields or the water didn't take away her pain but deadened it intermittently. Her feelings dovetailed with the things she looked at; every sight was a torment; she would turn to another, and that too would torment her. But in between there were dead points, when the whirligig world left her a moment's peace. At such moments, she was merely tired; thoughtlessly immersed in the water, she rested from the turmoil.

Then again everything in her clashed with the world around her; panic-stricken, she struggled to keep her balance, but the feeling was too strong and her peace was gone. She had to stand up and move on.

She had to walk very slowly because, as she told me, the horror strangled her.

She walked and walked until she was so tired she had to sit down again. But soon she had to stand up and go on.

So the time passed, and often she failed to notice that it was getting dark. She was night-blind and had difficulty in finding her way home. Outside the house, she stopped and sat down on a bench, afraid to go in.

Then, after a long while, the door opened very slowly and my mother stood there with vacant eyes, like a ghost.

But in the house as well she wandered about, mistaking doors and directions. Often she had no idea how she had come to be where she was or how the time had passed. She had lost all sense of time and place.

She lost all desire to see anyone; at the most she would sit in the tavern, among the people from the tourist buses, who were in too much of a hurry to look her in the face. She couldn't dissemble any more; she had put all that behind her. One look at her and anyone was bound to see what was wrong.

She was afraid of losing her mind. Quickly, for fear it would be too late, she wrote a few letters of farewell.

Her letters were full of urgency, as if she had tried to etch herself into the paper. In that period of her life, writing had ceased to be an extraneous effort, as it is for most people in her circumstances; it had become a reflex, independent of her will. Yet there was hardly anything one could talk to her about;

284

every word reminded her of some horror and threw her off balance. "I can't talk. Don't torture me." She turned away, turned again, turned further away. Then she had to close her eyes, and silent tears ran uselessly down her averted face.

* * *

She went to see a neurologist in the provincial capital. With him she could talk; a doctor was someone she could confide in. She herself was surprised at how much she told him. It was only in speaking that she began really to remember. The doctor nodded at everything she said, recognized every particular as a symptom, and by subsuming them under a name —"nervous breakdown"—organized them into a system. That comforted her. He knew what was wrong with her; at least he had a name for her condition. And she wasn't the only one; there were others in the waiting room.

On her next visit, it amused her to observe these people. The doctor advised her to take walks in the open air. He prescribed a medicine that somewhat relieved the pressure on her head. A trip would help, she needed a change. On each visit she paid cash, because the Workers Health Insurance didn't provide for treatment of this kind. And then she was depressed again, because of the expense.

Sometimes she searched desperately for a word for something. Usually she knew it, she merely wanted others to share in her thought. She looked back with nostalgia at the brief period when she had recognized no one and understood nothing.

As it wore off, her illness became an affectation; now she only played at being sick. She pretended that her head was in a muddle as a defense against her thoughts, which had become clear again; for, once her head was perfectly clear, she could only regard herself as an individual case and the consolation of belonging to a group was no longer available to her. She exaggerated her forgetfulness and absentmindedness in order to be encouraged, when she finally did remember or show that she had understood everything perfectly, with a "You see! You're much better now!"—as though all the horror had consisted in losing her memory and being unable to join in the conversation.

* * *

You couldn't joke with her. Teasing about her condition didn't help her. SHE TOOK EVERYTHING LITERALLY. If anyone started clowning to cheer her up, she burst into tears.

* * *

In midsummer she went to Yugoslavia for four weeks. At first she only sat in her darkened hotel room, touching and feeling her head. She couldn't read, her thoughts got in the way. Every few minutes she went to the bathroom and washed her hands and face.

Then she ventured out and dabbled in the water. This was her first vacation away from home and her first visit to the seashore. She liked the sea; at night there was often a storm, and then she didn't mind lying awake. She bought a straw hat to shield her from the sun and sold it back the day she left. Every afternoon she went to a café and ordered an espresso. She wrote cards and letters to all her friends in which she spoke only incidentally of herself.

She recovered her sense of time and awareness of her surroundings. She listened curiously to the conversations at the other tables and tried to figure out the relationships between the people.

Toward evening when the heat had let up she took walks; she went to villages nearby and looked into the doorless houses. Her amazement was real; she had never seen such dire poverty. Her headaches stopped and so did her thoughts. For a time she was outside the world. She felt pleasantly bored.

Back home, she was her old talkative self. She had plenty to talk about. She let me go with her on her walks. Now and then we went to the tavern for dinner and she got into the habit of drinking a Campari before her meal. She still clutched at her head, but by then it was little more than a tic. She remembered that a year ago a man had actually spoken to her in a café. "But he was very polite!" Next summer she thought she would go to some northern country where it wasn't so hot.

She took it easy, sat in the garden with her friends, smoking and fanning the wasps out of her coffee.

The weather was sunny and mild. The fir trees on the hills round about were veiled in mist all day, and for a time they were not as dark as usual. She put up fruit and vegetables for the winter, and thought of adopting a child.

* * *

I was already too busy with my own life. In the middle of August, I went back to Germany and left her to her own resources. During the following months I was working on a book. I heard from her occasionally.

"My head spins a little. Some days are hard to bear." "It's cold and cheerless, the fog doesn't lift until mid-morning. I sleep late, and when I finally crawl out of bed, I have no desire to do anything. And adopting a child is out of the question right now. They won't give me one because my husband has tuberculosis."

"Whenever a pleasant thought crops up, a door closes and I'm alone again with my nightmares. I'd be so glad to write something more cheerful, but there isn't anything. When I start a conversation, he doesn't know what I'm talking about, so I prefer to say nothing. Somehow I was looking forward to seeing him again, but when he's here I can't bear the sight of him. I know I ought to find some way of making life bearable, I keep thinking about it, but nothing occurs to me. Just read this and forget it as fast as you can, that's my advice."

"I can't stand it in the house anymore, so I'm always gadding about somewhere. I've been getting up a little earlier, that's the hardest time for me; I have to force myself to do something, or I'd just go back to bed. There's a terrible loneliness inside me, I don't feel like talking to anyone. I'd often like to drink a little something in the evening, but I mustn't, because if I did my medicine wouldn't take effect. Yesterday I went to Klagenfurt, I roamed around all day and caught the last local home."

In October she didn't write. During the fine autumn days someone would meet her walking slowly down the street and prod her to walk a little faster. She was always asking her friends to join her in a cup of coffee at the tavern. People invited her out on Sunday excursions and she was glad to go. She went with friends to the last church fairs of the year. Sometimes she even went to a football game. She would look on indulgently as her friends cheered and whistled, and hardly open her mouth. But when in the course of his re-election campaign the Chancellor stopped in the village and handed out carnations, she pushed boldly through the crowd and asked for one: "Haven't you got one for me?" "I beg your pardon, ma'am."

* * *

Early in November she wrote: "I'm not logical enough to think things through to the end, and my head aches. Sometimes it buzzes and whistles so that I can't bear any outside noise.

"I talk to myself, because I can't say anything to other people anymore. Sometimes I feel like a machine. I'd like to go away somewhere, but when it gets dark I'm afraid of not finding the way home again. In the morning there's a dense fog and then everything is so quiet. Every day I do the same work, and every morning the place is a mess again. There's never any end to it. I really wish I were dead. When I'm out in the street and I see a car coming, I want to fall in front of it. But how can I be sure it would work?

"Yesterday I saw Dostoevsky's 'The Gentle Spirit' on TV; all night long I saw the most gruesome things, I wasn't dreaming, I really saw them, some men were going around naked and instead of genitals they had intestines hanging out. My husband is coming home on December 1. I keep feeling more and more uneasy. I can't see how it will be possible to live with him. We each look in a different direction and the loneliness only gets worse. I'm cold now, I think I'll take a walk."

*　*　*

She often shut herself up in the house. When people started telling her their troubles, she stopped them short. She treated them all very harshly, silenced them with a wave of her hand or with her sudden laugh. Other people were irritating children; at best she felt slightly sorry for them.

She was often cross. There was something about her way of finding fault that often made people feel like hypocrites.

When her picture was taken, she was no longer able to compose her face. She puckered her forehead and

raised her cheeks in a smile, but there was an incurable
sadness in her eyes; her pupils were out of kilter, dis-
placed from the center of her irises.

Mere existence had become a torture to her.

But at the same time she had a horror of death.

"Take walks in the woods!" (The neurologist.)

"But it's dark in the woods!" the local veterinarian,
her occasional confidant, said contemptuously after her
death.

* * *

Day and night the fog hung on. At noon she tried
putting the light out and immediately turned it on
again. What should she look at? Cross her arms and
put her hands on her shoulders. From time to time,
an invisible buzz saw, a rooster who thought all day
that the day was just dawning and crowed until late
afternoon; and then at closing time the factory whistles.

At night the fog pressed against the windowpanes.
At irregular intervals she could hear a drop of water
running down the glass outside. She kept the heating
pad on all night in her bed. Every morning the fire was
out in the kitchen stove. "I don't want to pull myself
together any more." She was no longer able to close
her eyes. There had been a GREAT FALL (Franz
Grillparzer) in her consciousness.

* * *

(From this point on, I shall have to be careful to keep
my story from telling itself.)

* * *

She wrote letters of farewell to everyone in her family.
She not only knew what she was doing, she also knew
why she could no longer do anything else. "You won't

understand," she wrote to her husband. "But it's un-thinkable that I should go on living." To me she wrote a registered special-delivery letter, enclosing a copy of her will. "I have begun to write several times, but it's no comfort, no help to me." All her letters were headed not only with the date as usual but also with the day of the week: "Thursday, November 18, 1971."

The next day she took the local to the district capital and had the prescription our family doctor had given her refilled: a hundred sleeping pills. Though it was not raining, she also bought a red umbrella with a handsome, slightly curved, wooden handle.

Late that afternoon she took the local back. As a rule this train is almost empty. She was seen by one or two people. She went home and ate dinner at the house next door, where her daughter was living. Every-thing as usual: "We even told jokes."

Then, in her own house, she watched television with her youngest son. A movie from the "Father and Son" series was being shown.

She sent the child to bed; the television was still playing. She had been to the hairdresser's the day before and had had her nails done. She turned off the television, went to her bedroom, and hung up her brown two-piece dress in the wardrobe. She took all the sleeping pills and all her antidepression pills. She put on menstrual pants, stuffed diapers inside, put on two more pairs of pants and an ankle-length nightgown, tied a scarf under her chin, and lay down on the bed. She did not turn on the heating pad. She stretched out and laid one hand on the other. At the end of her letter to me, which otherwise contained only in-structions for her funeral, she wrote that she was perfectly calm, glad at last to be falling asleep in peace. But I'm sure that wasn't true.

* * *

The following afternoon, on receiving the news of her death, I flew to Austria. The plane was half empty; it was a steady, quiet flight, the air clear and cloudless, the lights of changing cities far below. Reading the paper, drinking beer, looking out the window, I gradually sank into a tired, impersonal sense of well-being. Yes, I thought over and over again, carefully enunciating my thoughts to myself: THAT DOES IT. THAT DOES IT. THAT DOES IT. GOOD. GOOD. GOOD. And throughout the flight I was beside myself with pride that she had committed suicide. Then the plane prepared to land and the lights grew larger and larger. Dissolved in a boneless euphoria against which I was powerless, I moved through the almost deserted airport building. In the train the next morning, I listened to a woman who was one of the Vienna Choirboys' singing teachers. Even when they grew up, she was telling her companion, the Choirboys were unable to stand on their own feet. She had a son who was one of them. On a tour in South America, he was the only one who had managed on his pocket money. He had even brought some of it back. She had reason to hope that he, at least, would have some sense when he grew up. I couldn't stop listening.

I was met at the station and driven home in the car. Snow had fallen during the night; now it was cloudless, the sun was shining, it was cold, the air sparkled with frost. What a contradiction to be driving through a serenely civilized countryside—in weather that made this countryside so much a part of the unchanging deep-blue space above it that no further change seemed thinkable—to a house of mourning and a corpse that might already have begun to rot! During the drive I was unable to get my bearings or form a picture of what was to come, and the dead body in the cold bedroom found me utterly unprepared.

Chairs had been set up in a row and women sat drinking the wine that had been served them. I sensed that little by little, as they looked at the dead woman, they began to think of themselves.

The morning before the funeral I was alone in the room with the body for a long while. At first my feelings were at one with the custom of the deathwatch. Even her dead body seemed cruelly forsaken and in need of love. Then I began to be bored and looked at the clock. I had decided to spend at least an hour with her. The skin under her eyes was shriveled, and here and there on her face there were still drops of holy water. Her belly was somewhat bloated from the effect of the pills. I compared the hands on her bosom with a fixed point at the end of the room to make sure she was not breathing after all. The furrow between her nose and upper lip was gone. Sometimes, after looking at her for a while, I didn't know what to think. At such moments my boredom was at its height and I could only stand distraught beside the corpse. When the hour was over, I didn't want to leave; I stayed in the room beyond the time I had set myself.

Then she was photographed. From which side did she look best? "The sugar-side of the dead."

The burial ritual depersonalized her once and for all, and relieved everyone. It was snowing hard as we followed her mortal remains. Only her name had to be inserted in the religious formulas. "Our beloved sister . . ." On our coats candle wax, which was later ironed out.

It was snowing so hard that you couldn't get used to it; you kept looking at the sky to see if it was letting up. One by one, the candles went out and were not lighted again. How often, it passed through the mind,

I had read of someone catching a fatal illness while attending a funeral.

The woods began right outside the graveyard wall. Fir woods on a rather steep hill. The trees were so close together that you could see only the tops of even the second row, and from then on treetops after treetops. The people left the grave quickly. Standing beside it, I looked up at the motionless trees: for the first time it seemed to me that nature was really merciless. So these were the facts! The forest spoke for itself. Apart from these countless treetops nothing counted; in the foreground, an episodic jumble of shapes, which gradually receded from the picture. I felt mocked and helpless. All at once, in my impotent rage, I felt the need of writing something about my mother.

In the house that evening I climbed the stairs. Suddenly I took several steps at one bound, giggling in an unfamiliar voice, as if I had become a ventriloquist. I ran up the last few steps. Once upstairs I thumped my chest lustily and hugged myself. Then slowly, with a sense of self-importance, as though I were the holder of a unique secret, I went back down the stairs.

It is not true that writing has helped me. In my weeks of preoccupation with the story, the story has not ceased to preoccupy me. Writing has not, as I at first supposed, been a remembering of a concluded period in my life, but merely a constant pretense at remembering, in the form of sentences that only lay claim to detachment. Even now I sometimes wake up with a start, as though in response to some inward prodding, and, breathless with horror, feel that I am literally rotting away from second to second. The air in the darkness is so still that, losing their balance, torn from their moorings, the things of my world fly soundlessly about: in another minute they will come crashing down from all directions and smother me. In these tempests of dread, I become magnetic like a decaying animal and, quite otherwise than in undirected pleasure, where all my feelings play together freely, I am attacked by an undirected, objective horror.

Obviously narration is only an act of memory; on the other hand, it holds nothing in reserve for future use; it merely derives a little pleasure from states of dread by trying to formulate them as aptly as possible; from enjoyment of horror it produces enjoyment of memory.

Often during the day I have a sense of being watched. I open doors and look out. Every sound seems to be an attempt on my life.

Sometimes, of course, as I worked on my story, my frankness and honesty weighed on me and I longed to write something that would allow me to lie and dissemble a bit, a play, for instance.

Once, when I was slicing bread, my knife slipped; instantly, I remembered how in the morning she used to cut thin slices of bread and pour warm milk on them for the children.

Often, as she passed by, she would quickly wipe out the children's ears and nostrils with her saliva. I always shrank back from the saliva smell.

Once, while mountain climbing with a group of friends, she started off to one side to relieve herself. I was ashamed of her and started to bawl, so she held it in.

In the hospital she was always in a big ward with a lot of other people. Yes, those things still exist! Once in such a hospital ward she pressed my hand for a long while.

When everyone had been served and had finished eating, she would daintily pop the remaining scraps into her mouth.

(These, of course, are anecdotes. But in this context scientific inferences would be just as anecdotal. All words and phrases are too mild.)

The eggnog bottle in the sideboard!

My painful memory of her daily motions, especially in the kitchen.

When she was angry, she didn't beat the children; at the most, she would wipe their noses violently.

Fear of death when I wake up at night and the light is on in the hallway.

Some years ago I had the idea of making an adventure movie with all the members of my family; it would have had nothing to do with me personally.

As a child, she was moonstruck.

She died on a Friday, and during the first few weeks it was on Fridays that her death agony was most present to me. Every Friday the dawn was painful and dark. The yellow streetlights in the night mist; dirty snow and sewer smell; folded arms in the television chair; the last toilet flushing, twice.

Often while at work on my story I felt that writing music would be more in keeping with its incidents. Sweet New England . . .

"Perhaps there are new, unsuspected kinds of despair that are unknown to us," said a village schoolmaster in a crime-thriller series. *The Commissar*.

All the jukeboxes in the region had a record titled WORLD-WEARY POLKA.

The first signs of spring—mud, puddles, warm wind, and snowless trees. Far away, far beyond my typewriter.

"She took her secret with her to the grave."

In one dream she had a second face, but it too was rather worn.

She was kindly.

Then again, something cheerful: in a dream I saw all sorts of things that were intolerably painful to look at. Suddenly someone came along and in a twinkling took the painful quality out of all these things. LIKE TAKING DOWN AN OUT-OF-DATE POSTER. The metaphor was part of my dream.

One summer day I was in my grandfather's room, looking out the window. There wasn't much to be seen: a street led uphill through the village to a building that was painted dark ("Schönbrunn") yellow, an old-time inn; there it turned off to one side. It was a SUNDAY AFTERNOON, the street was DESERTED. All at once, I had a bitter-tasting feeling for the man who lived in that room; I felt that he would soon die. But this feeling was softened by the knowledge that his death would be a natural one.

Horror is something perfectly natural; the mind's horror vacui. A thought is taking shape, then suddenly it notices that there is nothing more to think. Whereupon it crashes to the ground like a figure in a comic-strip who suddenly realizes that he has been walking on air.

Someday I shall write about all this in greater detail.

Written January–February 1972